I WANT YOUR LIPS

HOT EROTICA SEX STORIES,

EXPLICIT DIRTY COLLECTION

SWEET VANILLA

The same author of

"LUST"

20 erotic stories of eager and passionate men and women. Untold taboos will follow you in these hot stories.

You will be harshly excited or wet to the end.

...I want your lips.

CONTENTS

Original sin...Part1

Introduction:

Sunning in the pool I get surprised by my son

This all began two years ago at my home when I was alone and in our pool. This story continues to this day.

My name is Jill, 45 and I'm a married with three grown children ages 25 (son) 23 (son) and 20 (daughter). I really don't know where to start this or how to explain what happen to me last month but I think I need to tell someone just so I can get it off my chest I guess. I grew up on a farm with 4 brothers and three sisters in a home that I'd say was somewhat strict when it came to the subject of dating and sexual things. When we raised our children we tried not to be that way and nudity and seeing other family members nude was just normal for us. My husband and I didn't run around naked all the time but we didn't try to hide our bodies from the kids or raise them to hide from us or each other as they grew older. Well with that said I hope you'll understand my story better.

The kids are gone now and my husband and I live our own lives now on our small place in the country. We have enough land that we, but mostly me, go outside nude or semi nude most of the summer months. Well last month I was home alone and started out just sun bathing on the deck than jumped in the pool to float around for awhile to get more sun. I don't know if I fell asleep or what but I never heard my son's truck coming up the drive to the house.

I don't know how long my son, I'll call him Mark here, was by the pool watching me but when he said, "You look so comfortable and sexy mom ", I about jumped off the float mattress in the pool. I asked him how long he had been there watching me and he just said long enough. He said he wasn't doing anything so he thought he stop in to see us both. I told him his dad had gone fishing that morning with friends and probably wouldn't be back till late that afternoon or evening, but he was welcome to stay and visit with me. Now just so you all know, I'm in the pool topless with only my string bikini bottom on that really doesn't cover much. At this time I was semi covered because I was on my stomach but Mark was still getting a pretty good view of the one side of me, my ass and pussy.

We carried on with some small talk for awhile about what we both had been doing lately, just the normal mom/son stuff. While we talked Mark was sitting down on the edge of the deck with his feet hanging into the pool trying to cool off I guess from the heat but with a weird look on his face I thought. He was wearing a pair of nicer dress shorts when he arrived and at first I thought it was just my imagination or the angle I was seeing from floating in front of him, but I could swear he had a hardon poking up from his shorts. I suggested he get in the pool but he said the chemicals in the pool would ruin his shorts and added with a smile and that cute little laugh of his that it might not be such a good idea right at the moment. Well me being the mother I am, I had too question him why.

Not too my surprise because I know how he's like his father and they say what their thinking, he said he was aroused some by seeing me almost naked and that he did indeed have a huge boner and had hoped I hadn't noticed. Well all I could do was fake a little laugh for him because really the thought that the sight of me, his mother had given him an erection kind of made me feel sexy and sort of dirty at the same time. What the hell was I thinking? Here was my 23 year old son who I of course think is good looking, sitting not three feet, at almost eye level from me on the edge of the pool, with a rock hard cock that I had caused.

To try and put him at some ease I just said "don't worry sweetie, I've seen your penis many times when you was growning up and there's nothing that will surprise me or for you to be ashamed about so you can get up and get in the pool if you want".

Relaxed I guess by that, he stood and asked if it was OK if he removed his shorts so they wouldn't get ruined. I told him sure as if it wouldn't bother me at all. Well this is where I'm afraid I lost all my morals as a mother or it just brought out the slutty side in me as some things do. Mark stood and with a little trouble clearing that bulge in his shorts, dropped his shorts too the deck. Well there above me stood my son with a cock as hard as could be, just as thick and as big, if not bigger than his father's I thought, and looking just plan hot as hell. Without trying to look but not able to stop myself, all I could do was comment that he had grown into a very good looking and well-built man. Damn he was so hot looking and the site of his hard cock just sent chills through my body. Again, what the hell was I thinking, I'm his mother?

Mark got in the pool with me and spent most of the first 15 minutes or so trying to keep some distance between us and not get him in a position where he had a view of my behind, remember all I had on was the bottoms of my tiny string bikini. He stayed away from me up until I finally asked him if I looked like I was getting sunburned. At that time he came over close and checked my back for me. He said, "mom you look like your starting to get red so you better put some lotion on or something". Well now this was a problem, for who I don't know but that's when things started to get interesting.

Mark I said, would you please put some lotion on for me dear. I swear I could hear him swallow hard but with a little excitement in his voice he said sure mom. When his hands first touched me as he spread the lotion on my back I thought I was going to die. The chills and the thrill that went through me was something I had never felt before. As he spread the lotion along my waist and hips, that did it. I'm probably the one that sent this whole situation over the line but as good as his hands felt I asked Mark to put some lotion on my legs and butt so they wouldn't burn too.

At first I didn't think he was going to do it but after a few seconds of delay I felt the lotion being squirted along both legs and across both my butt cheeks. As before, as soon as his hands touched me that same shock wave went through me as before. The thoughts I was having being this boys' mother were crazy but at this moment in time as I lay floating in that pool, he wasn't my son and I wasn't his mother, just a man and a very horny older woman who was enjoying a man's hands on her.

Mark worked the lotion into my legs and across my ass at first very quickly but then to my surprise he squirts some more on my inner thighs and across my ass again. As his left hand rubbed the lotion onto my ass, his right hand was working the lotion on my thighs and up closer to my now very wet pussy. At first I thought he touched me by mistake but as he moved his right hand up my leg again I know he was touching my semi-exposed pussy that wasn't even covered by that small sting on purpose.

He continued touching my wet pussy as if by accident several times. To give him a signal and too let him know I liked it I made a couple of well-timed moans when he did. After about my fifth moan he asked me if it felt good and did I like what he was doing. My only replay now for him was that it felt wonderful and that he could do any kind of lotion on me anytime he wanted.

Well I guess that was the signal he was waiting for and all he needed to hear. On the next run up my thigh with his hand he keep coming higher and run his fingertips over the lips of my pussy. As wet as I was by now I know he felt it and sure enough he said, "Damn mom you're sure wet". He asked "Is this turning you on that much"? Without thinking about my answer I said, "Yes Mark it is and you can touch me more if you want baby". Well again that's all it took because the next feeling I had was Mark's left hand pulling the small strip of material and string of my bikini off to the side and a finger of his right hand going deep into my pussy.

His finger felt so good inside me that I almost came right then. As he worked his finger, than a second and a third into me I knew I was seconds away from cumming. Using his thumb he started rubbing my clit as he moved his other three fingers around inside me and as if I was hit by lightning, I had one of the biggest orgasms of my life. It seemed like I was cumming forever. I just shook and spasmed like it was the first orgasm of my life.

When I had finally calmed down Mark just gently withdrew his fingers from me and said how nice it was for him that he could make me feel so good and cum so hard like that. I told him that it was wonderful and yes he had made me feel good but added that I should return the favor since I had made him so uncomfortable since his arrival. With that said, I slid off the float and finally gave him a full frontal view of his now overly horny mom. With a big smile on his face he commented that I looked very sexy, that I had a great body, and that he really liked how nice my tits where. There not big by any means, just 34C's but still firm for my age.

Thinking I'd take advantage of my height of 5' 5" for once I told him to get up and sit on the edge of the deck again so I could be at the level I thought would be just right. Once in place I was just slightly above face level with his now again hard cock. With a look of being unsure on his face, I move in between his legs and took his cock in my hands. That surprised but satisfied look came to his face as I looked up at him and took his cock into my wide open and waiting mouth. His cock as I said earlier was very thick just like his dad's and just as big, which would make it about 8" long. I know because I've measured his father's before and he has an 8 to 8 1/2" cock. Pausing just for a second I told him that he sure grew into a very big man. Well I did my best to get as much of his hard cock as I could into my mouth and work him the best I knew how. I've sucked a lot of cocks in my days but this had to be the most exciting for me to date. I licked the head, up and down the shaft and even sucked and licked his balls off and on, but from the sounds coming from Mark I knew I was doing a good job and it wouldn't be long before he'd be giving me my reward. I had as much of Mark's cock in my mouth as I could get, trying to take all of him deep but as I was trying to get those last inches in, he fell back on the deck and yelled, "Mom I'm cumming, I'm cumming mom".

Well that was it. Time to show my son what mommy could do. As I felt his cock start too spasm I forced the rest of his cock into my mouth and tried to use the muscles inside to milk all his cum from his body, and I wasn't disappointed. Spasm after spasm Mark shot his hot cum into me and as hard as it was I didn't gag once. I let him fill my mouth with every last drop and when he had shot that last bit of his load, I gently slid his cock just to the edge of my lips and went down on him again to make sure he was finished. Let me tell you, he has some of the sweetest tasing cum I've ever had so far.

Mark just lay there on the deck as I got out of the pool and went over next to him. Looking down at him with his eyes closed but with that cute smile on his face, I said, "sweetie why don't you come on into the house, we'll get something cold to drink and see what else you can help your mom with today, OK!"

Original sin...Part 2

Introduction:

Mother and sons first time continues indoors

My story of the first time with my son continues here

After I told Mark to come into the house I went on in ahead of him leaving him still laying there at the side of the pool. Walking to the house and in the back door I couldn't help or for that matter understand the strange new feelings I was having inside me. I was torn between thinking, what the hell have I just done to OMG that was the hottest and best blowjob I've ever given. Thinking about what we had just done as I waited for Mark, plus the fact that it was my own son that I had just sucked off, I started to get horny again and I must admit a little wet also.

My first thought as I entered the house was to go put on some shorts and a top since I was still only wearing my thong. But as I started to get the mixes out for our drinks the same thoughts came to me again as they did in the pool. Those thoughts brought the wonder images of Mark's hard cock and how sexy he looked standing out there on the deck, the thoughts I was having as he put lotion on me, how good his fingers felt while bringing me to that great orgasm, and the final excitment of having his cock in my mouth and him filling it with his hot cum.

Unable or not wanting to control my thoughts I know right than I needed more from my loving son, my baby. Without any further thought I removed my last piece of material protection and threw my thong on the chair next to the dining room table. Here I was now, naked and making drinks for my son and myself as he finally came into the kitchen and to my surprise and happiness, he hadn't put his clothes back on yet.

Feeling somewhat weird and I think both of us not knowing what to say, Mark just stood at the far end of the kitchen counter. I finally broke the ice and approached him with his drink. As I did I couldn't help but look at him, his cute face, fit body, and of course his wonderful manhood. As I handed him his drink I asked if he was alright and was what happen outside in the pool ok with him. With a few seconds of thought he said, "Mom it was great and I've always wanted to touch you like that but never thought it would ever really be possible or ever happen. When you let me get you off in the pool it was a dream come true for me Mom."

I gave him a little kiss and told him that I loved him dearly and I was glad it hadn't upset him. I told him that what we had done wasn't what a

9

mother and son should be doing but that I couldn't help the thoughts he was making me have. I said he had made me feel beautiful and sexy again when I saw him aroused by my body and that the orgasm he made me have was one of my best. With that said I moved closer and kissed him again but this time more deeply and much longer.

After a very long, tongues in mouth kiss, I could feel his cock getting hard between us. Again maybe to give him a sign of what I wanted I let out a few moans of my pleasure and took hold of his cock with my hand. I heard him place his glass on the counter than felt his hands running up my thighs, over my hips and around to my ass. His hands felt so good as he explored my body and with each heated moment my pussy was getting wetter and wetter. Wanting him to touch me more I slide my right leg up around his hip and around behind him to give him access that I so needed now. In this position he eased his right hand between my legs and started rubbing my wet pussy and clit. The feeling was just as good if not better than when he fingered me in the pool. He probed one, than two fingers in and out of me causing a slushing sound each time. At this point I think we both know that him fingering me again wasn't going to be enough this time.

Breaking off our long kiss I simply pulled him by his cock and turned him so he was up against the dining room table. I pressed him against his chest so he would lay back on the table and as he did I bent to take him back in my mouth once again. The taste and feeling of him in my mouth was wonderful. I swear I was acting like some porn star I'd seen in a movie as I sucked every inch of his cock and sucked his balls like a pro. Believe me, I so wanted to taste his cum in my mouth again but the heat of the moment and between my legs was just too much for me.

Taking him one last time deep into my mouth I slowly withdrew him from my mouth and looking up over his chest said, "Take me Mark, fuck me right here, right now".

As he slide off the table I replaced him by just bending over the edge of the table so he could get behind me and take me doggy style. As he was positioning himself behind me the thought of, "what the hell are you doing Jill stop this now" went through my mind until I felt him rub the head of his cock across the wet lips of my pussy. As fast as that thought had come it was now gone and my desire to have my son's cock deep in me took over again. With just two or three wipes plus the fact I had just gave him a wet blowjob, I think his cock was lubed more than enough as I felt the head pressing against the opening of my pussy and slowly spreading my lips apart.

Ever so gently Mark slide his wonderful cock into me. With each forward push I let out a moan of satisfaction until he was fully inside of me. The thickness and his length made me feel so full inside and wished he could give me more. Slowly Mark worked himself out than slowly back in so I could almost feel every vein in his hard cock. In a rythem now Mark was rubbing his hands over my back, sides and hips, than up into my hair and stopping once or twice he'd grab a hand full of my hair and stroke in and out of me while pulling back on it like the reins on a horse. I like having my hair pulled when I'm being taken doggy style so I told Mark it was ok to pull harder and as he did I just blurted out, "harder Mark, harder baby".

Now with my verbal direction I guess Mark's pace increased and he was pounding me hard just like I had requested. His hardness was slamming into me with each thrust, hitting that special spot that needed it so badly. He was pulling my hair hard now also, so hard my head was pulled back almost up straight and Mark was pushing two fingers of his left hand into my mouth saying, "suck them mom, suck them good".

As he spoke those words to me and the way he was fucking me, I'd have never thought he was like this or known he was this good. My boy had grown to be a wonderful man and as far as sex, very talented and a real lady pleaser. Well he was pleasing me and I was at the point of no return by now. The harder he fucked me the faster my orgasm was coming. With the table and us both rocking like crazy I came again for the second most wonderful orgasm of the day. I remember not being about to control the spasms that was going through my body as I orgasmed. As my orgasm slowed and neared it's end, Mark's was just beginning. Still pulling my hair hard and driving his cock into me I heard him grunt something than felt the hot liquid of his sperm shooting deep into my now overly used and hot pussy.

With his balls now emptied inside of me, Mark leaned over my back and kissed me on the cheek saying, "That was perfect mom and your one of the hottest women I know. I love you!" All I could say in reply was "I love you too Mark and thank you".

In a few minutes I could feel Mark getting soft so he slowing pulled out of me and helped me up from the table. As I said he emptied his balls and that he did. As I stood up next to the table his cum almost gushed out of me, drops falling onto the dining room rug and running down both my legs. Damn I didn't think a young man could cum that much.

I went to the bathroom and cleaned up while Mark cleaned up in our other bathroom. When we met back in the kitchen we kissed one last time and decided to go back outside on the deck, finish the drinks we should of had earlier and talk about what had happen before my husband Nick got home from fishing.

A party whit my hot wife

Introduction:

Wife has fun after years of begging.

This is what happened one night at a party. Wendy my wife is 35 weighs about 135 pounds and is 5'11" her tits are a D cup. We have been married for 15 years and have two kids but from the way here body looks it is hard to tell. She has always been very conservative about her dress and showing off her body.

I had always wanted her to show off more and had even tried to get her to talk about it while we were having sex but she would always say she couldn't. It was always in the back of my mind and I would fantasize about it all the time.

I had to go to a party for my work and I told her she really needed to wear a short black dress we had bought a few years back that she never wears. She complained about it but gave in eventually. The party was at a hotel about 4 hours from us so we had drove down that day and checked into the hotel. When it was time to leave she walked out and looked so good I almost did not want to go to the party any more.

We arrived at the party a little late and we were met at the door to the ballroom of the hotel by one of the guys from work who just kept talking to Wendy and brushed me off. I gave her a kiss and said "I am going to the bar and get us some drinks". Wendy stayed there with Steve. I worked from home most of the time so Wendy had never meet most of the people from work.

From the bar I watched as they got a table and were just chatting Wendy looked so good setting there here long brown hair in contrast to here milky white skin she kept laughing at whatever Steve kept saying to her. I took our drinks back to the table and Wendy said "I wanted a Coke". I just smiled and said "it's a party just have a couple of mixed drinks". Now Wendy who never drinks said "no, that's ok I will get a Coke in a while". As part of my job I had to talk to some potential clients and got up to mingle Wendy just stayed at the table.

After about 20 minutes I looked back at the table to see Wendy talking to a couple of guys and sipping a drink. I wondered what she was doing, I never thought she would actually drink anything as she never does. I walked back over to the table to check on her and saw she was ok and talking to guys from one of our other offices. She and I talked for a minute. She knew she would be without me most of the party because of me talking to clients and told me to go on she was fine. I left her and went back to making my rounds.

I kept glancing over at her and she seemed to be getting more relaxed as the night went on. I even saw her get up and dance a couple of times something else she never does. I stopped back by to check on her and she was feeling no pain and talking away, did not even notice I was there she was too busy talking to the guys setting with her. She was laughing and seemed to really be enjoying herself.

The party was really crowded and I noticed Wendy was not at the table. As I walked around looking for her and saw her dancing with a guy I had not seen before. He was holding her very close and his hand kept moving to her ass. She did not even try to move it but looked up at him and they started kissing. When the dance was over they went back to the table. I was actually I little jealous, but turned on. I walked over to the table and introduced myself. The guy was a client I had not met. We talked a few Minutes and Wendy got up to go to the restroom. He started talking about how she was letting him do whatever he wanted to her on the dance floor and he was sure it was going to be a good night. I let him know that Wendy was my wife and he turned red as could be. I explained to him how it was ok and not to worry I did not mind. I always wanted to watch her flirt and play around but never thought she would do as much as she already had. While talking I think I got the point across to him that I was ok with whatever she would let him do as long as I got to watch but did not think anything would happen.

When Wendy returned I asked her to dance. Once on the floor we talked about everything that she had been doing. She told me how she had a buzz after the drink and just let things go too far. After a long conversation she knew I was not mad and that I had really liked the Idea and was getting turned on thinking about it. Then I said it "Do you think you might want to ask Gary to go back up to the room?" Wendy just looked at me like you can't be serious. All I could say was " I think you really enjoyed playing with him so far and you can have another drink and just flirt and when he leaves you will be turned on for me." Wendy said "if that is what you really want but just some flirting."

We returned to the table and Wendy sat down beside Gary and me on the other side of him. I said "you know this is calming down in here do you think you would want to come up to our room for a last round?" Gary looked at Wendy and said "sure why not." And to our surprise the guy Gary was talking to said "hey can I join." Gary said Shane this is Steve he works with me is that ok?" I thought great no fun now but Wendy said "Sure why not the more the merrier." The four of us headed to the room.

Once we went in I went to over to a small table and set down a bottle of vodka and rum I brought from downstairs and started to make some drinks. Wendy kicked of her heels and plopped down on the end of the bed. I gave everyone a rum and Coke including Wendy and we just kind of looked at each other not knowing what to say. Wendy whose drink I had mixed very strong turned her cup up and started to cough saying "oh my God I can't believe I just drank that yuk." We all started laughing thank goodness that had broken the ice and it was not long till we were all laughing and talking again. I gave everyone another drink and Wendy looked at me funny and just turned it up again. She looked up at me and said "are you trying to get me drunk?" I just laughed and we all went back to talking.

It was not long till Gary had got up to use the bathroom and when he came back he sat by Wendy. He would put his hand on her leg and rub while he was talking to her. Soon the conversation started to turn to sex. To my surprise Wendy was actually joining in and answering questions about does size matter and that kind of stuff. Then to my surprise Wendy looked at Gary and said "Well what about shaving do you like pussy shaved smooth or some hair on top or trimmed all over?" Gary not expecting it came back with "I like hair just above it and smooth below." Wendy looked at me and said "Wow he likes how I do it Shane is always asking me to shave it all off." Gary looked at her and said "I would love to see that." Wendy came back with "I think Shane would like for you to see it to." Then Steve chimed in with "Please there is no harm in seeing? Would you just give us a peek?"

Wendy said "maybe in a minute" and got up to go pee. As she walked out of the room Gary and Steve just looked at me. I told them "Whatever she will let you do but do not expect much I am telling you." About that time Wendy walked in and said "What do you mean do not expect much? What are you guys talking about?" Wendy sat back down on the bed her legs hanging off the end. She laid all the way back reached her arms above her head and pulled a pillow under her head. She closed her eyes and said" You can look but do not touch" and kept her eyes closed. She was now lying beside Gary and Steve got up and sat on the other side of her legs. Gary looked at me I got up and walked over and grabbed the bottom of her dress and lifted the hem slowly sliding it up her thighs. Just as it reached the top of her thigh she said again "No touching" and her pubic hair came into view. We were all just looking at her not believing she had taken her panties off. Gary asked "would you mind spreading your legs just a little so we can see it all" Without missing a beat Wendy spread he legs and we could see her now very wet inner lips glistening with her juices. Gary sighed and said "Yes that is just how I like it" I said "Why don't you take you dress off so they can see all of your great body including those great tits of your."

To my surprise Wendy stood up pulled the dress over her head took off her bra and then just laid back down. Gary slowly reached a hand out and touched her tit Wendy jumped a little but then moaned and kept her eyes closed. He started to rub more and more stopping to play with her very erect nipples. She kept her eyes closed and started to squirm a little. Steve then being a little bolder started to rub her leg higher and higher till he was coming close to reaching her now puffy lips. Gary then leaned his head over and started to suck her right nipple and play with her left with his hand as he got on all fours beside her. Wendy started to moan louder and Steve moved his hand all the way up till he was messaging her pussy on the outside. As Steve would reach her Clit she would squirm under his touch.

Then I noticed her reach out her right hand and start rubbing Gary's cock on the outside of his pants. I could not believe what was happening. Was my shy wife really going to fuck these 2 guys in front of me? Gary reached down and undid his pants and started to pull them down. Wendy laid back and spread her legs as Steve now inched his face between them. As his tongue started to lick he pussy Wendy let out a very loud moan and said "Is this what you wanted to see baby?" I said nothing and just watched as she grabbed her nipples and started to give them a little tug.

Now Gary was fully undressed and crawled on the bed beside Wendy's head. He laid his good size cock if I was guessing I would say 7 ½ inches long and very thick on her cheek. Wendy wrapped her hand around it and guided it to her mouth. She stuck her tongue out and started to lick the head and then as she moaned again from the licking Steve was doing tried to get it in her mouth. She was trying her best to get the whole mushroom shaped head in her mouth but it was so thick she was having trouble. She started moving her mouth up and down the side of it as Steve now had 2 fingers in her finger fucking her as he licked at her clit.

Steve pulled back away to start undressing and as he did Wendy pulled Gary's cock toward the bottom of the bed as if wanting him to take Steve's place. As Gary moved into position Wendy opened her eyes and looked at me and said "Are you sure this is what you want to see? You want me to be their slut?" By this time Gary was no positioning himself on top of Wendy and lifting her knees up to get in line with her soaked pussy. I just pulled my dick out and started to stroke it watching what was about to take place. Wendy Reached down and guided the head to her opening. As Gary started to push forward with his hips I could see her lips resisting the large head. They slowly started to part as Gary pushed harder as Wendy moaned loudly "Oh God that is big." That gave Gary all the motivation he needed has he pushed harder as the head disappeared inside her. Gary groaned out as he sunk more if his cock in her until you could just see his balls lying against her. He then pulled out until just the head was inside and pushed back in again. As he started to get a rhythm going Steve got on his knees beside her head and put his dick to her mouth. Wendy opened her mouth as she moaned and Steve shoved the head in.

This was now the wildest scene I had ever witnessed. Two guys were using my formerly shy conservative wife like their personal slut. Wendy would moan every time that Gary pushed in deep and suck as hard has she could on Steve's cock. Gary started to pick up speed And Wendy stopped sucking Steve as she started to scream "Yes fuck me, Oh God fuck me hard!!!"

Then Gary pulled his dick out which the head made a pop sound as it came out. He turned her over and got her on her hands and knees and shoved back in hard and pulled her head up by her long brown hair. Her tits were swinging violently as he took her hard from behind. Steve took the chance and got in front of her and shoved his cock in her open mouth and started to push it as far as it would go. As Gary would push from behind it would force more of Steve's dick down her throat. Tit was not long till his balls were on her chin. She was actually deep throating him but I did not know if it was by choice. Steve grabbed the back of her head and moaned as he dropped his seed deep down her throat. Wendy gaged at first but then it started to flow from around his dick down her chin. Steve lay in front of her and she laid her head on him moaning while Gary continued to assault her from behind. It was not long till Wendy was screaming "yes oh God yes." She just kept saying "yes" over and over again and her Body was shaking with the hardest orgasm I had ever seen her have.

Gary was slamming her so hard she would move forward till just her tits were on Steve and push back to meet Gary's next thrust. Then Gary grabbed her hips and buried himself to his balls in her moaning loudly I could tell he was unloading in her. She just stayed there with her head on Steve panting to catch her breath till Gary finally started to pull out. As he withdrew his now shrinking cock Wendy just kept her ass in the air.

Gary got off the bed walked to the side closest to her head lifted her by her head and guided it to his cum soaked cock and forced her to lick it clean and to my surprise she did without even blinking. After a few minutes Steve and Gary got dressed said their goodbyes and Kissed Wendy as they left.

Wendy had just stayed on the bed not even trying to cover up she laid on her back with Gary's cum still leaking from her wide open lips. She looked at me and asked "is that what you had wanted to see all this time?" I crawled up next to her and said "Well I guess but, but I am not sure I was ready for all that at once." She just laughed and said "If you are going to go, go big." I laughed as I moved in and started to kiss her. I could taste the mixture of both of them on her lips and tongue as we kissed.

She knew I was still hard and pulled me on top of her. My dick slid straight in with no resistance and as we made love she looked at me and said "I guess you were right, there is a difference between making love and being fucked." I looked at her with my dick inside her with Gary's juices providing all the lubrication I could need and said "What do you mean?" She said "Well they just fucked me the best I ever have been but they can never make love to me like you are now."

Remembering Melly

True Story

Introduction:

This is how I remember it!

She wasn't THE prettiest girl I knew, but she was certainly one of them. And to my way of thinking, Melly was the ultimate Girl Next Door – and I'm sure you would have agreed, if you happened to be (as I was at the time) an athletic, fun-loving, mischievous fourteen-year-old boy. She was a year younger than me; we had lived house-by-house since I was ten, when my family moved to that quiet suburban neighborhood of older homes, wide tree-lined streets, deep lawns and a large public park with its own woods that in spring and summer provided a private retreat.

Melly and I had been friends and playmates since word one; we were both only children of two-working-parent families, and the only kids our age for several blocks around. Her long brown hair and flashing brown eyes, ready grin and playful attitude -- not to mention practically inexhaustible energy and daring that matched mine -- made her as good as "one of the guys" in all kinds of adventures. At about 5'2" she was maybe a hundred pounds soaking wet; there wasn't an ounce of additional flesh on her petite but muscular frame -- except, as we grew (and I noticed!) for those two slowly emerging mounds on her chest. They weren't much more than the size of halved oranges at the time this story occurred -- an event that was to change everything between Melly and me.

It was a lazy June day, and she and I had spent the morning on our bicycles, racing through the trails in the Woods. We made it back to her house and scrounged some lunch – baloney sandwiches and chips we munched on in front of the TV. "I'm hot!" she complained. "Wanna swim?" I haven't mentioned that the previous year Melly's dad had put in a very nice 4-foot above-ground pool with a deck extending out their back porch, which increased his value to me tremendously. "Sure, I'll be right back!" I responded, and running next door, stripped and pulled on my trunks. By the time I got back she was already in the pool in a skimpy little bikini, and we began splashing and laughing and playing tag and wrestling around as we always did.

She was something to see! When she climbed out on the deck to dive back in, I couldn't help staring at her chiseled abs and lean, muscular legs -- and of course, those two areas of her wonderfully female body no boy my age could help but ogle, barely hidden under the thin cloth of her swimsuit. Maybe it was the cool of the water that was causing those little points in the centers of each side of her bikini top to jut out temptingly, and although I had at that time no earthly idea of female physical geography I could make out a vertical depression in her bikini bottom between her legs that was fascinating to a degree I could neither understand nor explain. All I knew was that the water certainly wasn't cool enough to keep my fourteen-year-old manhood – such as it was -- from twitching to attention as I began to allow myself to wonder what might happen if...

"What's wrong with you? Getting waterlogged?" Melly giggled. I had not even been aware of it, but I had been just standing in the pool staring at her for who knows how long. "Not me!" I retorted, and lunged for her. In a flash we were playing tag again. She was quick as an otter, and slipperier than a trout, and not above flailing those pretty little feet at me in escape, for I was the hunter in this game and she the prey. For several minutes of wild splashing she avoided my grasp, but finally she lost traction on the soft bottom of the pool and I grabbed her from below by her legs, pulling her down into the water and -- as luck would have it -- bringing my face into sudden contact with the very center of that mysterious crease in the fabric of her bikini bottom! She struggled -- she squirmed -- but I had won, and hung on by main force for another second or so, as was my right. Then I let her go amidst the cries of "You cheated!" and "No fair!" that usually followed. But I could tell she was intrigued. There was a redder-than-usual flush on her face, and as she panted from the exertion I felt she was looking at me in a different way. "Well, I won!" I exclaimed "so what's my prize?" "Ummm -- a backrub?" she suggested. "Great!" was my response -- I'd had Melly's backrubs before, and they were downright heavenly. Her hands, although small, were firm and strong, and she wasn't afraid to "dig in" and do some good. Laying a beach towel down the yard behind the pool I stretched out on it and began to relax under Melly's experienced attentions. After she had worked her way down from my shoulders to the small of my back she said "Now my turn!" and, pushing me off, took my place. "Not too hard!" she said as I knelt over her. She purred like a kitten as I began gently massaging that wonderful little body, and believe me, I was enjoying it more than she was!

I had only just begun to get into this experience – I had never given Melly a backrub before – when (as often occurs in the South) out of nowhere a dark cloud appeared overhead with a bolt of lightning, a crash of thunder and a sudden downpour of cold, hard rain! Melly and I both scrambled for the shelter of the eaves behind the garage, and she nestled up with her back to me; I found my arms around her, holding her close to me, and the feel of her warm naked skin against my arms that were brushing up against the swellings in her bikini top once again brought my loins to attention – but this time her barely clad behind was pressed against it! As each flash of lightning made her squeal and squirm, she rubbed against my erection more and more, and I – too embarrassed to move, and too awestruck to the amazing sensation to want to – began to wonder if she was doing it on purpose.

As the rain fell harder, my question was answered; slowly she turned to face me, still wrapped in my arms. Our eyes met for a long moment, and without a word her head tilted slightly to one side and mine to the other as she lifted herself on tip-toe and I leaned down; our lips met, and for a while we stood there, unaware of the storm, slowly beginning to explore a new world of passionate affection. As if by simultaneous yet unspoken consent our mouths opened slightly and our tongues introduced themselves – at first with civility and curiosity, then with a growing hunger.

This went on – how long? I don't know – time had frozen for us. But the joy of our kisses began to overtake me, and I found my mouth straying from hers to kiss first her face, then her neck; she willingly and happily yielded to these forays, and began to softly moan with the pleasure of my lips on her neck. It was then that the real surprise came. She turned back around, pulling her wet tresses to one side, and as I began to kiss the back of her neck she guided my hands with hers to those tempting soft globes beneath her bikini top! Now her moans became soft sighs – I heard her involuntary "Ohhhhhhh!!" as I began to caress her breasts with both hands, while at the same time she began once again to again to rub her bottom into my now-raging hardness.

Her breath became shorter, and her sighs more frequent, and the pressure against my erection more constant, the circular motion against it more intense, and I found that my right hand was beginning to stray down from her breast to feel the tension of her hard, muscular abs. With each motion of her ass against my cock my hand made ever wider circles until it brushed against the fabric of her bikini bottoms, and then I felt her legs part ever so slightly, inviting me to explore further. The garment was loose enough after our pool-play for my hand to easily slide under it and in a flash of lightning I felt the downy-soft hair; as the ensuing thunder boomed I found the inner source of the crease I had observed earlier. Now her moans and sighs had become a series of panting sounds – "Oh! Oh! Oh!" on and on until my middle finger came to something wet and warm within the folds of softness – a slight swelling – and her legs parted even more as she cried "Yes! Oh, yes – yes – YES!" and we began to move in rhythm – the circles of her ass against my cock, the circles of my left hand around her breasts and stiffened nipples, and the circle of my finger around her tiny immature clitoris. Now she stiffened – her breath came in short catches – she arched her pelvis against my finger and then suddenly, at once, her legs clamped together on my hand, her arms wrapped tightly around mine across her breast and a loud, impassioned "OHHHHH!" made its way out from deep inside her, and I felt wave after wave of some other-worldly ecstasy course though her, over and over and over, and with each wave another "OHHHHH!" – Part moan, part cry – forced itself from her throat. Eventually, after another timeless eternity, little by little the waves diminished, and then I felt her knees buckle. I caught her in my arms as she fell, exhausted, and gently I lowered us both to the wet grass and held her gently as she panted her way back from wherever it was she had gone.

26

After a while she began to move; I found myself asking "Are you OK?" She laughed a laugh I had never heard – a deep, relaxed, satisfied laugh, and then answered "Oh, yeah, Danny. I'm great. That was awesome!" Then she turned and looked at me with something brand new in her eyes – a look of wonderful contentment and joy – and in another instant there was a hint of mischief. "But what about you?" she asked coyly, and her eyes fell to the still-throbbing erection causing an obvious tent in my trunks. She pushed my shoulders to the ground, and in a moment had pulled my swimsuit down. I heard her surprised "Oh!!" as my cock sprang to its full six inches, and before I knew it her hand was on it. "Show me how" she breathed, and I placed my hand around hers and began to stroke it up and down on my shaft. Soon I was able to relax my grip, and did she ever take over from there. I lay with my face in the rain as she jacked me off – first gently and slowly til I moaned "Faster!" She did as she was told; the result was inevitable.

Now, I had been masturbating for over a year, but nothing could have prepared me for the incredible rush of that first orgasm from Melly's hand. I felt my balls begin to tighten as a burning sensation at the tip of my cock began to work its way down through my entire pelvis, and it felt as though a volcano at the core of my very soul had begun to rumble and shake throughout my whole body; my eyes squeezed shut as my breath turned to panting. As though from some distance I heard myself begin to vocalize with each heavy exhale, just as Melly had done minutes before – "Oh! Oh! OH! OHHH!" and then suddenly the volcano erupted with such force and such indescribable pleasure as I had never experienced in my young life. Rope after rope of white-hot semen burst from my purple member as Melly continued to pump faster and faster – and with each ejaculation came, one after another, wave after wave of amazing, overwhelming ecstasy. As lightning crackled and thunder exploded over me I cried out time after time, utterly lost in the most all-encompassing, earth-shaking, mind-blowing orgasm I had ever experienced or even dreamed of. Finally the eruption subsided and as I felt by body begin to relax, Melly fell beside me, pulling up my swimsuit as she stuffed my limp but satisfied cock back inside.

We lay there listening to each other breathe as the rain softened and the sounds of thunder moved farther and farther to the east, and in a few minutes a ray of sun broke through the western sky. The storm was over. I rose – first to my knees, then to my feet – and stretching out my hand I tool Melly's and pulled her up. Again we kissed – a long, deep, passionate, loving kiss; pulling slightly away I looked at her questioningly. "Have you – ever – before – umm..." and my voice trailed off, unsure of the words, but Melly understood. "No, never" she said simply, her eyes never leaving mine. "Have you?" "No, never!" I replied emphatically. We stood peering at each other for a moment, and a grin came over her face. "But you want to – again, don't you?" "Oh, man, are you kidding?" I gushed. "That was the best – the most – you were – oh, God, Melly, I don't even know what to say! Like you said, awesome!" She smiled sweetly, and in that smile I saw something so indescribably beautiful that I knew what had begun in a sudden summer storm would never, ever end. "Good," she replied, as though reading my thoughts. "We've got all summer left!"

We slowly made our way back to the pool, and spent the rest of the afternoon floating on the water, kissing and occasionally fondling each other, until we heard her mom's car coming up the driveway, and I went home wondering what we might discover tomorrow.

Mrs. Campbell

Fantasy

When I was in junior high school in the mid 1970's the administration made the progressive move of making, on a trial basis, two of the ninth grade PE classes coeducational. One was to be taught by one of the boy's PE coaches, and the other by one of the girl's PE coaches.

The boy's coaches were very selective in their choices for this project: they only picked the best behaved boys, not necessarily the best athletes. I was one of those boys chosen.

While my buddies and I were waiting for the teachers to be announced we speculated and discussed whom we wanted to be our first female PE teacher. The favorite was Miss Rodgers, a young and slender redhead. The least preferred was Mrs. Cole, a fat, elderly woman who liked boys about as much as she liked slime mold, and girls only slightly better. Mrs. Cole wore her graying blonde hair in a short and severe hair style that screamed 'Butch!' In the end it was Mrs. Campbell who was my first lady PE Teacher.

This is the story of Mrs. Campbell and me.

I got along well with Mrs. Campbell from the start. I was well behaved with good manners. Mrs. Campbell selected me to lead the group exercises that we did at the beginning of each class because I could bellow like a Drill Instructor. Also, I was entrusted with the running of little errands for Mrs. Campbell, and that helped be get out of some of the more onerous games, like paddle tennis. Where Mrs. Campbell and I really hit it off was with our enjoyment of running track. She had been on the track team when she was at university, and was glad to pass on some tips and pointers to me.

In those days the girl's coaches wore baggy navy-blue walking shorts and light blue polo shirts with the school logo on the left breast. Mrs. Campbell herself was tall, with long legs. She wore her medium brown hair short, with no real attempt to make in stylish. Her face, arms and legs were well tanned. She was not what would be called ravishingly beautiful, with a long somewhat angular, face. She had a sweet smile and her light blue eyes would sparkle when she did. One thing that I noticed early on was the surgery scar on her left knee. She told the class that she had landed badly doing a high jump and had torn the tendons so badly that that ended her track and field career. With all that said, I really liked Mrs. Campbell as a teacher and as a person.

The highlight of the year in the PE department was the yearly school track meet, and this year the highlight was to be a head-to-head contest of the 4x100 yard relay: Mr. Hannigan's coed PE class versus Mrs. Campbell's coed PE class. The ground rules were that each class would have two boys and two girls on the relay team, and they could run any leg. After try-outs and practice I was selected to run the anchor leg of this important race.

When the day of the track meet finally arrived I was ready. I did well in my other events: the standing and running long jumps; and the 50, 100 and 440 yard dashes. The 4x100 relay was the last event of the day. I won't bother with the detail of the race, just suffice it to say that Carla gave me a two-stride lead going into the anchor leg, and I never looked back.

I stuck around after the meet to help put away the equipment and bleachers. When that job was done I headed to the locker room to shower and change. When I was ready to leave school I went by the girl's PE office to say good-bye to Mrs. Campbell.

When I entered the office I didn't see anyone.

"Hello! Mrs. Campbell?" I called, "its Andrew."

"I'm here in the back," came her muffled reply. "Come on back!

If the girl's PE building was laid out like the boy's, I was headed towards the coaches locker room.

The door to the locker room was about halfway open, so I poked my head in. Mrs. Campbell was seated with her back to me on the bench in front of her open locker. She only had on her bra and full sized briefs: 'granny panties.'

I stammered an apology and started to withdraw. My thoughts were in a jumble. I was startled, embarrassed and turned on all at once. Mrs. Campbell looked over her shoulder with a smile.

"Come on in, Andrew. I won't bite."

I entered the locker room, still staying by the door, ready to make a hurried exit if needed.

"You did a great job at the track meet today, Andrew."

"Thank you, Mrs. Campbell."

"'Mrs. Campbell' is too formal for friends, Andrew. When we aren't in class you should call me 'Joan.'"

"Ah...Okay, Joan," I sort of stammered. She said we were friends, I liked that. I had always been fond of Mrs. Campbell. In a heartbeat I realized that all along I had a crush on her. Mrs. Campbell had shown me nothing but kindness, and I always wanted to please her. My mind was in a whorl. Here I was, talking with my PE teacher, in the coach's locker room, while she was wearing only her underwear. And she was acting as if it was the natural thing in the world to do.

"I've enjoyed having you in my class this semester, Andrew. You have always been such a nice young man.

"Thanks, Mrs. Campbell," I said falling back into formality. "I've liked being in you class."

"Just another couple of weeks and you're off for the summer. Any vacation plans?"

"I don't think so. Mom has to work, and I'm going to Summer School at the high school." My mom had a rule: unless I had a paying job I had to go to summer school.

"Andrew, would you be a dear and undo my bra?" she asked.

I would have walked on the ceiling if she had asked me to! I stepped over to Mrs. Campbell. I knew how bras were fastened, having helped my mom sort laundry. I undid the three hooks and gently let my hands fall to my sides.

Joan took the straps off of her shoulder and tossed the now empty bra into her locker.

This was in the days before sports bras had even been thought of, so Mrs. Campbell had to wear her bra tight to keep her breasts from bouncing too much. I saw the deep marks on her shoulders from the straps, and I felt sorry. I don't like to see anyone suffering. On impulse I reached up and started to massage her shoulder and neck. The simple act of touching her bare skin made my penis stir in my jeans.

"Oh, Andrew, oh...yes, that feels so good," she said rolling her neck in enjoyment.

I worked my way lower down her back. I started to really massage deeply. I could feel the tension squirt out of her muscles, like toothpaste out of a tube. Joan leaned over so I could reach her entire back.

After several moments she let out a deep, satisfied sigh. "Thank you, Sweetie," Joan said looking back over shoulder. "You do that very well."

"Thanks, Joan." I was looking at her panty clad bottom. Her briefs were of thin white cotton, so there was just hint of flesh underneath: a very intriguing sight for a fifteen year old boy.

"You've had a good look at my back, Andrew. Would you like to look at my front?"

34

I was dumbfounded! Here was a mature woman inviting me to look at her breasts. Not some furtive peeking at some classmates budding titties, just come on and have a look.

It took me a moment or two to find my voice again. "Yes, Mrs. Campbell, I would like to look at your front." I did not trust myself to say the word 'breasts.'

I sidled around the bench until knees were almost touching. I could not really take my eyes off of my shoes. I was embarrassed and scared that something awful was going to happen.

"Don't worry, Sweetie," Joan said in a reassuring voice. "They won't hurt you."

With that I looked up. All guys want to have something sophisticated or cool to say at a time like this. "Gee, Mrs. Campbell, what did you do to make them so beautiful?" is what I blurted out.

She threw her head back and laughed. I had the pleasure of seeing her breasts jiggle as she laughed. My penis was making its presence known by its incessant pulsing.

Mrs. Campbell smiled at me as she reached out and touched my cheek. "Andrew that is the sweetest thing anybody has said to me in a long, long time."

"What about Mr. Campbell?"

Joan sighed again. "He doesn't look at me all that often anymore." My parents had been divorced since I was five years old, and too young to read the signs. I didn't know that intimacy was often an early casualty of marriage.

I now took the time to have a good look at Joan's breasts. They were full, sort of pear-shaped, and low slung with large pale pink areolas and prominent nipples. She turned a little left and right so I could see them from several different angles. They were very nice. My penis was threatening to burst out of my jeans.

"Have you ever seen a woman's breasts before?"

"No." I was too absorbed in staring at her breasts to reply with more than monosyllables.

"Not even in a magazine?" Joan asked playfully.

"No...Well, maybe once or twice," I admitted.

"Sweetie," Joan said softly, "I want you to touch them."

I must have given her a look of blank surprise because she nodded her head at me and smiled again.

Slowly, in part wanting to savor the moment and part apprehension that I was going to wake up from a dream, I reached out to Joan's beautiful breasts.

The moment that I first touched Joan was an instant to remember. Her breasts were soft, yet at the same time firm. And they were warm to my touch. Purely out of male instincts I began to gently squeeze and caress them. My efforts were rewarded by the magical feeling of Joan's nipples becoming erect against the palms of my hands.

Joan moaned softy and put her hands on mine. "Oh Sweetie, that feels wonderful."

All I could do was give a gentle squeeze as answer.

"Kiss them, Sweetie, kiss them!" Joan ordered breathlessly.

Reluctantly I released her breasts and knelt down between her legs.

I bent slightly to start kissing Joan's breasts. I resisted the impulse to head straight for the nipple of her right breast. Instead I started my kisses at the base. With tender kisses I slowly inched my way across and down towards her nipple.

"Oh, Andrew," she murmured, "You have the softest lips!"

As I approached the areola, I started kissing around the edge, gradually spiraling closer and closer towards the nipple of her breast.

"Oh Sweetie, you are such a tease!"

When I eventually reached Joan's nipple, I gave it the lightest kiss, then another a little harder, and then I took the sweet jewel in my mouth.

Joan started stroking my hair. "Sweetie, that feels wonderful! Don't stop. It's been so long!" She then pulled me close, between her beautiful breasts. She kissed me on the top of head, and then she took my head in both hands and brought me up to kiss her on the lips. She gave me a very long tender kiss.

"We have to wait. We can't let someone catch us here."

I nodded dumbly.

"Can you come to my house, Sweetie?"

I found my voice again. "Sure, where do you live?"

Joan rattled off an address. It was only about two miles from campus in the opposite direction from my house. I nodded in agreement. It would not be too far of a bike ride. "I need to call my mom," I said as I stood up.

"Use the phone on my desk." Joan smiled again at me. "Now scoot!" she ordered playfully.

I had just settled in behind Mrs. Campbell's desk when Mrs. Cole came into the office. It was a good thing too: my penis making a huge bulge in the front of my jeans.

"What are you doing here?" she snapped.

"Mrs. Campbell said I could use the phone to call my mom, Mrs. Cole."

"All right," she said, "Just make it quick." She then did something very odd: she smiled at me. "You did an excellent job at the track meet today, young man."

"Thank you, Ma'am," I knew that it was best to be very formal with Mrs. Cole.

"I wanted to beat the pants off of Mr. Hannigan's class."

"Yes, Ma'am."

With a nod Mrs. Cole headed back towards the locker room.

I picked up the phone and asked the school operator for an outside line. I dialed my mom's work number.

"Hi Mom."

"Oh hi there. I'm glad you called. I was going to call you. Ray has asked me to go out to dinner and a movie tonight." Ray was my mom's boyfriend. I was not that fond of him, but that is another story. "You'll have to find your own dinner."

"Then I guess it's okay if I go over to Hal's house then?" I said giving a plausible lie. Hal was my best friend and I often went over to his house on the way home from school.

"Of course, dear."

"Maybe I can mooch a meal off of Mrs. Taylor."

Mom laughed. Mrs. Taylor, Hal's mom, had the well deserved reputation of being a really lousy cook. Hal often came over meals at our house. "Maybe you can, but there's a casserole in the freezer if you'd rather."

"Okay, Mom," I said brightly. "You and Ray have a good time."

"Sure thing. Bye"

"Bye Mom," I said as I hung up the phone. It was all set. I knew that Ray would keep Mom out until at least midnight, so I had no constraints.

I figured that it would take Mrs. Campbell another fifteen minutes or so to shower and change. I had enough time to go to my locker, get my book bag and then get my bike.

I rode over to the faculty parking lot, looking for Mrs. Campbell's car. I was very sure that she drove a Gold Duster, but I wasn't completely sure. I cruised around the parking lot trying not to look like I was loitering. Sure enough, Mrs. Campbell came walking into the parking lot and headed towards that Gold Duster that I had pegged as hers. She had changed into a nice pair of tan slacks and plain white blouse. I rode my bike over to her.

"Hi Mrs. Campbell."

"Oh hi, Andrew. Still here?" she said with a smile. She dug into the pocket of her slacks and pulled out a crumpled piece of paper. "Could you be a sweetie and throw this away for me?" she asked.

"Sure, Mrs. Campbell," I said taking the paper. I got up on the pedals of my bike. "Have a nice weekend, Mrs. Campbell."

"I'm sure I will, Andrew," she called after me as I rode away.

Once I had saw Joan drive away I un-crumpled the paper she had given me. As I suspected it was her address and the notation 'Give me ten minutes.' That was an easy enough request to follow, and I figured that it would take another ten minutes of so to ride over to her house.

I gave Mrs. Campbell the ten minute head start that she wanted, and then rode over to her house. I was right in my estimate of how long it took. Mrs. Campbell's house was a rather nondescript southern Californian late fifty's era tract house. It was white with yellow trim, and a nice green lawn in front. Mrs. Campbell's car was in the driveway. I pulled my bike up in front of her car.

I had a kind of odd feeling in the pit of my stomach as I walked up to the front door. I liked Mrs. Campbell, I was still turned on by what had happened in the coach's locker room, and part of me wanted to continue, but also part of me wanted to run away. I took a deep breath, swallowed hard and rang the doorbell.

Mrs. Campbell opened the door. "Well hello there, Andrew!" she said smiling at me, "Please come in. How nice of you to drop by."

She led me into the living room. I noticed that was dark because the blinds were closed. She reached out her arms. I stepped up to her and we hugged for a long moment, nothing more. It felt so nice just being held by Joan, feeling her breasts against my chest. My penis was making itself known again. We then kissed on the lips. I was surprised when Joan tickled my lips with the tip of her tongue. I was ignorant of French kissing. With a little prompting I opened my mouth and let her tongue slip into my mouth. It was a weird feeling at but I sort of got used to it after a bit. I returned the favor and slipped my tongue into her mouth.

When we broke that passionate kiss, Joan patted my cheek. "Very nice, Andrew. You're learning. Now, why don't you have a seat on the sofa? Take off your shoes and stay awhile. I would offer you something, but I'm not used to having guests over to visit."

I did as I was asked, and sat down on the sofa.

"I'll be right back, Sweetie."

I waited for what seemed like a long time, but was really just a few minutes.

When Joan came back in she was wearing a silky pink robe. She looked beautiful. She sat at the end of sofa.

"Come here, Sweetie," Joan said patting the seat next to her. I scooted over to her. I was quivering in anticipation. This whole thing seemed like a dream. If it was a dream I wanted it to slow down so I could savor every second of it before I woke up.

She leaned over to me and kissed me on the lips again. It felt wonder again. Automatically I took her in my arms. Locked in our embrace, Joan gently leaned back, pulling me with her. I reached out and took her right breast in my hand and we kissed deeply and passionately. Joan worked her gown open and guided my hand to her bare breasts. I caressed those two perfect breasts.

Joan slipped her tongue into my mouth again. I was expecting it this time, so I let myself enjoy the sensation. With all of the simulation my blood was coming to boil. I broke our French kiss. I started smothering Joan's face with kisses. My lips were everywhere: her eyelids, her ears, even the tip of her nose.

"Oh yes, Sweetie...Love me, Andrew, Sweetie, love me!" Joan murmured.

"I do love you, Joan!" I blurted out between kissed.

In her infinite wisdom she soon put her fingers to my lips. "Shush, shush, Sweetie. We have plenty of time. No need to hurry. Let's just cuddle for a bit."

Reluctantly I stopped my kissing. I rested my head on her shoulder, and she started stroking my hair, after she closed her robe.

"That's it, Sweetie, just let me hold you."

"You know, Andrew, dear," Joan whispered in my ear after a few moments of silence, "I've always found attractive, since that first in day class."

"I've always liked you too, Joan."

"I've known that too."

We just held onto each other for a while. To continue my cooking metaphor, I had clamed down to a gentle simmer, and I guess that Joan could tell it was time to turn the heat back up a bit.

"Andrew," she said with a mock seriousness in her voice, "You have been neglecting someone."

I gave her a baffled look.

She opened her gown to expose her left breast. I now knew hat she was talking about. Back in the locker room I only had the chance to kiss her right breast, and the way we had been reclining on the sofa it was my left hand that was free to do the feeling, so I was more inclined to reach out for her right breast. I knew what to do.

As before I started kissing the base of her breast and slowly worked my way towards the nipple.

"Sweetie, you just know how to please me."

She took my left hand and guided it to her right breast. "We don't want anyone to feel left out, dear." Joan then murmured and stroked my hair. "Oh yes, Sweetie, suckle my tittie!"

I decided to be a little bolder and I licked the sweet bud of her nipple. This seemed to hit a nerve.

"Oh yes, Sweetie, oh yes," Joan moaned softly. "Nibble on it, Sweetie."

I felt a little odd at this request, but I gently took her nipple between my teeth. I did not want to hurt her.

"That's...yes...that's perfect, darling, Sweetie, Andrew, lover, oh yes!"

Without any prompting I changed over to her right breast and started kissing, licking sucking on that nipple.

After several minutes of that Joan stopped me again.

"You know, Andrew," she said taking my head in both hands. "You have me at a disadvantage: you have too many clothes on. Let's start by taking your shirt off."

I obeyed and eased my OP polo shirt over my head and off. This was just the opening that Joan was waiting for. She kissed me on the right nipple. I almost jumped at the sensation. I had never thought of getting pleasure from my nipples, but the way Joan kissed them changed my mind.

"Oh, Joan," I murmured. "That feels wonderful!" It was my turn to stroke her hair and kiss the top of her head. Her hair was soft and fine. It felt good under my fingers.

Between kiss she asked: "Did you ever notice that when I assigned color to the teams, I almost always had your squad change to red shirts? I liked looking at your chest." She was referring to the individual squad teams in PE class. The boys wore reversible t-shirts: grey on one side, red on the other. To tell teams apart on team of boys would change from grey side out to red side out, or go with out shirts; and the girls, much as the boys would have liked to see them change shirts; wore these stupid looking red tie-on bibs. "I always liked it when you chose to go 'skins.'"

When Joan had finished kissing and caressing my chest, she leaned back in the corner of the sofa. She opened her robe completely. She was wearing a very pretty pair of white briefs. They had a lace waistband and panels of lace that framed her mound. Much as I liked looking at her breasts, I could not take my eyes off of her pubes. My blood was starting to boil again.

"Would you like to kiss me down there?" Joan asked, noting my interest.

"Yes," I whispered huskily.

"Then come here, Sweetie."

There was something that I had to take care of first: I took off my jeans and socks, so I was just wearing my briefs. My penis was straining at the front. There was even a wet spot where I leaked a little in my excitement. Joan smiled as I stripped off my pants. She reached over and patted the prominence in the front of my underwear.

"Very nice, very nice indeed!" she complemented me. "I'll attend to you later."

I leaned over to her and kissed full on the lips. Taking my time had worked well before, so I figured to continue with a winning strategy. I kissed Joan's lips for a few seconds, then I moved to her cheeks, the down her neck, down her chest with a slight detour to kiss under her right breast.

Joan who had been breathing heavily, jerked and giggled. "That tickles!"

I continued down her beautiful body. Joan was about fifty years old, so her tummy was a little soft, but I didn't care. On impulse I rubbed my nose against her navel.

I slipped myself off of the sofa and knelt between Joan's legs. By now I had reached the waistband of her briefs. I didn't take them off; I kept kissing her through the smooth material of her undies. I eased my under her and held her bottom. I moved my lips closer and closer to her womanhood.

I had heard the locker room jokes about women's pussies sMellyng like dead fish or rotten cheese. Joan had a very delicate scent, with just a hint of muskiness to it. I fell in love with the aroma of woman's pussies at that moment, although, never did I find one that had as sweet a perfume as Joan Campbell's. (Yes, over the years I've come across women whose pubic hair was a rough as steel wool, whose vaginal juices were as thick as used motor oil, and who did smell like rotten cheese.)

When my lips first touched the soaking crotch of Joan's panties, my penis felt like it wanted to burst. I knew that I would ejaculate in an instant if I so much as touched it. I kissed up and down the length of her vulva. I then kissed the crease where her legs joined her torso. There were wisps of fine pubic hair sticking out of her panty. I worked my tongue inside of her undies for my first taste of heaven. It's hard to describe the taste, but Joan was light, thin and sweet.

"Oh Sweetie, take them off! Take them off, you tease!" Joan moaned.

In response I started easing her panties off. I stopped kissing her pussy, and as each little bit of skin was exposed I kissed it.

I was slightly surprised. This was in the early days of 'The Penthouse Revolution' when men's magazines first started showing the pubic hair of their model. From the few times I had seen those types of magazines I knew that women had thick amounts of pubic hair on their pussies. As I've mentioned Joan was in her fifties, so instead of a thick, dark bush her pussy had a thinner coverage, as was graying a little bit. I didn't care, the hair was long and fine textured and it felt good as I kissed across and down her mound of Venus.

50

When I came to between her legs I paused to take my first good look at woman's genitals. Here the information from Sex Ed class was actually of some use. I did know the technical names of the various parts of a woman's anatomy. Because of her age a bit of Joan's labia minora were peeking out in what I would later to learn to a call a 'butterfly.' I thought it was a beautiful sight. Again I kissed up and down the length of her womanhood. The tastes and scents were driving me crazy. The pot was about to boil over, to continue my metaphor.

"Use your tongue, Sweetie!" Joan moaned. "Lick me, taste me, put your tongue in me, Sweetie."

I did as I was told. The textures of the skin and fine hair, combined with the ambrosial taste of Joan were heaven on earth for me. I didn't want to stop, and from Joan's moans and murmured endearments, she didn't want me to stop either. I parted her labia with the tip of my tongue. I licked deeper and deeper into the folds of her womanhood. The tip of my tongue found the sweet bud of her clitoris, and I caressed it lightly. I was totally surprised by the reaction.

Joan groaned, moaned, arched her back and clamped my head between her legs. She called out my name, and with an overarching 'Sweetie!' she collapsed.

I sat back on my heels. In my innocence I thought, for a brief moment only, that Joan had had a heart attack. I was reassured when she started breathing deeply. She looked so beautiful laying there naked except for her robe, which was wide open.

"Oh, Andrew, that was wonderful!" She said smiling at me. "You know what I want."

I got up and sat back down on the sofa and closed my eyes. I may not have had an orgasm, but I was emotionally fulfilled. I had taken great pleasure in giving Joan her pleasure. I opened my eyes when I felt Joan move off of the sofa. She was positioning herself in front of me, kneeling on the floor.

"Turnabout is fair play, Sweetie."

Joan leaned over kissed me on the lips. I reached out for her breasts. Gently she pushed my hands away. "Just lean back and enjoy, Sweetie. Let me do all the work now."

She rubbed my chest and nipples as she kissed me tenderly on the face. As I had done for her, she worked her way down my torso. I did as I was told and leaned back. At least until she got to the lower edge of my ribs. She hit just the right spot and it was my turn to jump from being tickled.

"Oh, you like that?" Joan asked mischievously, "How about this?" she asked as she tickled the other side of my ribs with her fingers. I convulsed with laughter.

She smiled at me yet again. "I'm sorry Sweetie, I just couldn't resist. Lay back again. I'll be good. I promise."

Joan resumed her kissing, studiously avoiding my ribs. When she got to my briefs she started easing the waistband down. My mind was racing and my heart was pounding. Joan was about to see my penis! No woman, except mom years ago, had seen my privates. I was struck with a sudden anxiety about my size, but I was enjoying myself too much to worry. I wanted Joan to see me.

Joan gently took my penis with one have and pulled my briefs out of the way. My fears were allayed by what she said next.

"Beautiful! Just like I've imagined, Sweetie."

Of course I had masturbated, and enjoyed it very much. Now, with someone else, a beautiful woman handling my manhood it felt better than it ever had when I did it. Gently, knowingly, Joan softly pumped her hand up and down the length of my shaft. I was in heaven again. I closed my eyes to enjoy the overwhelming sensation of pleasure.

I was startled when I felt something warm and wet on my penis. I opened my eyes. Joan had taken my erect penis in her mouth and was bobbing her head up and down while she fondled my testicles. It was a wonderful sensation but I didn't want it.

"No, Mrs. Campbell, no," I pleaded, "I don't want to cum in your mouth."

Joan removed her mouth from my organ. "I won't let you, Sweetie. When that happens I gag and it ruins the mood." She resumed gently masturbating me. "Besides, I want you to cum in only one place," she gave me another mischievous look, "And that place is not here." She took my briefs off the rest of the way and stood up.

She held out her hand to help me off the couch into a hug. Our naked, or almost naked, bodies touched. The sheer pleasure of feeling her soft, warm flesh against mine was magnificent. Her breasts were pressed up against my chest, and my penis was squeezed against her leg. We kissed again, my hands scrambling for her breasts and bottom, while Joan took hold of my penis again. I struggled with alternating hands to slip her robe off her shoulders. Shortly it joined the rest of our clothes on the living room floor. My manly instincts took hold, and I reached between her legs to touch her pussy.

"Yes, Sweetie, that feels so good." Joan whispered in my ear as I slipped my finger between her labia. I rubbed around until I found her clitoris. She reached a small orgasm quickly. I was amazed at how sensitive she was.

Joan backed out of my hug.

"Come with me, Sweetie," she beckoned.

I followed her gently swaying bottom down the hall and into her bedroom. It was obvious even to my inexperienced eyes that this was a woman's bedroom: nice curtains, soft carpet, various feminine type knickknacks on the dresser and such. What I really noticed was the bed had been turned down so it was open an inviting.

Joan lay down, and adjusted the pillows. "Come here, Andrew, lay next to me so we can cuddle some more." I took my place next to her and we eased into each other's arms. Our lips met, and our hands roved.

I could not resist the allure of Joan's breasts, so I wiggled down to kiss and fondle the while Joan played with my erect penis.

"Andrew, Sweetie," she whispered, "Are you ready?"

"Oh yes, Joan, I'm ready." My words belied my nervousness. The Sex Education unit that was part of the overall health class was useless at this time. I knew all about the difference between myosis and mitosis; the process of menstruation and a woman's fertility cycle; and how the sperm and he ovum would come together to produce a zygote; but the actual way of bring the two together was not covered in the course material. There were still things one had to learn hanging around on grubby street corners or the boy's locker room.

We rolled around so I was lying on top of Joan. She spread her legs and my penis touched her pussy. It was a marvelous and exciting feeling. I started to rub against her. Joan bent her knees and reached around and gently guided my expectant member into her vagina.

The sensation of entering a woman for the first time was, and is, an event really beyond the scope of words. It was warm, wet, velvety and a thousand other wonderful words. I knew what to do and I started thrusting. Ever the wise woman that she is, Joan wrapped her legs around my bottom to keep from falling out. Being hyper-stimulated I lasted only a minute or so before I had the most powerful orgasm of my young life. I groaned loudly and collapsed on Joan.

I was emotionally on edge. In the space of an amazing Friday afternoon I had been given my first adult kiss, felt my first woman's breasts, seen my first naked woman, tasted my first pussy and now had my first experience of sexual intercourse.

My breathing was coming in heaving gaps and my heart was pounding when the sound of Joan softly crying entered into my world. That pushed me over an edge and tears welled up in my eyes.

"I'm sorry if I did it wrong, Mrs. Campbell," I blubbered, "I'm sorry! It's all my fault."

Joan clutched me to her breast. She stroked my hair as she rocked me back and forth.

"Shush, Sweetie, no, no, no, you were wonderful. It's just that it's been almost seven years since I've had sex with a man. That's why I'm teary." She kissed me on the cheek. "Oh, Andrew, you did more that that, Sweetie, you made love to me."

"I came to fast," I whispered sadly.

"Sweetie, I knew that you would. It wasn't a disappointment." I could tell by the change in the sound of her voice that her tears were finished. "It's more that just getting inside a woman. It's all the wonderful things we did before. Now we have all the wonderful things that come after." She paused. "Besides, we still have more time. We'll have another chance."

"You mean it?" I asked earnestly.

"Of course I do, Sweetie. I'm trusting in the stamina of teenage boys." She pulled the top sheet over us. "Now why don't we just lay here and enjoy each other."

So we lay next to each other gently caressing each other, and softly kissing. Nothing strenuous or overly stimulating, just enough to keep the pot simmering.

"Tell me Andrew, do you masturbate?"

"Yes."

"Who do you think about?"

"Some of the girls," I said evasively.

"Like whom?" Joan asked teasingly.

"Well, Carla," I said naming one of the girls in my PE squad.

"She is a nice enough girl. I don't think she realizes what a teaser she is with her knickers always showing." Joan observed. "Anyone else? Like Terry?" she asked. "Her mother should buy her a stronger bra."

All of the guys were horny for Terry. She was very buxom and single handedly made jumping-jacks a spectator sport. "Yeah I've thought of her too."

"What about me?"

I swallowed. "Yes." I admitted softly.

Joan laughed and gave me a big squeeze. "I had a hunch that you had, Sweetie."

"I'll never think of anyone else!" I promised emphatically.

Joan laughed again. "You dear boy." She kissed me full on the lips again. "If you do ever think of someone else, don't tell me." With that she picked up the pace of our caressing and fondling.

I did not need much to arouse me again, and I got that arousal from caressing Joan's pussy. She was still wet from both of us, so I was able to slip my right middle finger into her vagina easily.

"Oh Sweetie, yes, that feels wonderful." Joan said huskily. Her breathing then became rapid and shallow. "Oh, oh, yes, Sweetie, lover, oh, don't stop, oh, oh, oh." She moaned, her words tumbling out faster and faster. She clutched me tightly and buried her head against my shoulder to muffle a scream of pure pleasure.

I was again taken aback by the intensity of Joan's orgasms.

"Sweetie, you do that very well." Joan said from my shoulder. "Now let's do something different." She rolled me on to my back. "You see, Sweetie, the woman can be in charge sometimes," she told me playfully.

Joan draped her left leg over my legs. She rubbed my chest and kissed my face and nipples while she gently fondled my penis. I loved the sensations of her lips on my nipples and her hand on my penis. When Joan determined that we were ready again she knelt over me and slowly lowered herself onto my waiting penis.

For the second time that afternoon I felt the extraordinarily wonderful sensation of being in a warm and loving woman. Joan slowly bobbed up and down.

"You see, Sweetie, this way the woman can control the pace to her liking."

What was to my liking was the face that her breasts were dangling in front of my eyes. I took hold of them and fondled and caressed them to my hearts content. I was able to take the nipples in my mouth as well.

"Oh yes, Sweetie, that is so nice. Yes...yes," she murmured in pleasure.

As our climaxes approached Joan picked up the pace. I answered by thrusting with my pelvis to meet her strokes.

I moaned my pleasure, and with a cry of "Oh Joan!" I ejaculated deep inside her.

The sensation of my semen flooding her was enough to push Joan over the edge of her orgasm. She gave an inarticulate yell of ecstasy and she collapsed into my waiting arms.

We lay quietly in each other arms for several moments enjoying the feeling of each other's warmth, and not wanting it to end. Regrettable things had to move on.

"Oh Sweetie, Andrew," Joan whispered "You were magnificent. It's been so long since I've felt this way. Thank you, Andrew."

"Thank you, Mrs. Campbell." I wanted to say 'I love you, Joan,' but I could not get the words out.

"Much as we might want to keep going, Sweetie, we have to stop." She smiled down at me. "We've made a mess of the living room and my bed. We need to tidy up before Jack comes home."

The mention of her husband made me feel sick to my stomach. I just cuckolded Mr. Campbell. My upbringing told me that it was a sinful thing to do. Joan noticed the queasy look on my face. She held me tightly.

"I know, Sweetie," she said softly and slowly. "It may not be right, but you are very special to me, Andrew. And Jack has given up his rights to me. I've been lonely for a man's touch."

This time I was able to get the words out. "I love you, Joan."

"I love you too, Andrew, my dearest, my Sweetie." We hugged tightly again. "Now come on, we've got work to do."

Joan directed me to have a quick wash in her bathroom while she stripped the bed. Joan brought me my clothes. I was a little disappointed that while I was washing up she had gotten dressed again.

Things were all quiet when Mr. Campbell came home from work. A load of laundry was in the washer, and I was sitting chastely with Mrs. Campbell on the sofa looking at scrapbooks from when she ran track at university.

A good neighbor

True Story

We had been neighbors since I was 5 and she was 7. We played outside together and were never really great friends, but got a long quite well. We used to play outside with the other neighbor kids and see each other all the time. As time passed we grew apart and saw each other less and less. She was a junior in high school and I was a freshman. She usually gave me rides to school in the morning. I never thought much of her to be honest; she wasn't bad looking but wasn't great looking either. She was about 5'7 with dark hair and light milky skin. She had very small breast and a nice round ass. I was about 5'11 with a decent build; I wasn't completely cut up or anything. We didn't run in the same circles in high school but were always friendly towards each other.

The fall of my freshman year one night she called me and said that they didn't have any hot water. Her parents like mine were out for the night. I told her I would be over in a few minutes to look at it. When I got there, she was still in a towel that barely covered her ass. I could tell her hair was wet and asked her why she didn't check the water before she

63

got in and she just smiled and said she didn't know. I went downstairs to check the pilot light. As I was looking through the little window to see if the pilot light was still on she came down and asked me what I thought was wrong with it. I was on my knees at that time and when I turned around I could see right up her towel. She had full hairy bush, that remind me of Kay Parker or and untrimmed Christy Canyon. As I stared at her full thick dark hair around her pussy it was the very first time I had ever thought of her in a sexual way. We made eye contact and as she started to adjust her towel, she knew that I had gotten a peak. I got up awkwardly and told her I just needed to relight the pilot light and everything should be fine.

I relight the hot water tank and told her that it would take some time for the water to heat up. I had my hand on the door when she asked me if I was going to tell anyone. I looked at her confused and said tell anyone what? That I don't shave my pussy she said. I started laughing and told her no, I wouldn't tell anyone, but I said why does it matter if you shave or not. She explained that boys don't like pubic hair and that if anyone found out she didn't shave she would get made fun of. I told her that not all boys are like that, but her secret was safe with me. I was just about to walk out the door when I told her from where I was looking; I thought it looked pretty good. She smiled and said thanks. She got me off guard when she asked me what I did with mine. I smiled and told her she would just have to wait until my hot water tank quit working.

I started for the door again, and was caught between staying and trying to see if this would take me anywhere or just going home and jerking it to what I just saw. I decided to offer to let her shower at our house, which to my surprised she accepted. We walked across the back yard and I couldn't stop thinking about her hairy pussy. I couldn't decide if I should try to make a move on her or not. I didn't know much about her sexually, never heard anything from anyone at school, so I wasn't sure if she was interested in sex or not. I had really done much with any girls before besides the occasional making out and titty grabs. I took her up to my bed room and told her she could use the bathroom between my brother's room and mine. It was a tile shower that was custom built, so it was slightly larger than the standard shower. It had several shower heads and a large bench in the back. I got her everything she needed and told her I wouldn't peak, to which she smiled and asked me why not. I knew at the point I was going to get something from her, just wasn't sure how much.

She told me she wanted to see mine because I got to see hers, and without hesitation I dropped my shorts. My dick stood at attention and she looked me over up and down. She asked me if I could give her a hand in the shower to which I smiled and said sure. She dropped her pants and began to head towards the shower; her lower body reminded me of Kay Parker, with that light white skin and nice round shape. I couldn't wait to touch it.

As we showered together I lathered up her back with soap and let it run into her ass crack. I slide one finger in and out of her pussy from the front and ran the edge of her asshole with the other. She was stroking by dick with both hands slowly and we made slight eye contact as she went down to her knees and began sucking my dick. In one swift motion she moved down and placed my dick in her mouth. I could feel her dragging her tongue across the bottom of my shaft. I could see her hand between her legs; no doubt she was rubbing that hairy clit. She had one hand stroking by dick between her sucks and was vigorously rubbing her clit with the other. Then she stood up slowly dragging me to the corner of the shower and placed her back up against the wall and placed her leg on the bench. I knew exactly what she wanted me to do. I got down on my knees and licked my lips I moved slowly towards her hairy entrance. I began licking her slit from bottom to top several times as she held my head tightly against her pussy. I stark sucking her clit and licking

65

it with my tongue. I had my hands wrapped around her round ass checks. I couldn't believe how soft and smooth her ass was. I slowly started moving my fingers towards her asshole. I rubbed it slowly for a few seconds before I slid it in part of the way. I felt her sliding down against the wall pushing my finger deeper inside her ass. Her breath began to get heavy and her moans became louder and I felt a warm rush of water squirt out of her pussy, down my chin and all over my chest. I couldn't believe I actually made her squirt.

She took a few seconds to catch her breath, as rolled back from knees to my butt. She looked at me and smiled and crawled over my knees and placed my dick right beneath her pussy. She told me not to worry because she was on the pill and slowly slid my dick in her. It was tight for a few seconds as she rocked up and down, but it finally went all the way inside of her. Our hips were right against each other's and she moved her legs behind my back and wrapped her arms around my neck. She slowly started humping me as I moved my hands back to her ass checks again.

She moved to the back wall of the shower with her ass facing me and placed both of her hands on the bench. I got up and moved behind her and slide my dick right into her pussy. I placed both hands on her ass and begin pushing her ass back and forth on my dick. I could feel her pussy getting tighter and convulsing on my dick. She took one hand off the wall and slid it between her legs and began to massage my balls. It didn't take me long after she looked over her shoulder and told me come inside her. I shot 5 solid ropes of cum deep inside her. I slid my now softening dick out of her and sat down on the bench in the shower. I watched her as she begin to wash her body and the suds slowly followed down her body and her pussy dripped out my cum. She smiled at me and said it was fun and made me promise not to tell anyone. I told her I wouldn't as I got up and began to wash myself off. We made a little small talk as we finished our shower. As we began to dry off she told me it was her first time and I told her it was mine as well.

Warm snow

True story

Introduction:

A young boy finally gets his dream girl

Snowball Fight

It all started when I was around 14 years old, just getting used to growing up and learning about my sexuality. I was interested in trying new things, especially with girls. I lived in a pleasant town, with lots of friends in my neighborhood. But one stood out. A few houses down lived a Stacey, who was a year younger. Though she hadn't developed fully, she was a striking figure with milky, smooth skin and fiery red hair that I couldn't stop thinking about. She was small, about 4 feet 8 at the time with petite tits, I would say A cup, and a tight but small little ass.

Every morning at the bus stop we would socialize, mostly just small talk and what not, but she never seemed to be too interested in me. This was very hard for me because soon she was all I could think about. The only problem was I didn't know how to turn our conversations into something a more than just "How's your morning been?..."

I was also afraid of what she would think of me, since we had been neighbors and not only did we know each other for so long but we lived so close. Also, our parents never really got along, the only reason I know of was that her family was a bit strange and her dad was a real asshole. This also scared me from making any further advances.

One lucky day, as winter was rolling in and we were all huddled up in jackets by the corner (which I hated because Stacey covered up her hair and covered her body in a thick jacket) she quietly came over to me and said, "Hey, would you like to come over after school today?"

"Yeah that would be awesome," I replied timidly, not knowing what to think or say in the situation.

"Great! See you when we get home!" she smiled showing off the most lovely expression I had ever seen.

All day at school I couldn't focus, nothing mattered, not my boring math class or geography or even science which I usually loved. The only thing on my mind was what I would do once I got over to Stacey's house. This was the first time Id been over to a girls house by myself, and I had no idea what to do or say. I was afraid her dad might be home or that I would make a fool out of myself just opening my mouth. But as the final seconds of the day ticked away, all I felt was excitement, hoping that this could be the start of something good.

The bus ride home we both sat awkwardly in separate seats, only adding to my fear that this would be a very strange experience for the both of us. We both just sat starring out the window listening to music, all the while I was hoping she was thinking about me the way I was of her. Just a kiss from those soft lips would make me the happiest boy, but maybe I was getting ahead of myself. She probably just wanted help with some homework or had a question about something trivial, the way girls often do.

The bus screeched up to our corner and after letting off a hiss, opened the doors. We walked off her looking back to check if I was coming with. Our eyes met and I was lost in her big dark brown orbs. We walked into her home, and walking up the steps she called out "MOM, DAD, ANYONE HOME!" No reply. "Sweet" she smirked, " lets go to my room." And with that she grabbed my hand and pulled me into her bedroom a place id never ventured into before in my life. As I sat down on the bed next to her I looked around, checking out the scenery. It seemed very nice with pink walls, a comfy pink bed, and posters of her favorite boy bands. Seemed pretty average to me.

"So…" she said coyly, "ever been with a girl?"

A little caught off guard I replied, "Uh like over their house?"

"No silly! Like kissed and stuff?"

"Of course not! I'm only 14."

"Hahah ok I was just wondering," she said seeming to leave the subject alone for now. We moved on to other things and I was getting more relaxed in the situation, which had a very strange start.

"Uh oh, my dads gonna be home soon! You gotta go or he'll think something's going on," she said urgently, looking at the clock.

"Going on? Like what?" I asked naïvely.

"Sex!!" she blurted.

Confused, we walked down the stairs and to the door. About to walk out, she said, "we really need to hang out again sometime soon."

"Sure that sounds fun," I agreed, taking any chance I had to spend with this beautiful girl. And before I could say anything else, she quickly kissed me, on the cheek. As her lips made contact to my skin it felt like an electric current was shot directly into me, coursing through my body, ending up with a stirring in my already temped dick.

"I uh, I gotta go," I said frantically, quickly walking out the door and jogging back to my house. That night the kiss was all I could think about, and naturally the only way I could even begin to fall asleep was to stroke my cock until I erupted in one of the biggest loads of my young life. I feel asleep with happy dreams of Stacey and me.

A week later, a huge winter storm rolled in, shutting down school for 3 days and to the relief of the every child in the neighborhood, giving the kids an extra long weekend. One of the afternoons I was sitting on my bed when I heard the doorbell ring. Since I was the only one home, I went to answer it. To my surprise and delight, on the other side of the glass door was Stacey, looking extra cute in her white coat, leggings and snow boots. Smiling, I told her to come inside.

"Hey wanna have a snowball fight!?" she exclaimed.

"With who?" I wondered looking around to see if she brought friends.

"Just me silly!"

Normally it would have upset me to be called silly so much but for her to say it I knew she was joking and if felt good for her to be playing with me. "Alright alright just lemme get changed first. Where do you wanna play?"

"Can we go in your back yard?" she asked.

"Of course, it'll be perfect we can use the deck for cover!" I said eagerly, ready to sow off my snowballing skills.

With a smile she ran right through my house and out the back door into the cold.

As fast as I could I got out there and ready to start. Of course she was already waiting for me, as soon as I stepped outside I was pelted right in the chest. "Not fair!" I yelled calling foul.

"Too bad silly! Better find some cover"

I ran to the side of the deck and immediately made a stack of snowballs. After about 10 minutes of fighting, I through a ball and with a perfect shot nailed her right in the face.

"AHHHHHH" she cried out in distress.

I ran over to check on her and make sure there was nothing wrong. Next thing I knew she grabbed my pants and dumped a whole handful of snow right onto my package. It hurt a lot and I started screaming in pain. Unaware of how sensitive a man is in that area, she just kept laughing. "Bitch!" I said, trying to smile through the pain and make a joke out of it. "That really hurt..."

"Aww I'm sorry, here ill try and make it better."

I wasn't sure what she meant by that, but she started taking off her gloves and stuck her bare hands right down my pants and wrapped them right around my cold cock. "How does that feel," she asked with a sneaky smile.

"W-what are you, d-doing?" I stuttered, not just because of the cold, but also out of pure shock.

"Just warming you up!" and with that she started to massage and rub my sore but swelling cock. Her warm hands felt incredible as they slowly fondled me making sure she felt and "warmed" every inch of it. "Wow its so hard!" she exclaimed. All I could do was blush as I was quickly loosing myself in ecstasy, feeling myself nearing an orgasm. To my surprise she brought one of her hands to my shriveled balls. Gently caressing them she asked, "wow is this what happens when you get cold?"

71

"Y-yeah," I managed to blurt out. It felt so go I thought I was gonna explode, and I did.

Stacey quickly pulled her hands out as I shot my hot cum all over her hands. I could see the sticky ropes of cum hanging from her fingers as she held them in front of her face, shocked and confused. "Oh my god I'm so sorry Stacey! I couldn't control myself. Come inside so we can get cleaned off."

"Hahah ok," she said with a chuckle, which relieved me greatly that she wasn't mad. As she walked up the stairs, right before she disappeared, I swear I saw her lick her fingers clean. After she came back, we both just sat on the couch.

"I'm so sorry I didn't mean to do that too you," I said to her, when in reality it was one of the best experiences of my life.

"Its ok, I've always wanted to see a boy cum," she said catching me of guard. "In fact, I really been wanting to touch you there for a while now, I think your really cute. I'm sorry if it hurt in the beginning." I just sat there completely dumbfounded. Me cute! She was trying to touch me? Its as if my world was just flipped upside down and everything was a million times better. "I was actually wondering, do you think we could do more?"

"Uh, well what did you have in mind," I said, eager to find out what she had in store for me. Without a word, she crept over to my side of the couch, and seductively kissed the side of my face, them moved her mouth on top of mine. As our lips locked I felt her soft tongue sneak out from her mouth and start to taste my lips and the inside of my own. I began to explore hers as well and our tongues got caught in a wet embrace, which I will never forget. Then to my delight she reached down into my pants once again and started to stroke my already raging hard on. She kept this up for a few minutes, and then broke our embrace, and pulling her hand from my dick. Feeling a little upset since I was so close to climax, I asked, "What's wrong?" All she did was give me one of her sneaky smiles and proceeded to work her way down so that her face was now mere inches from my cock. Blowing on it lightly, the cool air sent intense chills up my spine and put my hairs on end. She really knew how to get me excited. She stuck out her tongue, and slowly ran circles around the head flicking the bottom every now and then. She licked from the base to the tip, and then in one smooth motion engulfed almost 4 of my young 5-inch dick into her mouth. It was by far one of the best sensations I have ever felt in my life.

Her warm mouth contracted all around my cock sending heat rippling through my body. She continued to use her tongue to taste all side the new intrusion into her mouth, the sensation caused me to jerk my hips up towards her face. This pushed the rest of me into her and instead of gaging, she kept trying to fit it farther down her throat. At this point I was impossibly close to releasing my load inter her warm mouth. "Stacey, Stacey I'm gonna CU—," but before I could finish she pumped her mouth up and down quickly making sure to catch my sensitive head on each pass. I erupted into the back of her throat, sending more cum then I thought was possible into her mouth. Holding my cock in her mouth I felt her swallow as much as she could, but I could still see a small glob ooze out of the corner of her mouth.

She slowly pulled off of me, and wiped her mouth, getting every last drop into her stomach. It was probably the sexiest act I had ever witnessed. "Mmhmm, delicious" she said with a big smile. I was completely wiped, almost to tired to look up at her. "That was really fun! Can we do this again soon?" she asked sounding so innocent, although I knew better.

"Of course, whenever you want!" I replied knowing I would do anything in the world to make sure this happened again and again. "We'll probably be off school tomorrow too, want to come over and have another snowball fight?"

"Absolutely! Can't wait, but I gotta get back home now sorry," and with that she ran out the door just as quickly as she came. Leaving me spent and in disbelief if the event of the past hour had actually occurred or were a dream, and I drifted off to sleep...

Lust

Alison closed the door behind her and left a sigh of disappointment as she watched out of the window to see the car disappear. Another attempt to date, another failure. Jake was a great guy, handsome , smart and successful but that wasn't enough for Alison. In a couple of weeks it would be 7 years since her husband's death but she still couldn't find the strength to move on. She was a gorgeous woman, her juicy curvy body and her beautiful face were always the centre of attention everywhere she went. Being so wanted and knowing that every man was extremely jealous of her husband was very flattering for her.

All that before that terrible night. It was one day after her 32th birthday when that horrible accident changed her life forever . Their son, Eric, was only 10 years old when it happened and Alison had to struggle a lot to raise him all alone. She did well, now at 17 Eric was a handsome young man, excellent student and very polite. She knew she was a good mother to him and this made her happy despite her sacrifices.

Walking into the shower Alison couldn't stop but wondering if she made a mistake by ending the romance with Jake. Eric was always telling her that she deserves someone in her life and she knew that she needed to feel a man's touch again. While the water was slowly touching her beautiful skin, Alison pictured in her mind how this night could have gone if she had invited Jake in instead of sending him away. Her hand moved slowly on her breasts and she started caressing her hard nipples while thinking of Jake. She had never touched herself thinking of someone else other than her husband but now the sensation was taking over. The water combined with the warm feelings of her lust was too much for her and she was ready to give in to her naughty thoughts about another man. Her hand was moving lower and lower , she could now feel the warmth between her legs and that's when she heard Eric's voice out of the door, calling her.

"Mom, are you ok? You are home early."

Alison answered fast, blushing as if someone had caught her.

"Oh...Yes honey, I'm fine, Jake had to work early so he had to go. I am just taking a shower".

The tone of her voice was sweet as always when she was talking to her son, but the truth is that she was full of frustration and maybe a little bit of anger, being interrupted in that moment of enthusiasm. She couldn't concentrate again now, so she just finished her shower, disappointed but determined to finish what she started after her son went to sleep.

It didn't take long, Eric had a test in the morning so he went to bed earlier than usual.

Alison knew that her body was in need of an orgasm and for the first time in 7 years she felt that her mind was free to think of another man. Wearing her nightgown , which embraced her stunning curves perfectly, she layed in her bed and immediately started touching herself again. She took her nightgown off and needed no time at all to get where she was before, her body was so hot that she knew this wouldn't take long. Thinking that the hands touching her were Jake's hands , she started playing with her soft naked breasts and slowly moved down to remove her underwear. She couldn't even wait to take them completely off , she needed to feel her fingers, Jake's fingers inside her and that's what she did. Moving her middle finger slowly inside her warm pussy sent shivers through her whole body, this night would be different for her and she knew it. She started fucking herself faster and faster, with one, then two and then 3 fingers. Her soft sighs gave their place to wild moans of pleasure that she couldn't contain at all.

Eric woke up from the unusual sounds and got off the bed to see what was happening. Alison was losing control more and more by the second so her moans were very clear to Eric as soon as he opened his bedroom door. His mom was moaning with pleasure! It was the first time ever that he heard that noise coming from her bedroom. He was too young to have heard his parents having sex in the past and Alison was always very careful and masturbated silently in the rare occasions that she would think of her husband and their nights together.

But tonight was different. It was all about her, she needed this and her mind had blocked any other thoughts, even the thought of being heard by her loving son.

Eric took a few steps towards his mother's bedroom but he was hesitant. He didn't know how to react. His mom was pleasuring herself and although he knew he just had to go back to bed and try to sleep, he couldn't fight the urge to move closer. And that's what he did! With silent steps he reached his mother's bedroom and a gentle push was more than enough to slightly open her door and give him a glimpse of what would change his life forever.

Alison was fucking herself with her fingers while her other hand was rubbing her clit with great intense. Eric was speechless! He couldn't believe that his mother was so gorgeous . Her naked body was hotter than anything he had ever seen. Eric had seen naked girls before, he was a handsome boy and had a couple of relationships with some beautiful teenage girls, but Alison was a stunning woman that could put any young girl's body to shame.

Eric's heart was pounding strong and he felt his cock swelling immediately. He couldn't believe it, watching his precious mom masturbating was driving him insane . He wanted to go back but the sight was too intriguing . After a couple of minutes staring at his mother's body and watching her hands pleasuring herself, Eric concentrated on his mom's face. It was almost completely red, her eyes were closed and her mouth open and he could tell by her expressions that her orgasm was very close.

He couldn't help it anymore. He took his rock hard penis out and started stroking it like crazy, trying to catch his mother's orgasm. He was so excited that he knew it would be seconds before he came and although he wanted to wait for his mother to cum first, he knew it was too late now.

He felt his cock throbbing and he closed his eyes waiting for the first spurt of cum to come out.. but then his eyes opened wide again as soon as he heard a huge scream coming out of his mother's mouth. Alison exploded like a volcano and she took her pillow in one hand , placing it over her face trying to reduce her screaming sounds . Eric felt a moan of his own escaping from his mouth while he was cumming and he froze still for a moment, fearing that his mom could have heard him.

But Alison couldn't have heard him, she was only concentrating on one thing, enjoying these rare moments of pleasure as much as possible. When her body finally stopped trembling , Eric looked down and saw that the floor was drenched in his thick cum, thicker than ever before. He came so much, he couldn't believe it!

He got nervous and immediately went in the bathroom to take a towel and got back to sweep it before his mom got up and caught him. This would embarrass him forever! He cleaned it fast and took a final look at his sexy mother, now breathing heavily with a small grin of satisfaction on her face. He locked this image in his head and then walked silently back to his room. He had a test in the morning and as hard as it would be after what he had just witnessed, he knew that he had to go to sleep .

Alison was still in her bed exhausted ,almost unable to get up and completely unaware that her own son was cumming for her just a few minutes ago! She just had one of the greatest orgasms in her life, and it happened while she was thinking that another man was fucking her. The guilt was starting to fill her mind again, but she decided that the pleasure that she felt was too big to cause her such thoughts. Alison decided that there was no need to feel any doubts or remorse, her thoughts were her own and she could do whatever she wanted with them. She eased her mind enough and closed her eyes to rest from a very complicated day.

The next couple of days were a nightmare for Eric. Everytime he looked at his mother his mind went back to that sinful night . He couldn't take it out of his mind and masturbating again and again was the only way to deal with this. He knew it was wrong, so wrong but he had to do it. After 3-4 days he slowly started to finally get over it and was very positive that things would soon be back to normal for him.

CHAPTER 2

It was Alison's birthday today. 39 years old, still looking young and very beautiful, but these last years had been so hard for her that Alison felt that she was much older than she really was. And those last 7 years her birthday was always a very sad day for her and Eric, it was one day before the sudden loss of their husband and father. Alison was determined to do something different this time, so she arranged to go out with some of her friends. It was Friday so they wouldn't have to worry about waking up for work the next morning, they could stay out all night long and have a girl's night like they used to do when they were younger.

Eric was also happy with that decision, he knew his mother needed to have some fun and also he always enjoyed staying at home alone. His mom wasn't a control freak but once in a while he needed some alone time. Eric would usually go out at a Friday night but he decided to stay home and take advantage of his freedom. So tonight for him it was pizza, a movie or two and video games.

It was past 2 am when Alison got back from her night out, a little tipsy and very happy. She had a great time and she flirted a lot , like she used to do with her friends when they were younger and single. Her mood was very positive tonight and she wanted to make it even better. She decided to take a quick shower and then go to her bed to pleasure herself once more. This would be a perfect ending for her best birthday in years!

Eric had just finished his video gaming when his mother returned and he was about to sleep when he heard the shower running. Something in his mind told him to stay awake and as soon as Alison finished her shower and went to her bedroom, he decided to go out and take a look.

"I'll just go and see if she is ok" he said to himself, knowing deep inside that what he wanted was to catch his mom naked and pleasuring herself again.

And that's exactly what happened! Alison was already fully naked, her towel thrown on the side of the bed and she was touching herself again. This time it was different, slow and sensual. Eric went hard immediately and didn't think twice, he took his boxers off and his cock out and started stroking it slowly. His mother , his beautiful full of sexual desire mother was right in front of his eyes again, naked and touching herself. He wouldn't let the opportunity get away!

Alison was taking her time, enjoying every second. She was 39 now but after this night and the encouragement of her friends, she was more optimistic about her future. Her son wasn't a child anymore so maybe it was time for her to live her life again, find another man and enjoy love.

Those thoughts were making her so wet, she was moaning as she was slowly rubbing her already swollen clit. Eric could see her pussy lips shining, a sign that she was already very wet and horny. What a beautiful sight, they looked so inviting and he couldn't help but thinking about how warm and tight it would be inside of his mother. His own mother but he didn't care at the moment! There was a gorgeous woman in front of him masturbating, this was all that mattered.

Al of a sudden Alison freezed! Her hands stopped moving, her face lost the expression of pleasure and happiness and she stayed there without moving , looking at the ceiling. Her mind had betrayed her once again! It was already past midnight, one day after her birthday.

She started thinking about her husband again, the awful moments that she spent that night 7 years ago, the anxiety at the hospital... everything went black. She bursted into tears . How could she ever forget? This was the incident that destroyed her happy life, how could she ever get over it??

Eric knew what she was thinking. It was his time now to feel the guilt. He was masturbating for his own mother that raised him with so much love and care. And she was now crying over his dead father . Could he be more insensitive? He knew now that his mother needed him so he put his boxers up again , went back to his room and pretended that he just woke up.

"Mom!", he asked from the distance of his open door " Are you ok? Are you crying?"

Alison was taken by surprise, was she really crying that loudly? She immediately wore her nightgown , cleared her throat and answered to him.

"It's ok, honey! I'm ok I just drunk a little too much . Don't worry about it, go back to sleep, ok?".

Eric moved closer, hoping that his mom had enough time to put some clothes on. He didn't want to embarrass her , that was the last thing that he wanted. Alison didn't have time to put any underwear on but her night dress was covering her nakedness just fine.

"Mom", Eric said walking into her room " What's going on? Are you thinking about dad again?"

Alison tried to remain calm but only the mention of her husband was enough to bring tears to her eyes again.

"Sorry honey, it's just that this day.. you know?". Her voice was trembling , she couldn't even talk about it.

"It's ok mom, come here".

Eric sat on the bed and gave his mother a much needed hug.

"You have me mom, never worry about it again".

Alison immediately felt relieved, their mom-son moments had always been very strong after the loss of her husband.

"You are the one that kept me sane all these years Eric", Alison said to him" I love you so much you are becoming such a good man and I am so proud of you".

Eric felt proud of himself too. "Mom, you made me everything I am, I owe everything to you. You are the strongest woman I know and you are a hero to me!".

Alison was so happy to hear this that she pulled him near her again and held him in her arms with all of her strength.

"Oh, Eric", she whispered still with tears in her eyes but now from the nice words that her son said to her.

Eric could feel her breasts pushing on his chest, but what really excited him was his mother's smell of soap from the shower and sweet sweat from her wetness and he immediately went hard again. He felt ashamed and he was afraid that his mom would notice but Alison was lost in the moment. She loved her son so much and this was the exact time she realized that he is a man now, her job raising him was done. This was her top moment as a mother. She had succeeded.

But Eric was struggling with his own feelings now. His heart was pounding so fast, his mother's hug was so strong that their bodies had become one and he could feel her warm naked skin through her dress. He didn't even realise, his hand went subconsciously on his mother's thigh and touched her gently. Alison didn't mind, she took it as a sign of affection and just kept pulling him closer, talking to him in her soft voice.

" Look at you, you are so handsome, you remind me of your father", she said it with so much passion.

Eric loved what he just heard, he knew that she loved his dad so much so telling him that he looked like him was a great compliment !

"I love you Eric", Alison said, kissing him with affection on the cheek.

Eric was now moving his hand up and down on Alison's thigh, feeling her soft skin and moving it higher and higher every time. He started to feel the hotness that was coming from between her legs and he got so excited. His mother's mind was completely empty of sexual thoughts at that time but her body was still so hot and horny, Eric could feel it now.

This drove him crazy once again and his cock got harder than ever.

For the first time, Alison now felt her son's cock through his boxer shorts, rock hard as it was, touching her leg. She was left speechless for a moment. Did her son just get an erection by being that close to her? This was the time that she realized that her body was still so eager to feel a touch of pleasure ! Could Eric sense that? Is that what got him that hard?

She was so confused, but she decided not to break the hug just yet because Eric would be embarrassed knowing that she did it because of his hard on.

"Oh my God, he is so hard. I can feel his penis on me".

Alison was surprised of how hard he was. She hadn't been near a hard dick for so many years, the sensation was overwhelming. For a moment she wished that it was a complete stranger next to her and not her loving son.

"What a sinful thought", she said to herself and tried to take it out of her mind.

Eric had no idea what was going on in his mother's mind but he knew what was going on in his mind. He wanted to feel her mother's pussy on his hands, now all he could think of was the sight of her pussy lips while she was about to masturbate a few minutes before. And that's when he realized his mom's lack of reaction and thought to himself.

"Why is she not moving ? She can certainly feel my hard on now, could she maybe enjoy it? "

The thought of it was more than enough to confuse his mind. He wasn't thinking as a son now but as a man. And as a man , he decided to make his next move.

He moved his hand with speed and determination under her dress and touched her between her legs. The soft feeling of her well trimmed pubic hair and her wetness sent shivers through his body.

He knew what he just did was way over the line but the feeling was amazing, he knew it was worth it. Even if his mom slapped him, he would have something to masturbate to for many days to come!

Alison was indeed shocked but she didn't slap him. She immediately pulled away and looked deep in his eyes without knowing what to say. Her son just touched her pussy! Her precious boy did this? She couldn't believe it! Her mind was empty of thoughts so her mouth was empty of words as well.

"M..mmom...". Eric blushed and was so embarrassed.

" I am so sorry. I don't know what happened". Eric knew he messed up. He had to find a very good excuse.

"I... I don't know...I wasn't thinking at all. I am..."

Alison interrupted him but what came out of her mouth was totally unexpected

"It's ok Eric. It was only a moment of weakness, right? Didn't mean anything?"

Eric was surprised. She didn't yell at him at all! Why was that?

" Y..yes mom. I don't know what happened. I am so sorry it will never happen again. I promise it w.."

Alison interrupted him again

"Ssshhh, honey. Just forget it, you got carried away that's all right? Being close to a woman just reminded you one of those girlfriends you had is that it? But I am old , I shouldn't remind you at all of a beautiful girl right?"

What did Alison just say? She couldn't believe it herself! Instead of yelling at him she is trying to find excuses for him and also she is asking questions that she hopes will give her back a compliment?

"... yes mom.. Probably, I was thinking about another girl. But Mom, don't ever say it again". Eric said, falling into his mother's trap.

Alison knew that she was about to hear what she wanted

"Say what honey? " She asked eagerly, waiting for the answer that she expected.

"Mom, no girl could ever be as beautiful as you are, you are a stunning woman. And you are young and beautiful Mom, I wish my wife will look half as good as you when she is 39!" Eric said it and meant every word of it. She was that beautiful!

Alison got excited and smiled ! That's what she wanted to hear! She was being selfish at the moment but she needed this, a young man saying these words to her. What a huge confidence boost! After getting what she wanted, she decided to calm things down a little bit.

"Ok hun, but you need to understand, this can never happen again. There are so many women that would want you , you are a hot boy and you can get what you want from every woman! But not your mother , do you understand?" .

Her words were a little preachy but her voice was still so soft . She surprised herself again. She enjoyed it that much that she couldn't get mad at him, not even tell him that he did wrong!

Alison decided to end this awkward moment with another hug, to show Eric that all was good. Eric didn't even move this time, he was afraid to do anything. Alison kissed him on the cheek again and told him to go to sleep.

After Eric left , Alison let out a deep sigh and went to the bathroom to throw some water on her face. What an intense moment! Looking at the mirror she felt more beautiful than ever. A 17 year old boy just praised her so much, she felt wanted like she used to until a few years back. She was happy again and started to walk back to her room.

While she was getting past Eric's bedroom she decided to take a last look to see if he is ok with what happened. She opened the door and that's when she was shocked once again!

Eric was naked , had his big hard cock in his hand and was masturbating ! He thought that his mother was already asleep and went on to release himself from all the tension that took place that night.

Seeing his mother at the door he froze ! What a shame!

Alison didn't know how to react! In the end she didn't say anything, she just ran to her room and closed the door.

"Oh no what did I do? Was my own son masturbating for me? Is this my fault? Oh my god what kind of a mother am i?".

"And he was so big. Did he get that hard for me? He thinks I am sexy?"

Once again, Alison's mind was filled with complex feelings! Flatter and guilt!

"My own son... my own son". she kept repeating in her mind. She was trying hard to tell to herself how wrong this was but every time she said it her excitement grew stronger.

"Snap out of it Alison... Your own son!!".She couldn't convince herself anymore. She was getting horny!

She decided to let Eric calm down and they would talk in the morning. But her thoughts were still troubled. As it happened a couple of weeks ago while thinking of Jake, she decided once again that her thoughts are her own. She can think of anything she wants, as long as she keeps it to herself!

Her body was filled with erotic tension and she knew she had to take care of it. Before even finishing her thoughts she got naked and her fingers were deep in her pussy, her muscles pulsating and pulling them deeper and deeper with every move.

"Oh my God Eric", she couldn't get her son's cock out of her mind.

She was troubled but she decided it was too late to go back and she let herself go. She had just seen her son stroking his big dick for her and she would cum for that!

Eric , embarrassed like never before had pulled himself together and decided to go and apologize. For one more time he reached out of his mother's door and that's when he heard the familiar sounds of his mother's sweet moans!

This time his heart wasn't pounding like crazy. The shock was so big for him that it almost stopped pounding at all! His mother was masturbating 5 minutes after seeing him play with his cock for her!

"She liked it? My god, did mom enjoy seeing me masturbate? ". His 17-year old mind went completely crazy.

"I have to dare this! ". He didn't mind at all anymore, it was time to show courage without any doubts.

He opened the door and entered the room.

"Mom!!".

Alison lost it once again. How did this happen? Now she was the embarrassed one, she was left speechless.

" I wish I would die right now". Alison thought in despair .

How could she explain this? How could she convince her son that this is not what it seems?

Before she had time to think of anything, Eric was next to her. He sat down, staring at her mother's frozen eyes and put his hand on her thigh again, like he did earlier.

"ERIC!What the h...? " Alison couldn't finish her sentence when Eric's hand was on her pussy again!

She gasped, the unexpected touch was so pleasant that she didn't react immediately. Half a minute had passed and she managed to say some words.

"Eric, wha... why? What ...? Eri... noo.. Eric, stop!". The only word that came clear from her mouth was "stop" but that was the only word that she didn't want to say.

"You stop Mom, let me touch you. You were touching yourself for me, now let me do it ! You want this". Eric was so determined, his voice was steady. He was in charge now.

"But.. Eric.... No, it ...is .... so... I'm your mom, Eric!!". Alison kept saying no but all this time Eric's hand was gently touching her pussy , making it harder and harder for her to hide her excitement.

She was dripping wet now, Eric could feel her juices flowing down his hand and knew he was so close to getting what he wanted. How could she resist now?

"Eric, nooo, Eric stop! Erriiiccc..".

Alison's voice was getting so soft and deep, she couldn't struggle anymore. She knew she had to stop this right now or else she would cross the line with her own son.

"Mom, I love you. I want you happy, so let me take care of you!".

Eric's words made her feel so safe, she couldn't fight it anymore. She had to give in .

She didn't say a word, she just opened her legs more and arched her body back, showing her son that she was his now. Her mind was still saying no but her body had a mind of its own. She needed this and she would let it happen!

"Please forgive me Eric …Please forgive me..Oh god, it feels so nice.."

Her words made Eric even more confident and he knew his mother was melting under his touch.

He drove two fingers inside her tight pussy and went as deep as he could. Alison moaned with excitement, first time in 7 years that someone else is playing with her pussy. She couldn't think anymore, it wasn't her son it was just a man being there for her pleasure.

"Oh yeeeeess…ERIC, YEEES" That was it! Now Eric had her complete approvement and he wouldn't stop.

He kept fucking her pussy with his fingers, getting more and more excited by her loud moans. He started kissing her under the neck , driving her crazy. Alison was lost, she couldn't believe the feelings she was getting from her own son! Eric knew what to do, he started kissing her breasts and took her nipple in his mouth. Alison was now screaming with ecstasy, getting closer and closer to cumming for her son! She couldn't believe it !

" Eric, oh Eric, yes, honey, suck my nipple, make me cum, I am yours baby! Oh yeesss…". Alison's words were encouraging Eric once again and he kept sucking her nipple harder and harder while his fingers were moving furiously in and out of his mother's delicious pussy.

He was determined to go down and taste his mom's womanhood when suddenly Alison screamed , pulled his face to hers and kissed him deep while her body was starting to tremble.

With their lips locked firmly ,Alison was moaning with pleasure while her orgasm was taking over every inch of her shaking body. Eric could feel her pussy tightening more and more as she was cumming hard, and her juices were dripping all over his hand now! His mom was cumming on his hand, he couldn't believe it!

Eric was going crazy but he knew he had to control himself and surely he could get his reward!

With a last loud moan Alison exploded hard without taking her lips of her son's. What an orgasm she just had!

She was still kissing her son , softly this time trying to catch her breath at the same time.

"Oh God forgive me, what did I do?" She thought, guilty again...

She broke the kiss suddenly and looked into her son's eyes.

"What did we do? Eric?" She felt so satisfied but once again ,the end of her orgasm brought all of her guilt to the surface! She felt so bad!

Eric saw the concern but he knew he had to encourage her some more.

"Mom, that was amazing, I love you!".

But Alison felt differently now, her body was starting to relax and now she was seeing the truth. Her son just gave her an orgasm!

"Mom?" Eric was concerned seeing his mother 's beautiful face getting dark from sadness.

"Honey, go away! Oh god Eric, this was so wrong! Please go away and forget this!"

Alison sounded a little angry now, more with herself than with Eric. But Eric got angry too!

"Mom, please! You are playing me! You got what you wanted and now you throw me away? That's not fair!" He needed the attention and he demanded it.

"Mom, what about me?" He asked.

Alison got angrier now. Her own son was demanding from her to make him cum?

"Eric, go to your room. NOW! What happened was wrong and you know it! We will never talk about it again, you understand? Never! Go now and forget it ever happened. I was drunk and you took advantage of me!".

Alison was sounding furious now!

" What? Mom are you seriously blaming me for what happened? How can you say this ? You weren't drunk, you wanted this you were teasing me all night! And took advantage of me, you had your pleasure and now you are yelling at me!".

With those words Eric left running from his mom's room and slammed the door behind him!

Alison was left alone, unable to think clearly or find some good explanation. She was the one that was right, she knew she was right. Her own son took advantage of her! How could he? ...Or maybe he didn't... Was it really her that started everything? Was Eric right? Alison was so confused. But it didn't really matter who started it. Eric was right in one thing. She took what she wanted but he was left with a huge hard on. What could she do? It's her son, she can't make him sad.

"Hmmm. Maybe a quick handjob will make things right? He needs to cum, he is a man. I remember his father when he needed to cum, there was nothing more important".

Alison was whispering to herself. Was it really the right thing to do? She didn't want to torture her son. She had to make him feel nice. It didn't take any more thinking, she decided to help him finish. This was the right thing to do.

She put on her dress and went to his door. She knocked first.

"Hun? Eric?" She was nervous , what would he say? Was he really that angry?

Eric was indeed very angry and didn't want to talk to his mom right now.

"Eric, open honey, we need to talk, maybe you are right".

This brightened Eric's face again! What did she mean, would she be willing to take care of him as well?

'Mom, come in i haven't locked". He answered , very curious to see what she would have to say.

Alison opened the door slowly, still hesitant about what she would do next. Eric was on his bed , wearing only his boxer shorts.

"E..Eric...Honey, I was too cruel with you before".

Alison's voice showed her weakness. Eric could see that she came to his room to make things right for him and decided to take advantage of it.

"Mom, it's ok. I understand. It is strange for both of us but I deserve your attention too. I feel stupid for what I did and it feels like you are just using me."

Eric wasn't believing a word he was saying, he just wanted to make his mom guilty enough to forget her insecurities.

"Eric, no , honey, I would never do that! It's just, what we did was wrong and going even further would make it even worse. But I know it wasn't fair so maybe..." Alison was hesitating.

"Maybe what mom?" Eric was enjoying it, his mom was the one acting like a young girl and he was the man!

'Maybe I could...?"

Alison didn't want to say it. Was it too late to go back ? Eric made sure of it. He took of his boxers fast...

"Mom, come here". Eric pulled his mother on him and took her hand and placed it over his already hard cock.

"Oh my god, Eric... a... are you sure honey?". Alison knew the answer.

"Mom, I am sure... just do it. I want it and you want it.. Touch my cock !".

Eric was sounding more and more like his dad now and Alison was getting excited again. Her hand was on her son's big and hard cock and she wanted it more than anything. She took it in her hand and couldn't believe how hard it was. She knew what to do, she started stroking it gently and slowly like her husband always wanted her handjobs. Eric seemed to respond to that gentle touch too, he closed his eyes and looked to be in his own heaven.

"I can't believe it. My own mother is stroking my cock, this feels too good to be true". He thought, filled with enjoyment .

"Is this ok baby? " Alison asked caringly, knowing ofcourse that Eric was enjoying it a lot.

"Oh mom, it is the best feeling ever! I love it, keep jerking me off like that, make me cum!".

Alison kept stroking , focused and determined to pleasure her son and redeem herself for her selfishness. As she was moving her hand faster and faster, Eric was getting so horny that he already felt too close to cumming.

"Mom...mom stop for a while, I don't want to cum yet!".

Alison was confused, wasn't this what he wanted? What did he have in mind? Had she maybe lost her touch after all of these years?

"Honey, what is it? Am I doing something wrong? Please tell me, I promised to take care of you, tell me how to do it." Alison asked , worried that she wasn't doing a good job.

"Mom, it's nice i am enjoying it but I can't cum like this. I want something more". Eric didn't lose any time at all, he wanted more and decided to play for it.

"More? Eric, what do you mean more? I said I will help you cum and that's what I am doing, what else do you want me to do?"

Eric's new demands scared her but also excited her. What did he want?

"Mom, you are so gorgeous, I want you to use your mouth. Please suck my cock, please mom it will make me cum so fast! ".

Eric went for it, he knew his mom was getting wet again and wanted to try his luck. The thought of his mother's mouth pleasuring his big cock seemed like paradise to him. Most men would kill to get a blowjob from such a woman and now he had his own chances! He wouldn't miss it !

Alison wasn't willing to get this far though. Jerking him off was already too much of a sin, taking her own son's cock in her mouth would be way, way over the line.

"Honey, please don't go there, It will not happen.. What we are doing now is already too bad, please don't ask me again ok? It won't happen. Just enjoy the handjob baby, I like giving it to you. Relax and I will make you cum Eric, I promise".

"Oh...Ok, mom, keep doing what you do it feels nice." Eric said, disappointed that his mom took a blowjob out of the question without a single thought. But getting a handjob from her was still awesome so he concentrated on that.

While Alison was stroking his cock , she kept thinking about what Eric asked. Her husband loved her blowjobs , she knew how to please him well and always enjoyed the power that she had over him when his cock was in her mouth. Thinking back about these moments was making her even more wet, she could feel her wet pussy soaking her thighs again.

Eric was breathing heavier now, laying back with his eyes closed as his mom was speeding up her handjob , trying to make him cum. She knew that he was close, she hadn't touched a cock for so long but her son's reactions were very clear, he was a couple of strokes away.

"You are so beautiful mom, you are so sweet to me, oh please don't stop I am cumming. I love you mom!".

Eric was whispering while he was about to cum and Alison once again felt extremely proud because of the words that she was hearing.

"What a lovely boy" she thought again.

She knew that he deserved more than that!

She stopped stroking him suddenly and that made him open his eyes and look at her with extreme frustration.

"Mom, no.. I am so close!". Eric started to protest but his mom had the control now.

"Sssshhhh...." That was all that Alison said .

She smiled at him and while still looking deep into his eyes she lowered her head and wrapped her wet lips around his hard cock. Eric went crazy.

"Aaaahhh! Mom...!"

That was it! Eric made it! He had his mother's mouth all over his young cock and he felt this was his personal triumph!

"Yeeeessss". Eric whispered with extreme satisfaction!

Alison felt his cock getting even harder in her luscious mouth. She let out a moan of pleasure, she had forgotten how amazing it was to have a dick so deep between her lips. She closed her eyes and just enjoyed her son's huge member filling all of her mouth, slowly moving her tongue up and down making sure that she is getting it wet and sloppy. She started caressing the tip of her son's cock with her tender tongue, knowing that this would drive Eric crazy.

"Aaaaah….".

Eric was feeling things that he never felt before. His mom's mouth was so warm and wet, he was the happiest man on earth! He moved his hand on Alison's long and silky hair and started pushing her head deeper and faster.

Alison always hated it when her husband did that, but not now. She loved it! "Mmmmmm…". she couldn't stop moaning softly every time her son pushed her deep making her feel his beautiful cock touching the back of her throat.

"Ooooh, mom!". Eric tightened his legs, feeling his orgasm closer than ever.

Alison was enjoying everything so much that she didn't realize that Eric couldn't hold back anymore. She heard a loud moan and then she felt a huge jet of cum splashing on the back of her throat!

"Oh my God, he is cumming in my mouth!" Alison couldn't believe it! As much as she loved sucking, very rarely she would let her husband cum in her mouth, she didn't enjoy it at all.

This was no exception, Alison immediately tried to take Eric's cock out of her mouth and she pulled her face away just fast enough to avoid getting the second splash of her son's love juice on it.

"Ohh, oooooh mom, I am cumming..! "

Eric was having the orgasm of his life. Big spurts of cum were coming out of his cock, flying everywhere uncontrollably. Alison could not believe the amount of sperm that her son was giving to her, she kept watching in awe while it was coming out and landing on her thighs , on Eric's legs and on the sheets.

When it was finally over, Eric looked at his mother, enjoying the sight of her beautiful face and eyes staring at him. Alison smiled seductively and then slightly opened her mouth letting the first amount of cum that Eric shot in it slowly drip down her lips and onto his cock again.

This was all too much for Eric, he took his mom in his hands and kissed her passionately!

Alison was surprised, her husband would never kiss her after she had sucked his cock, much less in those rare occasions that she had his cum in her mouth. She loved it !

Alison broke the kiss, looked into Eric's eyes and whispered.

"I love you son. This was my gift to you!". Before Eric had the chance to respond she got up fast and left for the bathroom with a smile on her face.

Eric was trying to catch his breath watching his mom slowly walking away and he knew he never felt more satisfied in his life.

This was better than he had ever dreamed of and he had a secret desire that this would just be the beginning of a beautiful story. Could his mom think the same, or was it just a moment of weakness for her?

Alison cleaned Eric's cum off her thighs and hands and looked up on the mirror again. Her face looked such a mess, her eyes had tears from all the sucking , her hair was scruffy and she still had small signs of cum on her chin. But her eyes were shining with happiness! She chose lust over logic and guilt, and it was the best decision she ever made...

Alison took a very fast shower to clean herself well but she kept wondering what was going on in her son's mind now. Did he sleep , was he happy , did he feel any guilt? ..

"Or maybe he is masturbating again, thinking about his mom". She said to herself and giggled like a school girl.

What a night! It was the hardest day of the year for her but she wouldn't think of her husband anymore. Her son was more important!

" The past is the past. The future is what matters". That's what her friend Sophie always said to her and for the first time Alison agreed with it.

Walking out of the shower Alison noticed that Eric had his bedroom lights out so she knew he was asleep.

"Well...Time to rest I guess!" Alison thought and headed back to her bedroom.

She turned on the lights and walked towards the bed.

" Hey , Mom!".

Eric's voice scared Alison and made her jump a little bit! Eric laughed.

"Eric...what! I thought you were sleeping and I w…. OH MY GOD! Why are you naked honey?" Alison gasped, looking at her son on her bed, completely naked and his cock rock hard again!

"Mom, come on, the night isn't over yet, is it?"

Eric was saying these words playfully but not as confident as he was before. He wasn't so sure about his mom's reactions now.

"Eric, are you crazy? We did what we did honey, isn't it enough? How come you are hard again? You are not satisfied yet? Is mommy making you that hard?".

Alison was answering in the same playful way, although her intentions were to flirt a little bit and then end the night.

"Mom, be serious, I really want to know how you feel about what happened!". Eric 's voice got serious again.

"What did it mean to you Mom?", he insisted to get an answer.

"Eric, we had a deal, I satisfied you as you satisfied me, that's all, the end! ".

Alison's words were like a dagger in Eric's heart. He didn't say anything but Alison could sense that. Even his cock was starting to get limp. She didn't want to make him sad again , but what was he thinking?

"Aw Eric, come on. What more do you want honey?" Alison asked again worryingly.

"You need to cum again? Is that it?"

Eric looked at his mom and nodded.

"Mom, I can't stop feeling horny, and look how hard I am again". Eric said in frustration.

Alison looked at his cock and it was again so hard. She couldn't believe it, it didn't take him more than a few seconds to get that big. How could she say no to that?

"Oh Eric, what more do you want? I just had a shower but if you want...". Alison stopped talking and looked at him. His eyes had widened so much. Alison didn't know what he expected to hear but her next sentence wasn't what he wanted.

" I will get naked and let you masturbate next to me, is that ok?"

'Oh... yes mom.. ok, thanks". Eric expected so much more, but well, better that than nothing.

Alison could feel his disappointment so she wanted to make him feel better.

"Oh honey, I already sucked you once, maybe I would do it again if I hadn't taken a shower but I don't want to get messy again".

'Mom, I won't grab your head this time, please. I will be gentle. And I will tell you before I cum ok?"

Eric was almost begging!

"Baby, no, let's control ourselves ok? " Alison asked her son to behave and Eric nodded again.

She dropped her towel and layed next to him fully naked.

"Wow, nice way to control yourself Alison", she thought to herself sarcastically. She knew what Eric wanted and she knew what she wanted. She wouldn't hold back this time!

"Play with it honey, does it make you hot that I am that close to you again?" Alison went playful again.

"Oh yes mom, so hot! But mom...." Eric wasn't happy. He wanted more again!

"You can touch me too ok?" Alison interrupted him again and let him touch her. Eric didn't want more encouragement, he groped her breasts squeezing hard.

"Heeey... easy!". Alison laughed to her son's roughness.

"Be soft honey. Take your time."

Eric followed her advice and caressed her slowly with one hand while the other was slowly stroking his dick.

Alison felt excited again.

"Yes, Eric, like that... Nice and slow... take your time."

Alison's voice was so sensual now, Eric loved that. He was getting his mother wet again!

She moved her face closer to her son's and Eric needed no instructions. He kissed her deep, his tongue swirling with his mother's like two crazy dancers in love .

The kiss they were sharing was so passionate that both of them were moaning and breathing heavily. Alison felt loved for the first time in 7 years.

"Eric, I love you".

"I love you too mom". Eric responded and looked at his mom again, before kissing her again with all of his passion.

"Mmmmm.. " Alison was loving this . Her desire for her son was too strong and she didn't want to wait anymore, she decided to cross the line for good!

"Baby... Take me! Do whatever you want with me!" Alison said with her most sensual voice.

Eric was stunned! Did his mother just say what he thinks she did? He broke the kiss, looked at her ..

"Mom?"

Alison had no doubts. She knew what she wanted. She wanted to feel love tonight and her son was giving it to her. She placed her mouth on Eric's ear and whispered passionately.

"Take me Eric! I am yours tonight. "

Eric was losing his mind. He was really waiting for a blowjob but he didn't expect his mom to go even further! His heart was pumping like crazy as he asked again.

"Mom, what do you mean? You want me to .."

Alison put her finger on his mouth before he finished his sentence and said seductively.

" I want you to take me. I want to feel you inside me. All of you".

It was clear that she had lost control. But she knew it and she loved it.

"Make love to me Eric! "

Finally! Eric had all he wanted now! He took her in his hands and kissed her with all of his strength. This was more than he could ever dream of. He felt like he just won the jackpot.

"I love you mom!" .

"I love you too baby!". Alison answered with motherly love.

She turned slowly and got on top of her son, kissing him, rubbing her sexy body on his and feeling his erection pressing against her.

The game was on, and there was no turning back. Two players, two winners! No inhibitions, no guilts, no worries. Just two lovers ready to live their extreme passion for the first time.

Alison looked into her son's lustful eyes and gave him a smile full of meaning as her hand moved slowly onto his big young penis and grabbed it strongly to guide it into her pussy's warm entrance.

Feeling his mom's pussy touching the tip of his cock Eric left out a moan and relaxed himself, getting ready for his dream to come true.

Alison didn't want to torture him or herself anymore, she moved her hips back and let herself sit down slowly, feeling the gorgeous cock of her son penetrating her dripping pussy.

For 7 years she hadn't felt a dick in her but as soon as she took Eric in, it felt like they belonged together. Her son's cock was right where it needed to be, inside her welcoming pussy. She moved a little bit up and down and then took a deep breath and sat herself all the way down to the base of Eric's huge throbbing erection.

"Aaaaahhhhhhhh..." Her moans were so full of pleasure, Alison knew right then that she needed this more than anything in the world!

"Oh, mom, this feels so good. I can't believe it is happening!". Eric was feeling like a kid in the playground, he was inside his mom's pussy and she was enjoying it so much. He felt proud!

Alison kissed him again, smiling at him to make him feel more comfortable in case he had any second thoughts about it. But there was no chance , Eric was all for it! The movement of his hips started to match Alison's hips and now she could feel him even further inside every time she moved her body down .

Once again, this was driving her insane.. Losing herself completely, Alison felt her orgasm getting closer and closer . She was about to cum, and 7 years after her husband's, it would nowbe her son's dick to bring her to a wonderful climax.

"Oh, Eric, like that, don't stop baby! Keep pushing like that! Fuck me Eric, fuck me! Fuck me hard". Alison was now riding her son's cock like an experienced cowboy riding a tireless bull.

" Fuck me hardeerrrr, please! Push your cock deep in your mom's pussy Eric, make me cum!".

Talking dirty like that made Eric so eager to give her what she wanted that he started pounding her as hard as he could going deeper and deeper and faster than he ever thought he could.

"Ahhh, Ahhhh BABY!FUCK ME! Oh my god it feels so good!!".

Alison once again surprised herself. She was never a fan of hard sex, she wanted it slow and passionate. But her son was pushing her boundaries and she was experiencing something completely new for her.

She couldn't hold it anymore, with big long screams she welcomed a powerful orgasm and sat down taking Eric's long hard cock as deep as she could, staying there still as her body spasms caused her whole body to tremble.

Eric was overwhelmed! He was staring at his mom's face, lost in her own world , as he felt her pussy on his cock shaking rhythmically while her endless orgasm took her over completely.

"Mom, are you ok?" Eric asked as his mom stopped moving and let out a big sigh of relief.

"I have never been better. This was.." She had no words. This was the best orgasm of her life and she couldn't find any words to describe it.

"I love you !" She tried to say again with a voice that barely came out, as she fell exhausted on Eric's chest, trying to catch her breath .

Her pussy was calming down but she could still feel Eric hard inside her. She knew it was his turn and now she wouldn't make him beg for it.

She kissed him and whispered to him.

" I want to suck you honey, I want to take the cock that made me scream like that in my mouth and make it cum. I will take it all in my mouth Eric, I'll do everything you want".

"Will you let me cum in your mouth mom?" Eric asked with anticipation.

Alison looked at him, smiled and nodded her head slowly.

She knew that he deserved it and she actually felt eager about it. She wanted to give Eric back all the pleasure she received from him and letting him cum in her mouth would be the best way to do it.

Eric couldn't wait to cum in his mother's mouth now. He was in a rush to cum so he took Alison's head in his hands and pushed her gently lower.

"Honey, we said no pushing!".

Alison pretended to scold Eric but her expression gave away that she didn't mean it . She just wanted to do it her way. She took Eric's hard erection out of her satisfied pussy and she could feel the wetness on her hand as she started stroking it very very slowly. She moved her mouth over the tip and just stood there looking at Eric's impatient face.

"Oh mom, you are driving me crazy. Suck me please, don't tease!" Eric couldn't wait , he needed this so bad.

Alison laughed but didn't want to prolong her son's agony anymore. She opened her mouth and took the head in. She could feel the hot juices of her pussy mixed with the sweat and the sticky precum of Eric's cock and she loved the taste of it. It was so naughty and she loved it! She started sucking slowly but deep , knowing that Eric wouldn't last long.

Eric also knew he would cum very fast so he opened his eyes to watch his mom's beautiful face while she was about to swallow his hot sperm. Alison had placed herself between Eric's legs and while she was moving her head up and down his long shaft, she was giving Eric a wonderful view of her perfectly shaped perky butt.

"My god, her ass is incredible like that". Eric was impressed by the sight of her butt and that gave him new plans.

"Mom, stop!!" Eric pulled away from his mother's mouth as he was too close now.

"Honey what happened why did you stop me?" Alison looked confused and sad. She had given all of herself to that blowjob , she really wanted to make him happy but he stopped her.

"Mom, please… I want to fuck you again… I want to fuck you doggy!" Eric wanted it too much.

"Please, will you let me mom?"

Alison really wanted to finish this blowjob but her son wanting to fuck her again made her flattered again.

" Doggy? Are you sure you want to look at your mother's old ass while you fuck me Eric?" She asked teasingly, knowing that this was the exact reason why Eric wanted to take her like that.

And she wanted it too, Eric's dick in her mouth, with the strange taste of their fluids mixed together made her horny again. She needed it!

"Mom, your ass is phenomenal, I will cum just by looking at it! You know it, stop teasing. You have the best ass I have ever seen you should be proud" Eric would say anything to fuck his mom again, but this time he meant it completely.

"Ok, baby… I said I am yours and I mean it. Fuck me honey but promise me, you will take it out before you cum. Promise me, that's important!"

Alison wanted it so bad now, but she wanted to make sure that Eric wouldn't cum in her.

"Honey you are already close, if you feel like cumming pull it out and I will take it in my mouth again ok? Don't cum in me no matter what!!" She was nervous to make this safe!

"Mom, I am not stupid! You didn't even have to tell me, ofcourse I will pull out! Come on!"

With Eric's words, Alison felt safe enough and got herself in all fours, waiting for her son to penetrate her again.

Eric pushed her head down softly, making her ass get even higher as he admired the view.

"Oh my God!" Eric was mesmerized , he could now see her whole womanhood in all its glory, her pussy lips open and wet with anticipation, her tight asshole and her soft butt cheeks moving slowly as she was waiting impatiently for his cock.

Eric didn't lose time, he moved closer and put his dick deep in his mom's pussy. Once again, they had become one. And while Eric was enjoying the glorious view, this new angle of the penetration was giving Alison new sensations and she was getting even hornier than before!

Eric felt his mother pushing back with every stroke and knew he would cum soon enough.

"Mom, I can't last anymore!"

Alison didn't like that, she was just starting to feel her own pleasure building but she didn't show it.

"Ok, love, take it out though, cum in my mouth as we said ok?"

"Mom..." Eric was about to ask something and Alison could feel it.

"What is it Eric?"

"Mom, I would prefer not to cum in your mouth. Can i....?" Eric was so hesitant that Alison feared for the worst and started yelling at him.

"ERIC, NO! You can't cum in me, you could make me pregnant are you stupid? We already said it, take it out now! I will nev..."

"MOM! Stop, I would never cum in your pussy..". Eric interrupted her.

"W...what then baby? " Alison found it weird, what did he want this time?

"Mom, can I maybe cum in your ass? It looks so beautiful I really want to put it in, just to cum mom, please!"

Alison felt a little shocked! In her ass? No, no way! Her husband had tried to convince her to try it a couple of times in the past but it never worked. She was never comfortable with it .

"How dare he ask me something like that? I am his mother not a stupid slut he met at a club!" Alison felt frustrated by this request, anal sex had always been a taboo for her and she knew she would never do it.

She didn't want to show how annoyed she got though so she answered to him calmly.

"Eric, baby, no, I don't like it. I never did it and I don't want to ok? It is very wrong. "

"Oh, mom, I am so sorry, I didn't mean to insult you it just looks too beautiful and thought..." Eric really felt bad, what was he thinking? Putting his dick in his mother's ass?

"Sorry, mom!"

Eric thought he messed up and ruined the moment again but Alison gave him his confidence back.

"Eric, it's ok honey, I am flattered that you like my butt but we won't do that ok? Just fuck my pussy baby and remember to pull out when you cum ok?"

'I promise mom, can I cum in your mouth then?" Eric didn't know if his mom was still up for it.

Alison laughed and looked at him .

"Ofcourse baby. Nothing's changed! Fuck me and cum in my mouth! That's what I want! Fuck me hard!"

Eric felt powerful again and started fucking his mom deep and hard. This small break was very helpful because his penis lost it's sensitivity and he knew that he would last much longer than he was going to before. Full of confidence he started pounding his mother hard and steady.

Alison wasn't ready for that , she thought that Eric would cum in less than a minute and this took her by her surprise. A very pleasant surprise no doubt! Her boy, her young stud was now fucking her like crazy and she loved every stroke of his big dick more and more.

"Fuck meeeeee. Fuck me Eric, yeees, fuck your mother hard like a slut!" Alison started talking dirty again. A sign for Eric that he was doing a great job!

Feeling even more comfortable than before, Eric pushed his mother to lie out flat on her stomach and got on top of her with his full weight.

Alison was surprised at first but she loved feeling her son's skin rubbing on hers. She opened her legs slightly to help him enter her more easily and that gave her a new surprise as her clit was rubbing on the sheets while Eric was pounding her pussy harder and harder from behind.

"Oh Eric, this is amazing. Keep fucking me like this, yes. Fuck my pussy, do it hard baby, make me scream!" Alison became vocal again, as Eric kept fucking her like crazy.

Once again, she would be the first to cum.

"Ooooh yes I am cumming Eric".

She didn't expect her orgasm to be that sudden but she wouldn't complain. Eric's deep thrusts and the sensation on her clit send her to sex heaven and back. She exploded again and again, as Eric wouldn't stop pounding her even while she was cumming for him.

"Keep fucking me Eric, don't you stop!"

'Oh, mom, I love your pussy! I love it when you cum, it feels so great inside you!"

It was the first time that Eric talked dirty to his mom. He was hesitant before because it was still his mother but now he couldn't help it.

Alison LOVED IT! Hearing her sweet son talking to her like that filled her with desire again and she knew that another orgasm would soon be on the way!

"Eric, you like fucking your mom honey ? You like my sweet pussy?"

"Mom, it is perfect, I love fucking you, I love tearing your pussy apart with my hard cock! Take it all slut!" Eric responded to his mom's invitations to talk dirty and this made him approach his own orgasm.

"Mom, I am so close , are you ready? Come take it in your mouth mom, take my cum!" Eric had a little bit more in him before he would cum but he wanted to make sure he would follow his mother's orders to pull out in time.

Alison didn't respond, she just kept moaning as Eric was fucking her ! She couldn't control her feelings anymore.

"MOM!" Eric shouted to bring her mind back from the pleasure world where she was travelling.

Alison turned her head and with an expression of total pleasure on her face she looked at him and said in her sweetest voice.

"Eric.... In my ass baby... In my ass!"

Eric lost it!

"What? Mom?"

"Sshhhhh.." Alison reassured him..

" Just put it in honey!. Take my ass, I want to give it to you. Take me in the ass my love!"

Alison was in a trance and she just wanted to give every inch of herself to her precious lover!

She didn't care about anything else right now! Her son wanted her ass and she would give it to him! She wanted to , didn't care if it would hurt

.

"I am yours and so is my ass baby. I am yours for tonight and forever"

Alison said those strong words and she meant them! She never gave her ass to her husband but she was about to do it for her son! She loved him more than anything and anyone ever before. Pleasuring him completely was her only goal at the moment.

Eric was still reluctant, sitting there without moving.

Seeing that, Alison put her hands on her soft buttcheeks and opened them wide to reveal her tight asshole to her son.

"PLeeaseeee… put it in my ass and cum in it baby!".

Eric didn't think twice! He spit on his cock to make it as wet as possible, placed it in the entrance of her warm butthole and slowly started pushing it in. She was so tight that he felt his dick would break from the pressure.

"Ooohhhh" Eric was moaning with pleasure, this was an extraordinary feeling!

Alison felt the first wave of pain filling her but she wouldn't stop now. Her son was enjoying this!

"Go on, fuck me. Fuck my ass" she said as Eric was slowly moving deeper and deeper.

"AAAaaahhhh, god,…Eric!". Her voice was cracking as the pain was too much for her.

"Mom, you want me to stop?Mom?" Eric was nervous, it felt amazing but he would never hurt his mom on purpose!

'Nooo… never… this is for you. I am doing this for you! Don't stop baby, I want it!" Alison felt uncomfortable but her mind was determined! She would take it all the way until Eric had his satisfaction.

Alison's words made Eric push even deeper and deeper and deeper. They were both moaning, Eric from immense pleasure, Alison from the pain. With one last deep and strong push Eric went all the way in.

This was too much for Alison! She sank her face in the pillow and let out a loud scream of pain as she felt the tears forming in her eyes.

"Eric" she said with her voice shaking " Please don't move honey!Don't move for a while!"

They both stood there still while Alison was trying to get used to the pain.

"Mom.. I'll stop ok? I will pull out, it is too much for you!" Eric felt extremely disappointed saying this, it felt amazing in her butt and cumming in her would be a dream but he had to stop.

"Nnnnooo.. no Eric honey.. It's getting better, just move really slow ok? Slow baby!"

Alison meant it. Her muscles were starting to relax and a weird sensation of pain mixed with intense pleasure was starting to overwhelm her.

" Aaahhh.." Alison screamed again as Eric went in and out carefully. It was still very painful but she could take it. She knew she could!

"Mom, I am getting close".

Eric couldn't take anymore of this. His mother's anal muscles were crushing his penis between them and her moans were too much for him. He would cum so soon, with no breaks this time.

Alison wanted this to end but with as much pleasure as possible for Eric so she started talking dirty again.

"Fuck me Eric, fuck your mother in her tight ass... Put your cock deep in me , I want to feel it!"

His sweet mom's naughty words drove Eric crazy and he started fucking her hard now as he reached his orgasm.

"God it hurts so much, what did I put myself into?! " Alison felt some regret as her son was now fucking her a little harder but then she felt him go deep again and stay there.

"Aaaaahhhhhhhhhhhh.i'm cuuumminngggggg!". Eric screamed as his orgasm hit him like a hurricane. Spurt after spurt after spurt of hot sticky sperm flooded Alison's anus as Eric couldn't control himself. His whole body was shaking, pushing his dick even further into his mom's ass.

He was so deep that Alison could feel his balls hitting the entrance of her butt while they were pumping her inside with huge amounts of warm cum. The feeling was incredible, all this cum made her feel like the dirtiest slut in the world. And she loved it! She loved it because she knew this moment made her son happier than ever and that's all that mattered to her.

Eric collapsed on her with his cock still in her ass . Alison could feel it getting softer and softer. The warm cum was easing her pain and her ass wasn't feeling that bad now.

"God I feel so relieved. ..almost ... satisfied."

Almost? She did something extreme for her personality and it was totally worth it!

She enjoyed it and she knew it!

"Mom, I can't believe you did this for me! I love you so much!" Eric found his breath and immediately wanted to thank his mother.

"You enjoyed it hun? I hope you did!" Alison asked in her serious voice, wanting to let Eric know that this was a big sacrifice for her.

"Mom, are you joking, this was perfect beyond my imagination. I will do anything to thank you mom, anything, I will even clean my room by myself" Eric joked but this was the least he would do. His mother gave him the perfect gift, he would really do ANYTHING for her now.

"Eric, I did it for you, I don't want anything in return. Seeing you that happy made me happy! Just don't get used to it!"

With that, Alison pushed Eric away tenderly and got off the bed. She could feel the cum running down her legs now. It was too much for her ass to hold! She put her hand on her asshole to stop it.

"What a mess Eric! " Alison said with her strict voice and looked at her son.

They both laughed knowing that this mess was too small of a price to pay for such a wonderful evening.

Alison headed to the bathroom but stopped before leaving the room and turned around.

"Are you coming lover?" She asked in her sweet girly voice!

Eric got next to her, kissed her gently on the lips and then lifted her in his arms to carry her in the bathroom.

The night had ended but their life had just started.

Me, my sexy sister and the shower

The shower door burst open and I felt a playful slap on my bare butt. I yelled out, but more for effect than anything else. I would never let on, but I was thrilled to death.

"Move over Shrimp." My Sister said slapping my ass again smartly. I turned and grabbed her. My body was wet and soapy and we wrestled playfully, gloriously naked, mock fighting, growling and moaning as we turned, pushing and pulling under the water. She became wet quickly and her body slid against mine, wonderfully slick. We wrestled and moved against each other. I loved the feel of her slick skin against mine. I pressed hard against her, my pussy pushing against her hard muscled thigh. I wanted to hump it!

I was very conscious of her two breasts pressing against my face. I'm two years younger than she is, and as I bent forward wrestling with her, her young firm breasts were almost even with my face.

"Get your huge tits out of my face. You Big Fat Cow!" I yelled out. This had the desired effect - for me! She rubbed her sexy breasts hard against my face, pushing them firmly against me. I turned and my lips were against her erect nipples. I pressed my face against them again and again as I turned my face in mock horror, but in truth I loved it.

I really wanted to suck on them. My breasts hadn't fully developed yet and I loved the look and feel of hers. I just wished I could suck them for even a short moment. Her soft slick flesh pressed against my face and her nipples mashed against my lips. I turned back and forth like I was fighting her, but I really loved every second of it. Her erect nipples raked my face, my lips. God, I was in heaven.

With her superior weight and strength, she turned me around, took my arm pulling it back and upward in a hammerlock, while she held me close against her. She had me! My arm hurt and I quickly yelled "Uncle! Uncle! You're hurting me!"

"Say you're sorry!" She growled.

"I'm sorry." I repeated, giggling.

"Say you're sorry you called me a Big Fat Cow!" She giggled too, easing up on my arm twisted up behind me. I could feel her stomach muscles jump against my back as she giggled.

"I'm sorry I called you a Big Fat Cow, you Big Fat Cow!" I laughed back. She released me, hugged me to her and slapped my butt several times, stinging slaps, but her delicious breasts against my face made it all worthwhile. We laughed and giggled, hugging each other under the shower. God I loved her!

She released me and I went back to soaping my body. She took the soap from my hand and began to lather her body. 'Fat cow' - there was not an ounce of fat on her, or on me for that matter. She was tall and muscular from the gymnastics she did. Her muscles rippled under her skin, her body was well formed from all the exercises she did. I looked at her body with the pride of a sister who loves her big Sister to distraction. My body is smaller, slender and has the long muscles of a competitive swimmer, my specialty.

My breasts were smaller than hers. I hoped when I filled out fully, they would be as large as hers, or even better, as large as Mom's beautiful full rounded breasts. I'd seen Mom's full low-slung breasts many times; we were never shy around each other when we were naked. I had stared at hers and loved the full globes of her breasts with the huge brown areolas that were almost as large as the palm of my hand. When she was cold, her nipples would stand out at least a half-inch or more. I would salivate thinking I had sucked on them.

Mom would catch me looking at her breasts, and didn't seem to mind. She would sometimes turn a little toward me and thrust them out as if she was very proud of them. I would be too if I had beautiful full breasts like hers. Her motto was "If you've got them, flaunt them!" I'd sneak peeks at her pussy too, covering by her lovely brown fine, neatly trimmed curly hair.

As we washed I stared at Sis's breasts. They were nice and pear shaped and she has, what she said her boyfriend Ronnie called "puffy nipples." The areolas – she taught me that term – were almost three fingers wide, and bulged like swollen bee stings. I wondered if they would stretch as large as Mom's when she had children. The nipples were long and prominent like Mom's too, and so hard! I felt a stirring as I remembered them against my face, my lips, all too fleetingly. I hoped mine would look as sexy when I grew up.

She reached down and soaped her pussy. I loved that term "pussy." Her pussy hair was a lovely brown, trimmed neatly in an inverted triangle, and the lather swirled around in it as she washed herself. She looked down and saw me watching her.

"Have you washed your pussy?" She asked looking into my eyes.

I had several times, but lied innocently, with a straight face. "No, not yet"

"Ok, wash it like I showed you." She nodded toward my sparser pussy hair.

My heart jumped. I was going to do it in front of her. "Show me again how you do yours and I'll do mine at the same time.

She shook her head like I was a dunce. I think she knew I just wanted to watch her wash her pussy too. "OK, Little Dummy. I'll show you again. You sure aren't the swiftest fish in the stream are you?"

I dropped my head in mock shame. I had to hide a grin. She took the soap and lathered her hands; she spread her legs wide and ran her fingers down and in between her pussy lips. I watched fascinated as she slid a finger up and down her slit over and over, then inward and I could tell she had slid it up inside her pussy. She did it again and again. She closed her eyes a little as she rubbed her finger up high on her pussy. I knew how that felt!

She seemed to catch herself, opened her eyes and caught me avidly watching. "Now you do it." Her voice was just a little hoarse, or was it my imagination?

I took the soap and lathered my hands and repeated her actions over and over. I loved the feel of my slippery fingers on my pussy, and especially with her eyes watching me.

"Wash at the top real good, where your clit is! Make sure it's very clean." She eyed me and her hand went back to her pussy and her lather-covered finger moved up and down her slit. We stood inches apart, fingers playing up and down our pussies, "washing" them.

I didn't need any encouragement to clean my small but firm clit. I could feel it grow harder and longer under my finger and, God, it felt wonderful! I watched her fingers moving up and down - "washing" her

127

pussy. I think we both knew what we were doing – almost masturbating for each other.

"Now up inside. Careful, you don't want to scrape yourself with your fingernails." She said as she slid a finger way up inside herself again. I mimicked her every motion, my thighs spread wide, and I squatted a little. I slid a wonderfully feeling soapy finger up inside my tight wet pussy. My finger felt wonderful inside me. There was no barrier there now as my fingers had long ago pushed aside and broken the membrane there. I was no longer a "virgin," technically that is!

My finger inside myself felt so good. A tingling feeling deep inside me was growing, my pussy ached, and I was getting so close. I looked at my lovely Sister and saw she was feeling the sensations too.

"Now your backside, wash it good too." She said, coming back to the real world for a moment. She turned a little and slid a soapy finger up and down between her rounded butt. I did the same. Mine was smaller of course, but I slid my finger up and down between my small ass cheeks, over my little ass hole. It felt nice there, but not as good as it did when I ran it over my clit. I watched as her hand moved up and down, knowing her fingers were moving over her butt hole. I did the same.

"Now make sure it's good and soapy then slide your finger inside. Relax your muscle back there and slip it inside. You want to get your ass good and clean too." She said watching me. She turned me around a little and pushed gently on my shoulders, making me bend forward so she could watch. I loved that! I spread my legs wide bending from the waist. I knew she could see my exposed asshole the way she was standing behind me. I pushed and made my little hole pout. I found the small opening and slid my finger inside carefully. Mnn, it felt so nice. I slid it in and out slowly. I knew she could clearly see my finger moving in and out of my ass. It made me even hotter.

"Good, soap your hand once again and do it over. You want to make sure you are clean back there. One more time!" She said her voice a little hoarse now. She had turned slightly and I could see her hand moving in front, and her hand in back pushed a finger in and out of her ass. By the motion of her other hand and arm, I could tell she was rubbing her clit. My body got real tingly and ached as I watched her. I turned my head away a little but watched her out of the corner of my eye; she was rubbing her pussy faster and faster. Her finger was sliding in and out of her butt at the same time.

I could see the flesh of her anus; move in and out as she slid her finger in and out. Her flesh seemed to pout outward as if not wanting to let go of her finger as it slid outward. As she slid it in, it pushed the flesh inward slightly. I imagined my own finger was doing the same while she watched me. Her body gave a little shudder and I heard a soft sigh, almost covered by the running water. I knew that wonderful feeling. I guess it felt really good for her too.

She straightened up a little unsteadily. "OK that's probably clean enough. Be sure and do that real good, every time you shower." Her voice was a little throaty. She took the soap and washed her hands well, then took some shampoo and began to wash her hair. While she had her eyes closed I looked at her body. I leaned close, looking down at her pussy, and could see her pussy lips parted as she stood, legs spread. The water streamed down her body and her pussy was like two pouting lips. They were spread slightly and very red. That ratfink, she had rubbed them till she came. They gleamed with the water running off of them. It looked liked she was peeing. I would love to watch her do that up close. That thought sent a shiver up my spine. I was really getting excited. "Horny" as the fuck books said!

I turned my body a little and ran my soapy finger up and down my slit over and over, moving it over my clit. She had showed me her pussy very intimately one day, and named each part of her pussy as she opened herself up to me. I was fascinated and it really gave me a tingly feeling in my pussy watching her do it, my face inches away from her spread sex. I could smell her delightful odor. It almost drove me crazy. Her flesh had been gleaming wet from her pussy juices. Her odor had surrounded me and I remember salivating like mad.

I rubbed faster and faster, my body becoming more and more excited. I was close to it, almost there, close to that wonderful feeling I got when I really rubbed it till I almost fainted it felt so good, a climax, a cum!

"There, now wash my back, little Sis. Please. "She said straightening up, finished with her shampoo.

Crap, I was almost there! Reluctantly, I took the washrag, soaped it well and washed her back carefully with it. My hand was shaking a little from my excitement; I had been just on the edge of a climax. I ran the washrag up and down her back till it was clean. She took it out of my hand and washed her front. I watched as her breasts bobbed and swayed as she washed them. All too soon, she was finished. She turned me and washed my back all too quickly. I wished she had done it with her hands.

"Let's get out; you'll look like a prune!" She laughed as she slid around me, her slick body rubbing against mine. I loved the feel of it against my skin.

"I still have to wash my hair." I lied. I had already washed it once.

"Boy you sure are slow!" She gave me a quick hug and then a playful swat on my rear.

She got out and closed the shower door. I saw her take a towel and begin to dry off. Her back was to me. I took the soap and lathered my hand. I was facing the door watching her. I spread my legs a little giving my hand more room. I slid a finger up and down my slit while watching her dry off. If she turned I could turn quickly too. As long as she was facing the other way she couldn't see me rubbing my pussy. I thought of her fingers rubbing against her pussy, her other hand with a finger sliding in and out of her ass. I put a finger deep inside my ass, pushing it in and out. My other fingers played over my clit, faster and faster.

I watched her, seeing her sexy body through the glass, slightly veiled by mist and water, but still plainly visible. Her cute ass wiggled as she toweled off. My fingers flew faster and faster. She turned to the side a little and I saw her beautiful cone shaped breast bounce slightly as she moved. What lovely breasts, I wanted to kiss them, caress them, and suck her long nipples.

My clit seemed to grow under my fingers, feeling more wonderful each second, my breathing became faster and faster and then my whole universe seemed to explode. I bit my lip to keep from crying out as the fantastic feeling swept through my body. I saw stars and had to keep from yelling out it felt so wonderful.

It seemed to go on and on till finally I gasped and fell against the side of the shower. I managed to stand panting for a moment, my knees shaking. Then I straightened up and took some shampoo and made a pretense of washing my hair. I looked around when I was through, and she was gone. I wanted to see her beautiful naked body some more. Drats! I was disappointed.

I got out and was standing there drying off. I was facing the way she was when she had dried off. I looked in the mirror, and the angle was such that she could have seen the whole shower door from where she had been standing, with her body turned away from it. I could see rather clearly inside the shower stall.

Had she watched me? I blushed. She probably knew I was lying, and excited, and watched me climax, cum, explode! I had read those words in some of the dirty fuck books she kept hidden in her closet. Mom would have a fit if she knew they were there, and Sis would have a real hissy fit if she knew I had been looking through her things.

I dried off. She had watched me, I was sure of it! The thought kept running through my brain over and over. I was positive! I was spent now, totally relaxed. Feeling fantastic! Sis had watched me bring myself off! Wow, taking a shower with Sis was really wonderful.

Friday evening finally came; our parents had left after work and were going to be gone all weekend. Sis and I hadn't taken another shower together. I wanted to, but our schedules didn't match. Seems she was either up earlier or later than I was when we had to take a shower. Maybe we could take another one together, a long one. I really hoped so. My pussy tingled at the thought!

Our parents had left strict orders that Ronnie, her boyfriend, could not come over that weekend or she's be grounded for the rest of her life. Mom had asked Brandi our next-door neighbor, and her best friend, to watch over us while they were gone, so Sis knew that having Ronnie come over was out. She was really disappointed.

We were watching TV, in our nightclothes on Sis's bed. She had on a sexy frilly top with a bottom that was almost transparent. I had on a t-shirt and, plain cotton panties, not sexy at all, but then I didn't have very many sexy under things.

The movie on the pay TV channel was pretty hot, a man and woman kissing and making out. There was nudity in it, and the man was kissing her large sexy breasts. Hot! I looked over at Sis and could just make out her erect nipples poking up against the thin material. She would rub her hand over her breast from time to time when she didn't think I was looking. It was getting to her too. I hoped I could start some sexy talk with her. No harm in trying!

"Does Ronnie like to kiss you?" I grinned, looking over at her.

She giggled. "Kiss me, where?"

"On your lips." Suddenly it struck me, the man was kissing the woman's breasts. "Oh, on your breasts too? Does he do that?" I said wide-eyed.

"Yes Silly, he loves to kiss them. I told you he calls my areolas 'puffy'. How do you think he knew to call them that?" She laughed and cupped one breast.

Damn that was sexy looking! "Do you like for him to do that? Does it feel nice?" I asked my tummy doing flip-flops.

She was silent for a while looking at the TV screen. She finally turned to me. "Promise to never tall a soul if I tell you? If you ever breathe a word I'll fix you good! Promise?" She said very seriously.

"Cross my heart and hope to die!" I turned and scooted closer to her. My bare arm touched her warm arm and it felt so nice.

"Well, we got to kissing one night and he was French kissing me, had his tongue way in my mouth. We were in the back of his car out in the boonies. He really got me so hot; finally he pulled my top and my bra off, licked and sucked my nipples and breasts. God it got me so damn hot! Thought I would die. He'd suck and tongue them over and over while his hand cupped my breast and played with it.

"He put his hand in my panties but I made him take it out. He kissed my nipples and breasts for the longest time. He got a hard on, I could feel it against my leg. He was kind of humping my leg. No way was he going to fuck me. I don't want to get pregnant. I almost came I was so hot, so was he. My panties were damp I was so excited. Finally we had to quit as it got so late, and he brought me home. I came in and got myself off. I almost exploded I was so excited."

"Like you came in the shower the other day when we were there together?" I teased her.

"Yeah, like that, except hotter, more explosive. You little Fink you! I watched you get off in the shower too; you are a fine one to talk. I saw you with your finger in your ass and rubbing your clit." She got a huge grin on her face and laughed out loud. "Not that I blame you. I did get you hot didn't I? Making you wash your pussy and ass over, and over, and over. It was fun wasn't it? You have a cute little bod."

I blushed. "Thanks, yours is fantastic. I loved watching you rub yourself. And I loved seeing your pussy up close while you were shampooing." I grinned back at her.

"I saw you peeping, Shrimp!" She giggled. "We are bad! Mom said we could take showers together. She said she and Aunt Pat did it when they were young. She got this naughty smile on her face, like, you know, she knew what we were doing in there and didn't mind. She's something else!"

"Does Ronnie kiss your pussy too?" I asked seeing how far I could go.

"Why you little impertinent Imp! Where did you get that idea?" She asked shaking her head and pointing her finger at me. "You little Rat, you have been in my fuck books haven't you? I thought it looked like someone had been going through them. I wondered if Mom had found them. If she had, I think they would have disappeared, or I would have gotten a long boring lecture. They are pretty raunchy! I got them from Dottie, not Ronnie. Her folks don't mind if she reads them. I ought to tan your cute little ass for snooping in my stuff." She pointed her finger at me again, grinning down at me. "Did you get off reading them? Some of them really are hot and – oh God - really raunchy!"

We laughed together. She wasn't as mad as I thought she'd be. "Well, does he kiss your pussy?" I asked again giggling.

"You are a Scamp aren't you? Promise never to tell a soul? This is just between us, OK?" I nodded. "Yes he has, and it was fantastic. I flat won't let him fuck me even with a rubber on. He can finger me all he wants but I don't want to get pregnant or catch something. Oh, he wants to fuck me soooo bad!" She laughed, rolling her eyes.

"He kissed your pussy, really?" I gasped trying to think of his lips there.

"That's not all!" She giggled lowering her voice. "He put his tongue inside me, licked my pussy over and over till I came. God, I thought I'd go crazy."

I gasped, I had read a little about men kissing women's pussies in her fuck books but thought it was just fiction. "He actually licked your pussy, and put his tongue inside you? Jeeese!" I was flabbergasted. It was making my clit hard and my pussy so wet thinking about his tongue inside her cute pussy. The girls laughed about it, but I didn't know any one who said they had been "eaten."

"And it was fantastic. He licked my pussy for the longest time and sucked and licked my clit. He put a finger inside me pumping it in and out and I came like there was no tomorrow. It was out of this world, I almost fainted it felt so damn wonderful.

"He made me promise not to tell any of the other girls he ate me. Some guys think it's nasty and they make fun of 'cuntlappers.' I won't tell anyone, I don't want to get a bad reputation. The next thing they would say was we were fucking, which we definitely haven't and I'd get a reputation as a slut. Don't you dare breathe a word about it! OK? You do and you are D-E-A-D! You got that Missy?" She said very seriously.

I promised and was thinking about him sucking her breasts and licking her pussy. My mouth watered.

"Is it like French kissing? Betsy and I do that lots. It's fun. We like to do each other. It feels so good doesn't it?" I giggled.

137

"You and cute little Betsy Frenching each other. You two are really naughty! Do you do anything else?"

"Like what?" I asked not knowing what she meant.

"Oh come on! You know. Playing with each other's tits, or pussies while you French each other." She said tilting her head, a lopsided grin on her pretty face.

"No. We just kiss each other. It feels really nice." I said, then my mind kicked in. "Do you and Dottie play with each other's pussies." Dottie was a close friend and had stayed overnight in our house many times. They always locked the door and I could hear giggling and laughing but never thought too much about it.

"What do you think, Shrimp?" She laughed, rolling her eyes up dramatically, giving me her answer.

I sat looking at the TV screen, but not really seeing it. My mind was running a mile a minute. She and Dottie? Dottie was a cheerleader and drop-dead-gorgeous. This was some heavy shit she was laying on me. My Sister and her best friend making love! Damn!

"Sis, I really like taking showers with you." I said in a small voice. My throat had tightened up at the thought of telling her this.

"I like it too." She said absentmindedly, not seeming to pay too much attention to my statement her eyes on the TV screen. The sexy action on it had slowed down a little.

"You know what I like best about it?" I asked my mouth feeling like it had cotton in it. I could feel my whole body tingle. She didn't say anything but turned her head to me and looked at me, giving me her full attention. "I like to feel you against me, you feel so nice when we are wet. I really like to feel your tits against my face. I - I - well, I wanted to suck on your nipples. I loved seeing your pussy too. It's so pretty and so sexy too."

"Really? It feels so sexy having you against me too, when we are wet. I got hot the other day when you were washing your cute little pussy. God, I got so hot I had to cum watching you fucking your ass with your finger and rubbing your clit. You gave that cute little asshole of yours a real work out. Watching your soapy finger sliding in and out was so damn sexy. I know how good it feels when I do it to myself or Dottie does it to me!

"I was mean. I should have let you bring yourself off while I did myself. I don't know why I did that? We could have watched each other. But you did cum while I was outside. I watched you in the mirror. I almost brought myself off again watching you, but I went into my room and made myself cum on the bed, thinking about you slipping your finger up your cute little ass. I watched you cum and ran out and did it to myself. I shouldn't have done that. I'm sorry! I tend to be a fuck-up sometimes. Forgive me little Sister?"

My tension gone, I grinned and stuck my tongue out at her, we laughed. We sat in silence, neither of us talking, and not really watching the TV either.

"Would you like to kiss my tits? I'll let you if you want to." She asked softly.

I couldn't talk, I just nodded dumbly. She sat up and pulled the top off and sat there in just the thin bottoms. Her breasts were beautiful; the nipples were erect and sticking way out. I loved the puffy swollen areolas. My lips almost puckered looking at them.

She moved to the edge of the bed and hung her legs off of it. She motioned for me to get on the floor between them. I slid off the bed onto the thick carpet and kneeled between her spread thighs. I could make out the shadow of her brown pussy hair through the thin material of her sexy panty bottoms. It was pulled up tightly in her pussy, right along her prominent crevice. I stared at it.

I wished she'd take them off. I moved closer and kneeled up in front of her, between her spread thighs. She reached out and pulled me to her. Her breasts pressed against mine, her nipples seemed to be drilling two holes in my skin. Her body was hot as could be. She bent her head and kissed me softly on the lips. I almost melted. Her kiss was so soft and her lips warm against mine. Her tongue slid out and played along my lips. God, I almost died!

Betsy and I had kissed lots of time. I finally managed to meet Sis's tongue with mine, and our tongues played against each other. My hand was on her arm and I felt her take it and move it. She put it on her breast and rubbed it over the firm globe. I almost fainted it felt so wonderful. I let my hand roam over her hot breast, her hard nipple pressing against the palm of my hand. She pressed her chest forward against my hand as our tongues played. It was so erotic.

Kissing Betsy was never like this! I was kissing my big Sister and playing with her breast at the same time. I had died and gone to heaven! My heart was beating a mile a minute. I pulled back and looked at her sexy breasts. The nipple I had been fondling was very erect, it was longer too. I had done that! Me!

"You are really a good kisser Sweet One. You and Betsy must have been doing a lot of practicing!" She chuckled, then leaned in and kissed me lightly on the lips. I took both hands and ran them over her soft breasts. The skin was so soft, yet beneath the skin, her breast was firm. I squeezed them and stroked them. It felt wonderful. I felt a hot tingling sensation run through my whole body.

"I hope when my boobs get larger, they are as sexy as these." I grinned up at her. I stroked them over and over, and then played with the nipples, pulling and rolling them between my fingers. I could feel them swell and become even harder. It was making my mouth actually water and my pussy began to tingle while I looked at them.

"Kiss them. I love to have them kissed and the nipples sucked on. Come on Baby, I want you to suck them for me. Please?" She asked a little breathlessly.

I bent and kissed the tip of her neglected breast. I took the long nipple between my lips and sucked on it. It was warm and the tip hard. I ran my tongue around the hard tip and against her swollen areolas. Jeeez, I was actually sucking my Sister's breasts. I couldn't believe it! I sucked on them like I was nursing, while my hands cupped and stroked them. My body went hot all over.

Her eyes were closed and she seemed to really be enjoying it. I pressed in a little and took more of her nipple and breast in my mouth, opening my mouth wide, sucking harder. God it felt so fantastic, and her skin tasted so good too. I could taste the powder she used on them. Her skin tasted so sweet. I cupped her breast with both hands, squeezing it, molding it, trying to get more of it into my mouth. The pear shape of it helped me, but my mouth was too small and her breast too large. I tongued her nipple like I do when I kiss Betsy's tongue, flicking it around and around the swollen areola and using it against her hard nipple. It seemed to get even longer as I sucked.

I pulled back a little and saw she had a hand down against her pussy, rubbing it through the thin cloth. Her finger ran along the furrow, pressing the cloth deeper into her pussy. I sucked her nipple again and put my hand down over hers while she moved it up and down her slit.

"Take your bottom off, please Sis. Let me see your pussy. I want to watch you play with your self. Oh, please?" I begged her.

She stared at me a moment then nodded. I moved back as she lifted her ass and pulled her bottoms off. I noticed the crotch material was dark, wet with her juices. Her eyes were very wide open, almost as if she were in a trance. She kicked the flimsy bottom aside and sat back down. She spread her thighs and I moved back between them and kissed her breasts, going from one to the other. I moved my head sideways so I could see her pussy out of one eye. Her fingers played up and down her spread slit. The odor of her excitement surrounded me. It was the sexiest thing I had ever smelled, another girl's excited pussy; spread wide, open inches from my face. I could feel the heat from her thighs and pussy. I actually trembled as I inhaled her sexual odor.

One hand went to the back of my head and pressed me against her breast a little harder. I felt her fingernails dig in to my scalp. I didn't mind at all. I sucked harder, tongued faster. Her fingers moved faster against her clit, making little circles around her pink clit. I could see it momentarily when her finger moved out of the way for a split second. I was so close I could hear the little liquid sounds her fingers made against her wet pussy. She began to moan and whimper. I cupped her breast harder and sucked hard on her nipple. It tasted divine. I put my hand on top of hers carefully feeling the motion of her hand. I moved it a little so as not to obstruct my view, so I could see her clit and her fingers playing over it.

She began to gasp and she cried out as she came. She moaned, then screamed out as her body went into shivers of delight as she climaxed. I was glad the folks weren't home! My pussy was on fire and I wanted to rub it so bad, but I wanted to help her cum. I sucked and tongued her nipples going from one to the other, back and forth. She gave one last long undulating scream of joy and fell back on the bed, her breast pulling from my lips.

She lay panting. Her legs were spread and I could see her wet pussy, it was beautiful. I had only seen it wide open like this once before, but I leaned in and looked at it close. The lips were swollen and puffy, her clit a small pink bean at the top. Below, her neat brown ass hole looked inviting too. But her opening was like a red rose. There was a little of her juice in the middle, a small pool. My mouth watered as I looked at it.

"Ohhh, thank you little Sister. That was fantastic. I came like gangbusters. Wild! I loved your lips and tongue on my nipples. You are some lover. Come up here and let me hold you."

I moved up on the bed and she pulled me on top of her, holding me against her hot body. I kissed her lips and she kissed me back softly. I lay on top of her hot heaving body. I had helped my Sister get off. I had kissed my first breast and loved every second of it. I felt like a million dollars.

My Sister and I lay kissing softly. I was lying on top of her hot body. She was still breathing heavily from her climax. I nestled my body down against hers. I shook my head slowly. I had just kissed her breasts while she rubbed her pussy and made herself cum. I had done it! I had dreamed of doing that while we were in the shower, but now I had really, actually done it. I had gotten to suck and kiss her nipples and helped her cum. My hand had been on top of hers and I had felt the motions as she played with her clit. I was so happy, but my pussy was tingling and I wanted more. My hips seemed to have a mind of their own. They pushed downward against my Sister's body. I was nestled between her thighs and my pussy pressed downward against her spread naked pussy. My clit seemed about to burst.

She giggled. "Why little Sister, I think you are horny. You're dry fucking me. Poor Baby, is your pussy hot?"

"It's on fire, my clit seems like it will explode, it burns so. I have never felt it like this before." I said frowning, my voice a little strained with the sexual tension in my body.

"Well, you helped me cum, now it's my turn to help you get off. I'm glad Mom and Dad aren't here. I would have just scared them to death when I screamed out just now. You sucking my tits really got me going. Thanks. Now it's your turn to cum. Want to?" She laughed. Of course I did.

She rolled on her side and dumped me on the wide bed. She took my t-shirt and pulled it up and over my head. Before I knew what was happening she had pulled my panties down and off. She did something unexpected, she took them and put them to her nose and breathed in, sMellyng my odor on them. The crotch was wet! Her eyes sparkled above them. I lay on the bed beside her, totally naked, like she was. My panties flew across the room. She began to stroke my body. God it felt so wonderful to have her hands move over me. She kissed my face, my neck, my ears; I never knew that could feel so nice.

When she got to my breasts, she sucked on my nipples. I knew they were sensitive, but no one had ever sucked and licked them. My nipples came to life and she gleefully sucked them to two hard points and nibbled on them with her teeth. It made chills run down my spine and my pussy ache like crazy. She took them between her fingers and rolled and pulled them till they really stuck way out, rock hard. She licked my breasts too, sucking on them back and forth. They are more champagne glass sized and she was able to get most of one in her mouth. My areolas were large, but not as "puffy" as hers. Her hands were moving slowly over me. I lay on my back my thighs spread wide. My pussy felt about to explode.

Finally her hand cupped my pussy mound and she squeezed it. She ran her fingers through my brown hair, twirling it around her fingers. I moaned it felt so good. "You like that little Sister? It feels good to have someone else caress you. Dottie and I have done it for several years. We got to French kissing each other and it kept going further and further. You'll love what I'm going to do to you next. Just relax and enjoy it. You have never felt anything like what I'm going to do to your little sweet box. I'm going to eat you till you cum like you have never cum in your life." She almost growled her voice had dropped so low. She was obviously anticipating it too.

I shivered wondering what she was going to do to me. I thought I knew, but it was never clear in the fuck books just what the women did to each other. They "ate" each other, but didn't really go in to much detail. Now my big Sister was going to "eat" me.

She got off the bed. She took two pillows, had me lean forward, and put them behind my back and head, propping me up. "There, that's so you can watch me. It makes it so much more fun that way, you can see me eating your sweet little virgin pussy." She moved down to the foot of the bed and got on her knees. She leaned on the bed and spread my legs wider. She was looking up at my spread pussy. My pussy tingled and I almost couldn't seem to get my breath.

"Ohhh, your pussy is so pretty. So clean and neat! Damn, Sis, why didn't we think of this before? Your little pussy is so virginal. We'll have to trim your pussy hair a little though. That can really be fun. Dottie and I trim and shave each other. We usually wind up making love when we do.

"Mnnn, I've wanted to eat you for so long. But first I want to really look at your sweet pussy, tease you a little, and make you and me both want it so bad we can taste it. Dottie and I do that to each other, and when we cum it is like the world has turned inside out." She said as she slid upward.

She took her fingers and slowly stroked my inner thighs, softly, slowly. I shivered and goose bumps popped up all over my body. I bent my head so I could see her better. My mind raced, she and Dottie eating each other! My God! Now I was going to learn what they did to each other.

She parted my pussy hair, then my pussy lips gently. Her face was inches away, her breath soft against my bare flesh.

"Oh, your pussy is so beautiful, a soft pink, wet and slippery. I can see your little vaginal opening, like a pale rose. Here's your little pee hole, small and neat. I'd like to see you pee sometime. Would you like to pee for me?" She asked looking up at me, eyes naughty and sparkling.

I could hardly talk, my mouth felt as if it were full of cotton. I almost croaked out, "Oh, God, yes but I want to see you pee too. I want to see you do it too, oh yes."

"It's fun to do it. Pee while someone is watching you, their face real close to your pussy. Watch the pee come out of that little hole. We'll do it together, soon!" She said her eyes riveted to my pussy. I jumped as her finger touched me there, pressing against my pee hole. My urethra, I think she had called it; I'd have to ask her — but later. It felt so strange, so good. She rubbed it around and around.

"God, your pussy is so virginal. The lips are small and so neat." I felt her fingers play over my pussy lips and spread them a little more. Her fingers caught my inner lips and pulled them upward. I looked down and her face was almost touching my spread pussy.

"Oh, there's your pretty little clit. Mnnn, so small and pretty. It will grow. Play with it a lot. I do and it will get larger. " She laughed. "Wash it very good every time you take a shower. I'll suck on it and maybe that will make it grow too. You'll have to teach Betsy to suck on it while you suck on hers."

I shivered at that thought, then I cried out as her lips found my clit and she sucked on it hard. Her cheeks bowed in and out as she sucked and released the pressure again and again. Her tongue played over the end of it. I loved running my slippery finger over it, but her lips and tongue were so much better. She had me right on the edge. I hunched up against her mouth but she backed up and removed her mouth. I almost went crazy I wanted it so bad.

"Patience Little One, remember what I said? I want you to be wild with need when you finally cum! Ohhh, your little pussy center is so pink and pretty, like a little pink rose. Have you looked at yourself with a mirror?" I nodded. "So pink and tender. Mnn, I have to taste your center."

Her head dropped slightly and her tongue came out. She cut her eyes up at me to see if I was watching. How could I not watch? I jumped as her tongue touched me. It felt as if she had shocked me. She flattened her tongue and ran it the length of my pussy, bottom to top, flicking my clit at the top of the upstroke, giving me sensations that were beyond anything I had ever experienced. My mind whirled, my body felt like a thousand wonderful needles were pricking me all at once.

"Oh, you taste delicious, your pussy is almost dripping. I'm going to love this too." She said as I felt her tongue slide from the bottom of my pussy upward. It felt like nothing I had ever felt in my life. Over and over her hot wet tongue moved up and down my slit. Thrill after thrill shot through my body. She moved her tongue back to the bottom and I felt it press inward just a little.

149

I cried out as she pointed her tongue and slid it slowly inside me. She wiggled it a little and pressed it slowly inward. Her hot breath seemed to set my pussy on fire. My fingernails bit into the sheet. I pushed my hips upward and her tongue slipped a little deeper inside me. She pushed and it tried to go deeper. Her tongue was large and my pussy so small. I felt her lips come down on my pussy and cover it. I cried out and heard her moan as she sucked hard on the opening. She was sucking my juices out! God, my own Sister. I wanted to do the same to her.

I jumped as she moved her tongue and slid a finger gently inside my pussy. She moved back a little and her lips were gleaming wet. She pulled at my pussy lips stretching them wide and looked inside.

"You naughty girl, you're not a virgin. I can't see your hymen. I'll bet you have been putting things inside here, haven't you? I don't blame you, I did the same thing. I want to put my tongue deeper inside, I'm going to stretch you a little, but stop me if it hurts." She said as she slid a finger inside me. It felt wonderful as it slid up inside. I moaned.

" I don't want to hurt you, just get your cute little pussy a little wider, so I can get my tongue deeper inside you. I love doing that. I can put my tongue as far as I possibly can inside Dottie. Her pussy tastes so sweet. You'd love it too. I really love it when she tongue fucks me. I want to have her join us and let her kiss your sweet pussy. Would you like Dottie to kiss you and suck your pussy?" She grinned up at me.

"Would she want to?" I asked not really knowing. She just laughed. I was a pest, the younger sister, always hanging around, they were always shooing me away. Dottie was so beautiful, a cheerleader, so cool, so sophisticated, and so much older than I was, it seemed.

I gasped as Sis carefully slid another finger inside me. She spread them slowly, opening me up. She reached across and using her other hand, put a third finger in me and spread my pussy more and more. It didn't hurt, just felt funny. I could feel her tug and watched her hands move apart a little now and she had two fingers on one side, one on the other side, spreading me open.

"Damn you are so beautiful in there. So pink. I can see clear to the back of your little pussy, Hon, it's gorgeous. So nice and 'pussy pink'. There, now I think I can get my tongue inside you. Ready, Imp?" She didn't wait for my answer. She leaned forward and her tongue slid out, long and pointed. She pressed it down into the opening while she pulled her fingers out of the way. It seemed to fill me up. I cried out it felt so fantastic. She pressed downward driving her tongue deeper inside me. She wiggled it inside me and I cried out with joy. She pushed it in and out again and again I guess that was why it was called 'tongue fucking.' My lovely Sister, her mouth on my pussy, her tongue thrusting inside me. Tongue fucking me. Me! She wiggled and thrust her tongue still deeper inside me. I closed my eyes and just let the fantastic sensations wash over my body.

Her lips covered my pussy, sucking as she thrust her tongue in and out. With my lovely Sister's tongue buried inside me, my thoughts turned to Betsy and her sweet, pretty pussy. I wondered if I could do that to Betsy, would she want me to? I could sure find out. We had never done anything except French each other, but we had always gotten hot Frenching. We hadn't even played with each other's breasts. I'd sure try it. I'd seen her cute pussy lots of times, we had looked at each other's pussies closely, but that had been all. Her breasts were a little larger than mine, her pussy very pretty. She had told me mine was pretty too. She was interested, I was sure of that.

I moaned as Sis slid her tongue out momentarily and flicked my clit. God it was so hard and ached so much. I had found it years before and loved to rub and caress it. I had first rubbed it against everything in sight, the stair banister, my pillow, and my stuffed animals. Then one day I put my finger along my young slit and it got wet and slippery. I moved it up just a little and got the wonderful feeling when it ran over my clit. I experimented more and more with it. I learned to rub it and tried all sorts of lubricants to make it really slick till my natural juices got to flowing.

Mom caught me masturbating one day and had a little talk with me telling me that was OK to do, but do it in only in private, and there was absolutely nothing wrong with rubbing myself. She cautioned me about putting things inside my puss and ass though.

Some years later I was snooping in Mom's lingerie drawers and found several vibrators of different sizes. I even tried one of them against my pussy and it almost made me come unglued. I had never known anything like it. I "borrowed" it quite often when she was out, and always cleaned it off and put it back exactly as I had found it. I had never gotten the nerve up enough to put it inside my pussy.

If Mom ever found out, she never said anything about it. Did she really use it on her pussy? I never thought about her masturbating too, but if she had them, she must. Wild! Did Dad know she had them?

I moaned out loud as Sis's tongue slid back inside me and she sucked my pussy hard. I was getting hotter and hotter. I felt her wet finger play around my ass and then press inward. God that felt so wonderful. Her lips moved up and she sucked my clit and began to flick it over and over with her tongue. Her finger slid deep in my ass and that felt fantastic too.

I began to cry out and moan and thresh on the bed. She had one hand holding my ass while the other slid in and out of my asshole. Her tongue flicked over and over my hard little clit and her lips sucked hard on it too. She stayed with me and her vibrating tongue flicked my clit harder and faster. I gripped her head and pressed it hard against my body, as my passion seemed to fill every fiber of my body.

I screamed out as I climaxed, came, exploded, over and over. Her lips and tongue lashed my hard clit and her fantastic finger thrust in and out of my ass, a totally new mind-blowing set of feelings for me. The sensations seemed to completely overwhelm me. I had never imagined a climax could be this wonderfully intense, but I had never had a mouth on my clit before and a finger buried in my backside thrusting in and out either. I don't know how many fantastic climaxes she brought me to. I seemed to go from one to the next without any let up. She sucked and tongued me till finally I went black as my wonderful world exploded around me in a million pieces of glorious color.

I came to with her bathing my face with a cold cloth. I managed a smile. I think my eyes were crossed from all the wonderful sensation she had given me. There was a thin sheen of perspiration over my whole body.

She smiled down at me and kissed my lips lightly. "Well, there was no doubt that you enjoyed the hell out of that, little Sis!"

I just shook my head and kissed her back. "God, I had no idea that a cum could feel like that."

"The first one with someone can really be something you never forget. I almost came with you. I tend to get hot too when I am making love to a person I really care about." Her eyes told me she really loved me, despite her sisterly taunts.

I managed to kiss her before I fell back exhausted. "God, that was beyond fantastic. I never dreamed it could be so wonderful. I couldn't stop. Your tongue on my clit was the most wonderful feeling I have ever had. I have rubbed my clit, but that was way beyond just a clit climax!" I laughed at the alliteration I had inadvertently put together.

She stroked my body slowly while I recovered. "Do you and Dottie make love together? I have heard you two in your room, giggling and laughing, but I had no idea you did – that together." I finally managed to get out, still short of breath.

She laughed. "Well, we don't advertise. We usually kiss and caress and get each other hot and wait till we think everyone is asleep then we make love. We have to be quiet though. We did it several times at her house when no one was home and we could really let go. God, she really moans and screams when she really lets go. I do too!"

I lay still a moment. "You want her to join us? Really? You aren't just teasing me, are you?" I asked incredulously, not really believing she meant it.

"When I tell Dottie you and I have made it together, I'm sure she will want to join us. We have only made love together, just the two of us, not with any other girls. We discovered we liked each other and got to kissing and feeling around. We wound up going from French kissing to kissing each other's breasts. Pussies were just one quick step away from there. It was so fantastic. We both go with boys but neither of us will let them fuck us. When we want to cum really hard we manage to get together. We even made it in the gym one evening when everyone else had left. The thought our coach might catch us made it hotter. We kind of think she likes girls too, from the looks we get from her. Dottie and I kind of tease her; let her see us naked, for just a moment, then cover up. You can almost see her drool!" She laughed.

I lay there on the bed, my Sister's hands slowly stroking my spent body. I looked at her beautiful naked body and thought of Dottie and my beautiful Sister making love, and that they might want me with them, made a wonderful thrill run up my spine. God, my Sister and Dottie, the drop-dead-gorgeous cheerleader wanting to make love to little ole' me. 'Fan-fucking-tastic!'

It was morning and I awoke feeling on top of the world. Suddenly I turned my head, remembering where I was, and my sexy older Sister's head was inches from mine. We had spent the night together in her big bed. The sheet had slipped down and her beautiful pear shaped breasts were exposed. I remembered going to sleep, both of us naked, with her snuggled up against my body, feeling her firm breasts against my back, her arm around me cupping my breast.

The memories of our lovemaking came back vividly and my pussy stirred. I thought of our shower together, then days later, of kissing her breasts while she brought herself off as I sucked her breasts. Then the glorious feeling of her making love to me, kissing and sucking my pussy till I exploded with lust. My pussy tingled remembering the erotic time we had enjoyed.

I bent over and lightly kissed her nipple. She didn't stir. I opened my mouth and sucked the beautiful nipple with its swollen "puffy" areola a little harder. It tasted wonderful. Slowly I sucked it again and again gently. It began to become erect and harden. I twirled my tongue around it, and reached down and slowly ran my finger along my slit, it was wet. My clit quickly hardened and throbbed.

"Mnnn, that's a wonderful way to get me hot and awake at the same time!" She said stroking my hair sensuously. I moved up and kissed her lips; she slid her tongue along my lips and probed it inward. We kissed for a while bodies pressed together. I cupped her wonderful breasts.

Mnnnn, I could get used to this very easily." She said squeezing me. "Too bad we can't do this all the time. Hey, lets get up and have a sexy shower together. We don't have to worry about anyone coming in on us. OK?"

I was absolutely thrilled beyond words. We rolled out of bed and almost ran to the bathroom, and got in the shower. Today there was no pretense. We kissed, hugged, and fingered each other. We let ourselves go wild, kissing, thrusting our bodies together. I sucked her gloriously wet naked breasts. She sucked mine too, which felt so hot. Our naughty fingers slipped into pussies and asses, lingering, sliding sensuously up and down and inside also. We had a fantastic climax fingering each other standing under the water. Her slick body against mine, humping against my finger was fantastic.

We dried each other and vowed to take more showers together. We dressed in shorts and t-shirts with much giggling and horseplay. Relaxed and refreshed, we made breakfast together and ate a hearty meal. We were both famished!

After breakfast Sis called Dottie and invited her to come over, but didn't tell her anything about my being there. Dottie arrived about an hour later and didn't seem too happy to see me there in the den with Sis. I eyed her sexy body, thinking of the two of them making love together. Damn, she was drop dead gorgeous, and had a really sexy body too.

"Dottie, you won't believe what we have been doing?" Sis happily told her while Dottie looked at me like she wished I would just disappear into thin air.

"Probably not. What's made you so happy?" She asked still a little miffed at my being there.

"Promise never to tell?" Sis asked her. Dottie nodded and said she promised. "Well, we made love and this little sister of mine is quite a good lover. Not as good as you, but I think she's a quick learner. Interested?"

"Wow, that is some heavy shit. You two made it together? Tess, you sure you are ready for this?" She asked, but her eyes taking my body in, said her interest in me had certainly got jumpstarted quickly.

"Well, Sis certainly had no problem with it!" I giggled. That got a laugh from both of them and set the mood.

"Hey, just remember we were about her age when we first started making love together." Sis said. "Want to see what a cute little bod she has? Her pussy is so sweet and virginal. Well, she's not actually still a virgin, but her pussy looks like it. She's had her fingers and God knows what else in her cute little pussy. Come on Tess, show her."

"I'm a little bashful, why don't you undress me?" I said, wanting to feel her hands on me. For Dottie, I would have stripped in a flash, but why pass up some nice caresses from my beautiful older Sister? Beside, I wanted her to undress me in front of Dottie. The thought seemed so much more wicked.

Sis stood up and pulled me to her. She kissed me and her tongue slid into my mouth. We tongue kissed for a couple of minutes while Dottie watched while I stroked and cupped Sis's breasts. Finally she turned me around facing Dottie and slowly slid my top off.

Dottie watched, sitting on the edge of the couch, her lovely brown eyes taking in my bare young breasts. Sis caressed me from behind caressing my breasts and tweaking my nipples and rolling them till they were erect and tingling from her touch. She squatted down behind me unfastened my shorts and slowly, teasing Dottie, slid then down my body. She hesitated just as they would have cleared my pussy. Dottie's lovely eyes were riveted at the hidden treasure.

"Now, feast your eyes on this cute little pussy." She said as she slid my shorts and panties down revealing my slit to Dottie. Dottie unconsciously licked her lips and her eyes were locked onto my pussy. Sis slid my shorts and panties off and I stepped out of them and at a touch of her hands, spread my legs apart, letting Dottie have a better look at my pussy. I was proud of it and rotated my hips a little toward her.

"Wow, you do have a beautiful pussy Tess. Nice little body too. When you fill out and get fuller breasts, you are going to be as sexy as your sister or your Mom. I'll bet your tits will be big too, like your Mom's. She has some really beautiful breasts. Your sister's are still growing a little too. Come here and let me see you closer, Sweet Thing!" Dottie said her voice a little hoarser now. I noticed she was squeezing her thighs together.

I was thrilled to death that she liked my body and was interested in it. I had always been the tagalong one, the one they always wanted to get

159

rid of. Now I was standing in front of her completely naked and both of them were interested, very interested, in me - in my body. It sent a delicious shiver up my spine.

I moved closer to her, stopping a couple of feet from her. She looked at my body and ran her hands up and down my sides. Goose bumps popped all over my body, and they both laughed.

"Doesn't take much to get her excited does it?" Dottie laughed and bent forward and kissed my breast. Her tongue slid out and licked my breast and nipple. She flicked my nipple and then took it into her mouth and sucked it. Sis had gotten it hard and she sucked on it and it seemed to grow still more. My breasts felt fuller too, like they did when Betsy and I kissed, they always seemed to get harder, fuller.

I felt her hand slide down between my thighs to cup my pussy. I spread my legs wider for her. Her fingers moved over my pussy. I moaned softly. She slid a finger along my slit, reaching under and pressing it into my slit, opening me up. I knew I was wet and her now slick finger slid effortlessly along my pussy. Dottie's teeth nibbled on my nipple sending wonderful shock waves through me. She bit down just a little harder and I loved the delightful little pain.

I felt hands on me, and Sis came up behind me and pressed her wonderfully nude body against mine. She had slipped out of her clothes and her hot breasts pressed against my back. She kissed my neck and licked behind my ear. Ohhh, these two were really getting me hot.

"Why don't we get in bed and do this thing right." Sis said.

Dottie pulled back and took her gleaming wet finger, and to my astonishment put it to her mouth and sucked it.

"Mnn, delicious. I love pussy juice. I'm sure ready to get in bed with this delicious looking thing. I want to explore this sweet little pussy of your sister's further." She stood up and pulled me to her and kissed my lips. I kissed her back and felt her firm full breasts thrusting against me. She had to lean down a little to kiss me. I felt like a million as this beautiful older girl kissed me, and her tongue slid into my mouth. I fenced with her tongue, sucked it and stroked it with my tongue. They wanted me to join them; they wanted to make love to me. Me!

Dottie pulled back. "Very nice. You are a good kisser. Did your sexy older sister teach you that?" She asked smiling down at me.

"Guess again. Would you believe she and little Betsy have been practicing Frenching?" Sis informed her.

"Damn, that Betsy is one cute little thing. I'll bet she would make a hot lover too. You two go any further then just kissing" Dottie asked. I shook my head. She gave me that look like she didn't really believe me.

Sis took my hand and led me upstairs. I thought we would go to her bedroom, but she went to the end of the hall and into the master bedroom. "Hey, with the three of us, why don't we use the big nice king

161

sized bed. Mom and Dad won't mind." We all giggled at the deliciously naughty thought of making love on their bed.

Sis went to Dottie and pulled her into her arms. They kissed, I watched fascinated as Dottie stroked Sis and their tongues obviously were thrusting as their mouths were open wide. It was so damn sexy watching the two beautiful older girls kissing passionately. Sis's hands moved over Dottie's still clad sexy body, stroking and fondling it. Dottie's hands moved down to Sis's ass and pulled her hips against hers, and their hips thrust and swiveled together.

I watched for a minute then I moved behind Dottie and without asking unbuttoned her blouse in the back. She put her hands down so I could slide it off of her. I unfastened the clasps of her bra and pulled it wide, then slid the straps down off her shoulders.

"Damn, you two are double teaming me. Kit, this little vixen is undressing me already. I think she's going to be a natural lover." Dottie said turning and looking at me. I moved in and took the bra and pulled it slowly forward and off of her breasts.

My mouth dropped open when I saw her bare beautiful, young breasts. They were larger and fuller than Sis's, more rounded too. I wondered if they were a D cup, they were larger than Sis's, which I knew, were a C cup. Mine were still an A cup but filling out. Her areolas were smaller, but the nipples were as long as Sis's. I couldn't help myself and leaned in and kissed the nipple and sucked on it. My knees want weak it felt so wonderful. I cupped one breast while I sucked the nipple, pulling on it, making it harder and longer. I licked her velvet smooth skin. I loved the

162

taste of it. Her hand went behind my head and pressed me against her sweet sMellyng breast. Her perfume enveloped me and my head swam.

"Wow, this little lady knows her way around breasts too. I think we are going to really have a wonderful day of it. Has she kissed and licked your pussy yet, Kit?"

"Boy, has she! She's a fast learner too. She took to it naturally. I think Frenching Betsy came natural for her. They haven't really discovered each other yet, other then kissing. We'll show her some tricks to teach Betsy, won't we?" Sis asked with a wink.

While I kissed Dottie's breasts, Sis moved behind her and slipped her shorts and panties off. She moved back a little and stepped out of them. I looked her body over and whistled out loud. Her body was gorgeous. Her cheerleading had rounded her body and she was well muscled and fit as could be. She wasn't as well muscled as Sis, but her body could have graced the centerfold of any man's magazine except for her age!

Her stomach was softly rounded. Below her pussy hair was cropped close at the top, amazingly in a perfect heart shape. It was shaved below, so that no hair on the lower part of her pussy would show when she did the acrobatics while cheerleading. It was so smooth looking. I guessed Sis had trimmed and shaved her. I loved the look of it and it made my mouth water. I'd have to get Sis to trim my pussy hair like that. I hoped I would get to try to lick her pussy.

"Little Sis, like my lover's body? She is in fantastic shape isn't she? I want you to taste her too. She has the sweetest tasting pussy, and she gets so wet when we make love. I think you two will make wonderful lovers for each other." My heart jumped at that thought!

Dottie moved to the bed and lay back taking my hand and pulling me on to it. She laid me back and moved over me to begin kissing my body. I shivered at her touch. She was so beautiful. Her shoulder length brown hair fell over me, caressing me. She stroked my body slowly and gently. Her touch was feather light. She took my nipples between her fingers and rolled them and pulled gently at first then a little harder as they grew longer and harder. She bent and took one breast in her mouth and sucked and licked it. It felt wonderful! Would they get more sensitive as they grew larger?

I stroked her shining hair and reached under and cupped and squeezed her superb breast feeling the hard nipple against the palm of my hand. God, it felt so wonderful to have her make love to me. I had been a bratty kid before, now both the older girls wanted to make love to me. I moaned as she nipped my nipple. The delightful pain seemed to go straight to my hard clit.

Dottie moved upward, and she put her breasts against me and rubbed her hard nipples against mine. Damn it felt wonderful. She rubbed her hard nipples over my chest, her full breasts pressing against my skin. I wished I had larger breasts to push back against hers! I loved the feel of her hot full firm breasts pressing down against mine. Finally she moved downward and kissed and licked my stomach and then moved between my legs.

"Ohh, your pussy is so beautiful. Just like your sister's when she was your age. I licked and sucked hers, and was the first person to ever make love to her. Beautiful, absolutely mouth watering!" Dottie said as she kissed my thighs and licked them, making me almost wild with passion. Her tongue slid out and ran lightly along my slit parting the hair and running along the lips. Gently she pressed it downward splitting my pussy open. I spread my thighs giving her more room. Her fingers spread me even wider and she pushed her tongue down into me. I moaned out loud and Sis moved up close to me and leaned over to kiss my lips and her hand slid over my aching breast cupping it.

I was trembling it felt so wonderful, with a skillful pair of lips at my pussy and my Sister's lips and tongue playing over mine while she caressed my breast too. I had never dreamed this was possible. Never in my life had I ever thought it might happen to me! Sis tongued my mouth and one hand played with my breasts and nipples, pulling and rolling them.

Below, Dottie's tongue was working its magic inside me. My pussy was on fire and when her tongue flicked my hard clit I exploded. My hips came upward mashing against her mouth. I cried out and screamed my joy as my body went wild. Having the two of them making love to me was hotter even than just Sis making love to me. They redoubled their efforts and I came in a long series of climaxes till I was totally exhausted and begged for them to stop. I didn't faint this time, but came close.

They slowed their assault on my body. Dottie moved up beside me with Sis on the other side of me, and her lips were still wet from my pussy juices. Her eyes were shining with mischief.

"Well, Little Bratty One, you have an absolutely delicious pussy. Kiss me and taste it off of my lips. I love that." She leaned down and we kissed. I licked her lips and tasted my juices on her. I felt Sis move and her lips and tongue joined ours and we tongued, and licked each other in a frenzy of three-way kissing. A fantastic way to end my first, and I hoped, not my last lovemaking with this gorgeous friend of Sis's.

We three kissed and hugged and I caressed both their sexy bodies and wonderful breasts. Their hands roamed over me sensuously. I felt so loved and wanted between them as their bodies pressing against me.

"Didn't I tell you she had a fresh little delicious pussy?" Sis said kissing Dottie. Finally Sis got off the bed and went to Mom's wardrobe. "Hey Lover, I want us to try something really hot I found. You will never believe this! I still am not sure why she has it."

She opened Mom's lingerie drawer and reaching in, ran her hands way back under Mom's frilly, sensuous underwear. I had looked in it a number of times, even trying on some of Mom's sexy panties and used her vibrators on myself. The panties were too large for me, but I got a strange sexy feeling putting them on. I even rubbed my pussy through them, being careful not to get the crotch wet or leave telltale stains.

"Voila!" Sis said pulling out several assorted vibrators and even some fake cocks. She handed them to us and our eyes went wide, we looked and felt them, giggling and laughing. "Now the piece de resistance." She said with a little flourish pulling it from behind her back, where she had been hiding it. Our eyes really grew big as she showed us a rather large, long dildo with a vinyl panty-like attachment at the bottom to firmly hold the fake cock.

"Good Lord, your Mom has one of those? Why would a married woman want with one of those?" Dottie asked, taking it from Sis's hand and feeling of the large long dildo.

"I don't know, maybe she and Dad play games and she fucks him up the ass!" Sis laughed. "Turn about is fair play?" They laughed uproariously.

I didn't laugh, my head rocked back in shock at the thought. Surely not! My parents? Damn, that was wild, but I remembered how shocked I was the first time I heard how babies were made – no way would my parents do that nasty sounding thing, or so I thought at the time!

But I later found out they did have sex, no doubt of that. I had heard them a number of times when I was supposed to have been asleep, had heard the bedsprings creaking, the slap of flesh against flesh, the moans and groans, and Mom's long gasps and quavering sobs of what could only be ecstasy. I had stood in the hall listening, my fingers playing over my clit as I tried to imagine in my mind exactly what they were doing. I'd have a wonderful, cum then hop back in bed. Fortunately, I never got caught.

"Hey, I remember thinking that my parents would never do that dirty fucking thing, not even to make babies." I finally managed to laugh. Dottie and Sis laughed with me. I felt the fake cock. It looked and felt like real skin, and the plastic, for some reason, even felt warm to the touch. It even had blue colored veins on the sides, a large reddish-purple head, and a scrotum at the back.

Sis took the fake cock and put it up to her mouth. . "I hope she washed it the last time she used it!" She ran her tongue along the head. "Yep, tastes like plastic!" We laughed. "Lover, you want me to fuck you, or do you want to fuck me?" She said holding the device up toward Dottie.

" I don't know, neither of us has ever been actually fucked. You decide, we can sure take turns." Dottie said running her hand up and down the long cock caressing it. It looked really huge to me, and no way would that big thing go into either one of their pussies, I thought!

"OK, I'll try it. Good thing the panties are adjustable. Have to remember to wash it and put it back to the same size when we are through. Don't want Mom to find out we used it! I just can't imagine Mom fucking Dad in the ass is all. Wild! But what else would she have one for? It looks like it's been used, it's certainly not new." Sis said as she slid the latex panties on. It had Velcro adjustable straps, and she pulled and tugged till she had it snugly fitting her hips. We laughed as we saw her, beautiful breasts above and a long cock jutting out below.

"OK, Doll, where do you want it? I'm The Big Stud, and am going to fuck the Shit out of you!" Sis said in a passable imitation of Bogart!

"How do I know? In the pussy obviously, you are not putting that in my ass, no way Jose! Let me roll over and get on my knees. You can come up behind me. We've seen them do that a lot in the porn videos. Doggy fashion! I'll be your little Bitch." She laughed. She rolled over and got on her hands and knees. Sis got behind her and put the dildo against her pussy and pushed a little. It didn't want to go in.

"Sis, look in that bedside drawer and see if there is any lubricant there, Vaseline, or KY jelly, or whatever is in there. There's always some there." My Sister said, looking rather funny sporting this huge male cock in front of her.

I opened the drawer and found a small container. How did she know there was always some lubricant in the drawer? I guess she snooped a lot! I read the label then held it up for them to see. "Can you believe this? 'Anal lube!' I guess Mom does fuck Dad in the ass." I opened it and put some on my hand and lubed up the dildo, then put some along Dottie's pussy lips. I loved sliding my slippery fingers along her spread pussy lips applying the lubricant. She patted my hand and winked at me. My pulse rate went way up!

Sis took the dildo and slid it up and down Dottie's pussy as I watched. She pushed a little and the large head spread her lips wider but hesitated a moment.

"Wow, that is really big. Easy, Love, you stay still, and I'll push back against you. Let me do the work for a moment. Ooooh, it's really stretching me!" Dottie said as she bent her head and her lovely ass moved back just a little.

I moved very close and watched fascinated as the cudgel pressed against her gleaming pussy lips, spreading them wider then slowly began to move inward. The bulbous head slipped past the tight opening then seemed to pop inward. She gave a sigh of relief. I took my finger and ran it around her lovely pussy and spread the excess lubricant along the shaft.

"Now Lover, fuck me slowly. I'll have to get used to this. I'm not sure how much of that thing I can take in my pussy. This is the first time for something that big. It's a lot larger and longer then my vibrator. Go easy, please?" Dottie said looking back.

That got me to thinking and I reached over and found one of the slender vibrators with a long flexible tip on it with small rubber whiskers and a knobby surface. It was kind of ridiculous looking, but it had to be for the ass.

I turned it on and it throbbed powerfully. Mom even kept fresh batteries in them. My eyes lit up. Little Sister was going to join the fun! I took some of the lubricant and put it along the full length, and a little more on my finger. I watched as Dottie's cute ass pushed backward making the dildo slide deeper inside her pussy. I watched in fascination shaking my head thinking surely it would never all go inside her body. Finally I put my finger on her cute little brownish hole and ran it around in circles spreading the lubricant over it.

"Whoa, we have a novice player who knows the angles. Mnnnn, yes sweet Tess, put your finger in my ass. I love that. Damn, Kit, your sister is a real wonder. We should have gotten her in with us earlier in her young life! She's a natural." Dottie said smiling back at me. My heart soared. I was finally accepted by this gorgeous older girl.

"Oh, yes, Hon, that hit bottom. God that fills me up! Wait a minute and let my pussy get used to that inside me." Dottie said as her butt hit Sis's thighs and the whole dildo was inside her. I couldn't believe she had it all in her. I wondered how long a dildo, or vibrator I could take inside my pussy. I had just used the vibrations against my clit and that had sent me into orbit! I'd sure have to try one of the smaller ones, and find out how deep I could take it. I'd bet Sis and Dottie would help me find out!

Dottie wiggled her cute ass, a signal for Sis to fuck her. Sis didn't say anything; she was concentrated on moving the dildo in and out, slowly. I could tell she was worried about hurting Dottie, her best friend and lover! I ran my finger around Dottie's small brownish star, and pressed downward a little. I had put my finger in Sis's ass, and now I made sure my fingernails didn't scratch Dottie. It slid inside her tight little hole.

I loved the feel of her hot flesh around my finger. It was so tight. I pushed it deeper inside her and heard her moan. We both were making love to her at the same time. I let my finger move inside her hot rear tube exploring her wonderful ass. I pushed my finger toward the front of her body and was amazed, I could feel the dildo sliding in and out through the thin membranes of her ass and pussy. Wild!

While Sis fucked Dottie, I watched the dildo slide in and out of her beautiful pussy and watched the way her pussy lips moved in and out. When the dildo slid out, it pulled her reddened lips outward, then on the inward stroke they were pushed in. Her small neat asshole did the same for my finger. I slid it as far inside her as I could.

I laid my head against her shapely ass and nuzzled her soft skin. The wonderful aroma of her aroused sex filled my nostrils. She started to move her body with each stroke now as the dildo slid ever deeper inside her. I reached over on the bed and got the vibrating slender probe and as I slid my finger out, I replaced it with the rubber probe.

I slid it slowly inside her and heard her catch her breath as three, then four inches slid deep inside her backside. I didn't turn the vibrator function on just yet. I wanted to let Sis, with my help, get her really hot.

"Oh, wow, you hit bottom, Hon. Easy! That rubs against my cervix and it really feels nice. Fuck me slowly now, let me get used to the feeling of having that so deep inside me. It's longer and larger than my vibrator and takes a little getting used to.

"Wow, so this is what if feels like to get fucked! I still am not ready for some guy to fuck me. I'll wait a while. I'm like you Kit, I don't want to get pregnant or catch something. I'll hold off a few years. But I think we should definitely get one of these. Ohh, yes, Baby, like that!"

Dottie moaned loudly, as Sis must have hit an erotic part of her pussy. "Mnn, yes, love that thing. Ask your Mom where we can get one like it! Ohhh, yes Baby, fuck me slow now. I'm getting used to it. Your little sister had something way up in my ass and I don't think it's her finger. That feels so sexy, Tess. Slide it in and out in time with your sweet sister.

I looked at Sis, smiled at her, leaned up and kissed her lips then moved down a little to suck and lick her breasts. The nipples were long and hard in her excitement. I wondered if the base of the dildo was giving her any pleasure, I'd noticed small knobs on the base of it, or it was the thought that she was fucking her gorgeous girlfriend. I timed my thrust into Dottie's bottom to coincide with Sis's slow steady, deep thrusts. I loved watching Sis's cute well-muscled ass thrusting and moving. It was a fantastic scene with Sis fucking her from behind and the anal probe sliding in and out.

Dottie began to moan and wiggle her cute ass, as she got hotter. I moved a little and reached under with my free hand and began to rub her pussy. It only took one or two exploratory strokes till I found her very firm clit, and her gasp told me she loved it. I stroked it slowly at first till she was moaning louder. In a quick movement, I reached back and turned the vibrator on, then my hand went back to her clit. Her head went back and her body went taut as she neared her climax. Sis saw it too and her hips thrust harder till her thighs were slapping Dottie's delectable ass, and that noise and her moans filled the room. I pumped the vibrating dildo faster and faster in and out of her ass.

Dottie's body bowed forward, her head went down and she screamed out as the two of us brought her to a wonderful climax. My face was close to her ass and I watched her pussy and ass muscles contract around the two intruders. My finger flew over her hard clit adding to her ecstasy. I think she had two long sobbing, moaning climaxes before she finally told us to stop. I turned the vibrator off and pulled it slowly out of her lovely ass. Sis pulled back and the gleaming dildo slid out.

"Wow, you two, that was fantastic. Now I know how it feels to be fucked." She panted. "That was wild. And you, sexy little Tess; it was a stroke of genius to put that vibrator in my ass. We'll have to buy one of those too! Damn, we can have lots of fun, just the three of us. My Mom never gets home till after 6 in the evening and Dad about 30 minutes later. You two can come over any day after school and we can have a roaring good time before they get home. But you know what I want to do right now?" Dottie said rolling on her side and holding out her arms toward me.

"Uh oh, little Sister, I think she wants you. I know that look, she loves more than one cum." Sis said reaching over and giving my ass a playful slap.

I was thrilled beyond words. I moved into Dottie's arms and she kissed me and pulled me against her. Her hands pulled me upward and I slipped on top of her fantastic body. Her full breasts felt so wonderful against me. She slipped her hot tongue inside my mouth while she caressed my body. Her hands went to my ass and pressed me hard against her body.

She spread her thighs and I fitted down between them. She swiveled her hips and spread her thighs wider. A little pressure on my shoulders and I moved down just a little. My pubic bone rubbed against hers then I slid a little further down at her direction. I felt my pussy press downward into her very wet open pussy. My firm pussy mound nestled down into her hot wet flesh. It felt so erotic. She wiggled her hips a little settling me down into her pussy.

"Mnn, sweet Baby, yes, I can feel your pussy lips on either side of my clit. Move your ass slowly and fuck my clit." Dottie whispered against my ear. Her tongue flicked my earlobe.

I was almost shaking with lust. I experimentally thrust my hips, rotating them in little hunching movements and felt my pussy slide along her wet treasure. She moaned softly.

"Ohh, yes that sweet virginal pussy feels so good against mine. More! Make your hips thrust longer. Rotate your hips a little more too." She sighed. "Ohhhh, yes, sweet Baby. God, Kit, your sister is a wonderful lover. Ohhhh, shit, she's fucking my pussy so fucking good! We'll have to teach her in all the nasty things we have learned to do to each other. Ohh, yes, yes, faster Tess, Love. Fuck my clit, Baby. Mnnn, yessss, like that! It's fucking my clit; you are fucking me so fucking good, Baby! Yessssss!" She cried out.

My mind soared as I hunched my pussy against hers. I imitated the motions I had seen the men use in a fucking video I had seen once, unknown to my parents. Her hot pussy was spread wide and I could just feel her engorged clit slip along my pussy lips. I could imagine how it felt to her. I wished my clit were longer, so it would rake along her pussy lips too, but it was receiving almost no help. My clit just wasn't long enough. Rubbing against her felt wonderful, but didn't give me enough stimulation. I bent my head and kissed her breast and sucked the nipple. I hunched faster and her moans of joy filled the room.

Her body went rigid, she screamed out, and her hips thrust hard up against mine. I bit down on her nipple as I thrust hard against her pussy and clit. She screamed her joy over and over and I felt a hot wetness against my pussy, it was suddenly very slippery. Had she peed? I didn't know, but loved the slick wetness. My pussy slid delightfully along her slippery gash. She gave another long scream then she fell back spent. Her arms went around me holding me close to her. Her chest was rising up and down as she panted. I kissed her breasts softly and softly sucked her erect nipples.

"My God, that was fantastic. Your sweet pussy fucking mine was out of this world Tess. You have just graduated from the Bratty Little Younger Sister to a Full-fledged Lover. Right Kit?" Dottie said between gasps as she tried to catch her breath.

Lying on top of her I felt like I was on top of the world. I was finally accepted by the two beautiful older girls. I was IN! No longer 'The Brat' - the Brat to be gotten rid of!

"Your pussy got real slippery when you came, I felt something wet down there, it made your pussy so slick." I said, not knowing how to say it to her. If she had peed during her climax I didn't want to embarrass her. They started laughing and I was puzzled.

Dottie rolled me off of her and grinned over at me. "Little Lover, I didn't pee, if that's what you are thinking. Your sweet sister and I both spurt sometimes when we cum. It's not urine, we just get really hot and sometimes, not every time, but sometimes when we are really excited, we shoot out a nice tasting pussy juice. You just got me so damn excited. We have read about it on the net. Do me a favor, and lean down and lick my wet pussy. I think you will find it rather tasty. At least your sister thinks so!" She grinned at me and winked saucily.

I looked over at Sis, she grinned and nodded. I slipped down in the bed and brought my face close to Dottie's spread pussy. It was wet and gleaming, her inner and outer lips were swollen and red from the fucking and my pussy rubbing against hers. There was a small puddle of her juice at her vaginal opening. I sniffed in her wonderful odor. Then I leaned in and ran my flattened tongue along her wonderful wet pussy. The delicious flavor flowed over my tongue. So like Sis's, but slightly different. I licked again from bottom to top, lost in the odor and the flavor of Dottie's intimate flesh. I was making love to Dottie. I looked up at her and her face was a mixture of joy and pleasure.

"Ohh, yes, so nice. Keep licking. My pussy is still hot from your fucking. Lick me again sweet little Lover." She moaned.

I was only too happy to lick her delicious pussy. I would do anything for these two beautiful older girls. I licked over and over, sucked too, and tasted her sweet juices. I could get addicted to this, I thought with a grin. Would they let me?

"Damn that feels wonderful, Tess. You are a wonderful lover. I want to lick you too. I want to really make love to that sweet pussy of yours while you lick me. Want to do a 69 with me?" Dottie asked.

My throat was choked with lust. I couldn't have answered if my life depended on it. I had this feeling a little when Betsy and I kissed and

Frenched each other. But this was absolutely overwhelming, my Sister lying close beside me, and now Dottie wanting to 69 with me. I knew what that was! I only managed to nod dumbfounded. I opened my mouth but nothing came out but a croak.

"I think that means a 'Yes!'" Sis laughed. She reached over, kissed me and helped me turn in the bed. Dottie rolled onto her back and reached up and spread my legs on each side of her head. Her face was under my pussy, my thighs spread wide. My mouth watered as I looked down at her spread pussy, just below me. The thought that she was under me, her face inches from my wet pussy made my clit tingle and burn.

I leaned down and kissed her thighs and licked them. Her hands went to my ass and pressed downward wanting me to lower my pussy to her face. I repositioned my legs and let my hips drop. I moaned as her tongue slid up and down my pussy. I couldn't believe Dottie was making love to me and her pussy was just below my eager lips.

I nuzzled her sparse heart shaped pubic hair and then moved my head downward. She felt me and spread her thighs wider for me, giving me complete access to her very wet pussy. I saw a movement and Sis's head was close to me.

"Easy, little Sister, take it slow and easy. There is all the time in the world. Go slow. Part her pussy lips with your fingers. Lie down on top of her. That way you can use both hands on her pussy." She coached me.

I let my weight settle on Dottie's superb body. Her breasts cushioned my stomach. She smelled wonderful. I wondered what perfume she used. It, and the delightful odor of her pussy surrounded me, as my face was inches from her spread pussy. I just looked at it. Beautiful! Her pussy lips were neat and lovely; I spread them wider with my fingers and looked at the soft pink star of her vagina. A drop of her juice slowly formed there and her whole pussy was still wet from her cum. I began to lick her softly and slowly.

Her juices were slightly salty and so delicious. I had never tasted anything so sensual, so sexual as licking another girl's pussy. I loved the taste and smell of Sis's pussy, and now Dottie's. I would definitely have to try this with Betsy. We had gotten hot together Frenching and but never went any further. Now, I wanted to go all the way with her, lick Betsy's sweet pussy and have her lick mine. A thrill went through my body at that thought, and as Dottie's tongue played along my slit slipping into my pussy, pushing up into me.

I licked up and down Dottie's pussy then wiggled down a little and let my tongue find her center. It was hot and so wet. I licked it then pointed my tongue and slid it down, down into her center. It felt heavenly to have her wet flesh against my tongue. I pushed down still more, extending my tongue as far as I could. I have a pretty long tongue and can touch the end of my nose to the delight of some, the disgust of others. I ran it down into her.

My lips came against her pussy and I opened them wide to cover her hot wet opening. She moaned and I knew she liked it. I moved my tongue from side to side inside her while I sucked gently. I was delighted when her pussy juices spilled into my mouth. She tasted delicious. I sucked harder and thrust my tongue deeper inside her velvet-wet flesh. Her sweet juices flowed into my mouth. Delicious!

Damn this was fantastic! I could hardly wait to try this with Betsy, and have her taste me too. We lay there sucking and kissing each other. This was heaven to me, to kiss and suck a pussy while having my own made love to. No wonder I heard so much whispering about 69s!

Sis's face was close to mine and she kissed my cheek and whispered in my ear, "Remember her clit!" I had become so engrossed in tasting her and sliding my tongue deep inside her beautiful body, I had forgotten her clit. She sure hadn't forgotten mine and her lips found it and sucked on it gently at first, then harder. Thrills of lust ran through my body and it begged for release.

I put my fingers on her pussy and pulled upward at the top. Her erect clit slid out, reddish pink and extending out at least a quarter of an inch. It was larger and longer than Sis's or my own small one. I licked it and she shivered and thrust her hips upward toward my mouth. I put my lips around it and sucked on her hard nubbin. I ran my tongue over and around the tip, making her writhe with pleasure and her hips press against my lips.

I tried flicking my tongue back and forth across the tip and it set her wild. I tried to see how fast I could make my tongue vibrate over her hard clit, and whatever I did send her over the edge and she screamed out against my pussy. I held on to her bucking hips and tongued her clit till her body went rigid and she screamed over and over. Then suddenly I felt the juices pour from her pussy. I moved my lips just a little and was able to keep tonguing her clit while my mouth was opened wide against her spread pussy. I felt several pulses of her pussy juices spurt into my mouth. They were right, it was not urine. It had a wonderful salty-sweet flavor. She cried out one last scream and went limp under me. I lapped her pussy but when it came into contact with her clit she cried out.

"Don't lick her clit right now. It's always very sensitive just after a climax." Sis whispered in my ear and nibbled on my ear lobe. That felt wonderful, as I was so hot. It took a couple of minutes before Dottie was back to normal and then she started lapping at my pussy again in earnest. She slid a finger inside me and moved it in and out as she licked me. She went back to my clit and began to lick and suck it.

Wonderful waves of joy ran through my body as she made love to me. I felt a finger slip between my ass cheeks and move downward till she had found my nether hole. Her finger was wet and she gently pushed it inside me. Her mouth was on my pussy and her finger sliding deep inside my ass. She took my clit between her lips and began to suck on it rhythmically, in and out, over and over. Then she would flick my clit with her talented tongue from moment to moment.

She slid a finger into my pussy and curled it up inside and hit a place in my pussy that had never been touched. Only much later would I learn about the G-spot. That was the key that pushed me over the edge and I screamed out my ecstasy as my body went into spasms of pure pleasure. I saw stars and a million colored lights as I climaxed. Her lips sucked, her tongue flicked and her fingers pushed deep inside my pussy and ass. My climax seemed to go on and on. Finally I collapsed, completely spent.

I was aware of Sis moving above my head. I looked up to see the well-lubricated dildo, attached to her body moving close. I grinned and managed to guide the head to Dottie's pussy. I held the head steady, and she pressed it down into Dottie.

"Oh, God, yes, Lover, fuck me while your sweet sister licks my clit. I can lick her off to another cum. This is wild, I don't know how it could get any better!" Dottie's muffled voice came from between my thighs. Her tongue probed my pussy again. I raised my head slightly to lick her clit while the dildo slid in and out.

I saw a movement out of the corner of my eye, and looked toward the door. My eyes went wide in horror. Then all three of us heard a loud gasp from the doorway. There, hands on her voluptuous hips stood Mrs. Mason, our next-door neighbor, and Mom's closest friend. Her big blue eyes took in the spectacle of the three of us on the bed, naked. I was lying on top of Dottie, in a 69, and Sis behind Dottie with the long gleaming dildo, the large head already buried halfway inside her spread pussy.

"My God. I would have never in the world thought this of you two kids, or you either, Dottie." She gasped. Our hearts sunk. We had completely forgotten that Mom had given her a house key and told her to check on us from time to time. We were cooked, D-E-A-D, as Sis had told me earlier.

"I'm afraid I'll have to tell your Mother about this." She said shaking her head slowly. Her face looked very grim. We were totally, completely, fucked - dead meat!

182

"Mrs. Mason, Brandi, please don't! Please?" Sis pleaded, tears in her eyes thinking of what Mom would do to both of us, and to Dottie too. She pulled the pussy-wet dildo out of Dottie's spread sex, and rolled over facing Mrs. Mason. "We'll do anything you ask, but please, don't tell her. Please?"

It must have looked ludicrous to see Sis begging with that huge dildo poking up in front of her. Mrs. Mason's eyes dropped down to take it in. Her lip curled. Brandi looked up at her sternly, her full bosoms rising and falling at the sight of the three of us naked before her. Dottie and I rolled apart our faces red with embarrassment, our lips still wet with pussy juices.

"Anything?" She asked sternly. We all three nodded, still shocked by her sudden unexpected appearance.

Slowly she began to unbutton her blouse. Her magnificent full breasts came into view, covered by a frilly bra; her huge chocolate brown areolas were clearly visible under the sheer cloth, and her erect nipples tenting the ends were plainly visible too. I remember Mom referring to her once as zaftig! Damn, she really was! Her full breasts had to be at least a DD, my startled eyes estimated. She slid the blouse off and let it fall to the floor. We lay there, completely puzzled by her actions.

"Well, I'll think about it, but I still think I'll really have to tell your Mom. After all, you are using our favorite toys that we use on each other!" She said as she reached down to undo the front clasp of her bra. Her large breasts spilled out, magnificent in their fullness. They dropped just a little, large full mounds of beautiful flesh, her nipples hard, long, and erect. Even in our puzzled terror they still looked mouth watering.

"I'll sure have to tell her, or she'll never, ever, forgive me." She said with a smile slowly forming on her lips, and a wicked twinkle in her big blue eye as she let her sexy looking bra fall, and moved toward the bed. Her full breasts bounced and swayed as she walked toward us.

As she reached the edge of the bed, she was unfastening the buttons on her skintight shorts. She looked down on the three of us lying there, naked and confused.

"She'll want to enjoy all three of you lovely, sexy young girls too! She'd never forgive me if I kept you three all to myself, now would she?"

Nathan

My name is James, I'm 19 years old and I'm from a busy town with the usual life a teenager has. I spend most of my time working and playing football with friends. I have a best friend called Nathan, we've been good friends for 9 years or so now but since we left school a few years back I don't see him half as much as I'd like to with us both working. I have a fairly small build but because I'm into sports and I hit the gym I'm broader than most guys my age.

Around 6 months ago I was going through a strange stage in my life, I was horny all the time, I'm not sure if puberty hit me late or what but it was a very unusual time for me.

I woke up late on my day off from work, must have been around 11am, first thing I do every day due to habit is have a good cold shower and get cleaned up. I had nothing to do that day and thought I'd give Nathan a call. I don't know what it is about Nathan, I still feel it now 5 months later, he's the only guy I've ever looked at in a different way. I've had girlfriends on and off since I was around 13, now I've been with my girlfriend for 2 years so I'm pretty sure that I'm straight. So after calling Nathan he came round an hour later and we had nothing to do so we thought of a little plan, in the summer months we liked to go to a little village outside town which had a small river flowing all the way through it and it had some great flat grass in parts where we loved to play football. It was a nice day and the sun was out so we drove to the supermarket in his car and grabbed some snacks and pop. Then we were on our way, it took around 30 minutes to get there and park up then we took off down the hill to the river, it was a week day which meant most folk would be working and the kids would be at school so it was fairly quiet. We played football for abit then went down the banking to sit on an old tree which had become an L shape over time.

We messed around for an hour or so climbing the trees and skimming stones, Nathan thought it was a good idea to climb as high as he could up the tree, which did seem a fun idea at the time, as the tree got taller it had grown over the river, which meant that split second Nathan slipped from the tree I was going to get a front row seat on you've been framed. He managed to fall past every branch and splash right into the middle of the river, I was laughing so hard as he hit the water, he jumped up from the dirty water shouting all sorts of abuse at the tree which made me laugh harder than before. He started swimming towards the banking where I was sat, then as he got to the point where he could stand up he pulled his shirt off revealing his body. He was a little taller than me around 5' 8" and he has a great 6 pack with muscle showing in all the right places, the tattoos he had across his chest and arms only made him look better. Now I've seen him without a shirt on before many times but this time it was different, this time I was getting hard looking at him. He pulled a towel out of his bag and started to dry himself off, then looked around and pulled his trousers down leaving his boxer shorts which had love hearts on, I don't know what had come over me that day but I wanted to see his dick so bad. Eventually he dried off as best he could and pulled his trousers up, we set back to the car because he didn't want to stand around all wet, as soon as we got in the car he pulled his trousers off again laughing about how he had to drive home almost naked, all this time I hadn't said much as I was taking in everything he was doing, I wanted to pull his boxer shorts off right then but I resisted because I didn't want to turn all creepy on him.

We eventually got home around 11pm and went to my house as usual, he went straight upstairs and got a shower, I thought seen as he's going to be up there a while I sat at the computer and flicked up a porn site so I could quickly pull myself off, I always make the same mistake of getting too far into it and wanting to hold out as long as possible. I still hadn't done after 20 minutes and I heard him at the top of the stairs so I covered up and closed the browser window. I was hoping for him to walk in with just a towel wrapped round him but he'd already got dressed into dry clothes. I thought to myself "I gotta stop this, he's my best friend, why would I wanna ruin that?".

We sat down to watch a movie and I ordered a takeaway as we were both off work the next day and could lay in. We were talking about the usual stuff, girls, how much weed I smoked, how he always broke his car. After an hour or so into the movie I could see he was drifting off to sleep, I left him to it because I don't like waking people up and this could be my chance to have a wank. He slept like a log for the next 20 minutes so I stayed where I was and pulled my dick out of the top of my pants and started rubbing it slow, he was facing me but I was 100% sure he was asleep and I carried on, I kept looking over at him and thinking back to what I'd seen earlier that day, the thrill of wanking over him while he was sat next to me was amazing, and the chance of getting caught just added to it. I must have been wanking for 10 minutes when all of a sudden he started to move, luckily all he did was shuffle abit and put one hand down his pants, which got me going abit more. I kept going and noticed he'd started to tent the front of his pants, I was so hard right now and when you as horny as I was you do things you might later regret. I reached over and tapped him on the chest to see if he would wake up, he was in a deep sleep by now. I then pulled my hand down his chest and his stomach slowly, I don't know what made me do it but I kept going right to the band on his pants. By now I didn't realise what I was doing was a bad idea, I pulled the band of his pants right down to reveal his dick, he must have been dreaming about something pretty good to get as hard as he was. To my surprise he had no pubic hair at all, fully shaved all the way down his balls, his dick must have been 7 inch and fat too, it looked pretty much the same as mine in shape and thickness. I gently grabbed his dick which felt really weird holding someone else's, I slowly moved up and down hoping to god that he didn't wake up, he didn't move a muscle but he was still breathing deep with the dream he was having. I noticed he had a tiny bit of pre-cum at the tip of his dick and I couldn't help myself, I was so nervous because I'd never touched a guy like this before, I slowly moved towards him, I was now on my knees in front of him holding his dick with both hands, I closed my eyes and licked all the way up his hard shaft and round the end taking in the pre-cum he was leaking. I kept licking his dick up and down and stroking his balls, by now his breathing was getting heavier. Then I took it a step further, I moved my lips over his hot helmet and took his whole dick in my mouth slowly hitting the back of my throat, he twitched a little bit which almost brought me back to reality to realise what I was doing. I carried on sucking every inch of his dick and it felt so good in my mouth, after 10 minutes of sucking his raging hard on he was breathing really heavy, he must have known he was being sucked off but it didn't wake him. I kept sucking, by now I was really into it, circling round the head while wanking his dick with one hand, then taking the whole thing in, almost swallowing it, I started sucking harder and faster all the way down to his balls and back up, over and over then he inhaled hard and shot a huge wad of cum in the back of my throat, I sucked deeper making sure to get his whole dick in there, he shot again, thick cum in my throat, I had to swallow a couple of times to keep it down, he soon stopped shooting and I pulled my head back releasing his dick, I licked all the cum off and put his dick back in his pants. I was still surprised he hadn't woken up, I went up to the bathroom where I had an amazing wank which took literally 2 minutes after all the excitement that day had brought.

When I came back down he was awake, which shocked me abit, that's when I started to worry if he knew what I'd done, he didn't say anything to me so I presumed I was safe. We finished off watching the film and it was around 1am, Nathan decided it was time to go home so I stood at the door having a cig while he talked about some car show he was going to the week after. We finished chatting and he went to give me the usual man hug to say bye, I was expecting him to just say bye and leave, but he gently put his hand on my dick and said "same time next week?", he moved back, winked at me and walked towards the gate. I couldn't say a word back to him, I was speechless.

The end

Heavy artillery

Growing up I had always fantasized about sexual experiences with guys. In high school, on some occasions, my friends and I would jerk each other off. Sadly that was the extent of it. After graduation I was able to finally admit I was bisexual... at the least. I made some gay friends and was slowly introduced to the gay world but for an instance. With no work around I decided to follow a close friend and I enlisted in the United States Marine Corps. I loved it! Hot young studs to stare at for ages. But this was still 2005 and "don't ask don't tell" was in full effect. My brief time as bisexual was but an unfulfilled dream. I had only kissed a guy before joining. I moved around going through training for the first year until finally getting orders to Okinawa, Japan.

I spent an extensive amount of time in the gym. From 2005 to 2008, I had transformed my 5' 8" 135 pound toned body to 185 pounds of lean ripped muscle. I found any reason to work on my tan. My dark eyes would often find reasons to compare my physique to others.

I eventually managed to attain my own room in the four story barracks after being promoted a couple of times. It was hard not to check some of the other Marines out. They would often come out of there rooms wearing only basketball shorts. The shape of their manhood draped by the thin fabric that was those shorts. With fast promotions occurring rooms started to be doubled on. There was no way I was going to have an ugly roommate. Stephen had just been promoted so he had to be moved with someone of the same rank. He was 5'10" 165 pounds. He had a muscular swimmers build. He would joke that he could never be pinched on Saint Patrick's day because is eyes were a dark green. I would often watch as he would stand supervising his Marines. The sun making his light brown hair seem like a halo around this Greek god. I had heard stories from his former roommate that he liked to walk around naked and had a HUGE cock that he would often flash. So I gladly offered him the opportunity to move in to my room and the bottom bunk. All the while hoping that I could catch a glimpse of his cock. I first saw how big he was one morning we woke up to go PT. He woke up with morning wood and walked towards me to go to the bathroom and I could see the length and girth through his boxer briefs. The tip of it reached to his hip and the thickness of it made my mouth water. Oh did I want to see it!

We became as close as roommates could become. Everyday we would enjoy a beer together afterwork. On one night though one beer turned to twelve.... We were relaxing in our room lounging on his bunk watching a movie. With our backs flat against the wall and our legs dangling off the twin sized mattress, we watched a movie play with our beer in hand. I don't remember exactly how but we were just sitting there in our boxers watching the movie. Filled with liquid courage I started thinking of how I could see his bare cock.

He got up to go take a piss and I ran to the bathroom and proclaimed," Not before me!" But I knew he wasn't the shy type. And as planned retaliated with, "I'm gonna piss next to you I don't care if you see my dick."

Sure enough he pulled his cock out while I pissed and went right next to me. Of course I looked! It was huge!! It was about 6inches soft!

"Dude you have a huge cock!!!"

"You haven't seen it hard..."

We went back to his bed and we both sat down, pretty drunk already, and continued watching the movie. I don't know what got into me. Probably the fact that I was drunk and all inhibition went out the window. There we were sitting, and I looked over and his cock was sticking out the front slit of his boxer briefs. He must not have put it away enough when we finished pissing. In drunken blindness I reached over and grabbed it and told him it was sticking out. WHAT THE FUCK did I just do?!He just looked at me. We stared at each other for a moment.

Finally I asked if I could play with it. He nonchalantly responded," Sure it's just a cock."

Yesss!!

I began to fondle him. I tugged and pulled at it. Stroking it and jerking it making him get harder with each one. It was magnificent. His huge head followed by a thick veiny shaft beckoned me. I looked at him and asked, "Can I try something...?"

I had never done anything like this. I had only dreamed of this kind of stuff. Before he could respond I got down on my knees in between his legs and put his thick cock in my mouth. I sucked and licked all up his shaft. I loved the aroma that his balls gave my nostrils as I put each one in my mouth. I would look up at him and run my free hand all over his muscles as my mouth worked his ever enlarging cock. I tried to put as much of it as I could in my mouth but he was too big for my virgin my mouth and throat. I only managed about half. His cock was about 9.5 in and about 6.5 around. It was way to much for me to swallow. After enjoying myself and tasting him as much as I could handle, I remembered he had lube! I went to his closet and grabbed it. I poured some on his cock as he lay in his bed. I rubbed it all over and I knew what I wanted to do. I straddled him and I raised myself high enough I could feel his head at my virgin hole. I slowly let the tip slide in. Oh was it painful but it felt soooo good. I was only able to put some of him in me before the pain was too much. I got off of him and he grabbed the lube and ran it over my cock!!!Did he want me to fuck him?!He spread his legs and pulled me towards him... Oh fuck!!

"Be gentle its been a long time since I've done this."

I couldn't believe it. He actually wanted to bottom. Fine by me. I positioned my head at his tight little bud and slowly pushed in. I could feel his tightness surround my head and it going past his first sphincter and then him relaxing and allowing the rest of me to push in. I pushed until my balls were pressed against his soft ass and all 6.5 of me were in him. I let him adjust as he kept his hands on my hips to adjust himself. I slowly started pulling out and sliding back in. I could finally feel him relax completely and I began to slowly pick up the pace of my thrust. His hole felt so tight and warm it was amazing. With each thrust he would moan. I hoisted his legs from my hips to my shoulders and reached around and grabbed his muscled pecs.

"Oh you feel amazing inside me," he moaned.

That excited me even more and I pound harder into his hole making him moan louder. Thank goodness the movie was still playing if not we might have been discovered.

I looked down at him and watched in full amazement as my bare cock slid in and out of his magnificent hole. With each thrust I felt more like a man. His tightness sending almost an unbearable pleasure deep inside my loins. He grabbed his cock from bouncing on his stomach, the tip dripping with precum, and began to stroke it vigorously. His body began to tense. I could see almost every striation in his muscled body as his body neared orgasm. He moaned with pleasure before yelling "I'm about to cum!!!"Just as he let his load explode all over his chest and some hitting him underneath his chin. That's all I needed. Watching him blow his load and feeling him squeezing his ass around me brought me to orgasm. I quickly pulled out of his now gaping hole and stroked my dick to the sight of his cum covered body and let it spray all over his hole and balls. I collapsed on top of him and we held and kissed each other. Allowing our bodies to stick to each other with our own cum.

We got up and showered eventually, we had to be up in about four hours for work.

Loving my Daddy

My name is Katya. I was born in the Ukraine in 1980. My father was an engineer and my mother a nurse. In the early part of 1988 my father was part of a Soviet contingent that went to Sweden as part of a technology exchange program between the Soviet Union and Sweden. He had brought my mother and me along for the few months that we were supposed to be there. Well, he'd had enough of the Communist regime and he defected while we were there. We all soon moved to the United States, where he went to work at a large tech firm outside of Washington D.C. My mother never really took to her surroundings and refused to learn to speak English so, even when I was young, I acted as her translator when we went to the grocery store. She always seemed sad and wistful and often talked of our old home in the Ukraine.

I'll tell you a little more about myself. I am a natural blonde with ice-blue eyes. Even as a little girl I turned heads. As far back as I could remember I was a horny girl. Of course, I didn't know that at the time. When I was 7 years old, I discovered that humping a pillow or climbing a pole felt really good. By the time I turned nine, I had given myself my first orgasm, the intensity of which initially scared me half to death. I soon got over my fears and was diddling myself pretty regularly. One day, after I turned 11, I'd come home after playing with friends. At first, nobody seemed to be home, but then I heard some soft moaning, so I went to investigate. The door to my parent's room was cracked, and my mom was lying on the bed, legs spread, with a dildo in her hairy pussy. I watched with fascination when she started moaning louder and started jerking as she reached an orgasm. I knew immediately that my mom was masturbating, but I'd never thought of putting something inside me when I did it. The next time I masturbated I put my hair brush handle, which was smooth and rounded, in my little pussy and had even better orgasms. My hairbrush and I had a lot of exciting moments together after that!

Unfortunately, after I turned 12 years old, my mother, who never really got over being home sick, moved back to the Ukraine. Of course, by then I had friends in school and loved my life in the U.S. and I had no desire to go back to the Ukraine, so it was decided that I would stay with my dad. My dad and I both really missed mom, but we had always been close, and we spent even more time together after she left. Dad got a new job at his company that allowed him to work from home at least three days a week, so we spent a lot of time together. We'd go to the movies, watch TV, and go camping and fishing together. My best friend's name was Sarah and we were always getting in some kind of trouble together. Her parents always worked so we'd spend most of our time at my house. During the summer we rarely left my backyard pool.

Sarah also had an older brother, Steve, who was about a year older than me at the time. His was the first erect penis I'd ever seen. One day when I was at her house she asked me if I'd ever seen a "boy's thing" before. I told her no. She told me her brother would show us his. Show it he did. Fully hard his little cock wasn't much bigger than my pinky finger, and I couldn't help but compare him to the size of my trusty hairbrush handle. I even touched it, but then I blurted out "wow, it's so tiny". Suddenly Steve turned beet red, yanked up his pants, and ran out of the room. I guess that wasn't what he wanted to hear. He rarely ever spoke to me again.

One thing I learned from having Sarah as my friend was that I looked different "down there". We had both just started to really develop and grow hair, but where Sarah had only a straight little slit, my hooded clit poked out of my little slit about a quarter of an inch. Maybe that was why I was always so horny. It seemed that even riding a bicycle or wearing my swimsuit, which was a bit too small on me, really got me going.

One time she told me that another girl from school had told her how much boys like a smooth, shaved pussy. We had both started shaving our legs, so one day while she was at my house, we got out some fresh razors to shave our pubic hair. First I shaved Sarah's dark, curly, but sparse pussy fur very carefully. I was really afraid that I would cut her, but I didn't and I thought it looked better afterwards. Then it was her turn to shave me. She squirted on the shaving gel and carefully went to work. As she worked around my swollen lips I realized just how horny I was getting. As she shaved around my clit, she put her thumb right on my clit and pulled it over to the side almost immediately I started to have an orgasm that caused me to shudder and moan. She looked at me funny and asked "Are you OK? Did I hurt you?" I just laughed and told her no. That was the first time I'd ever cum with somebody else touching me, but it was years before I told her what had happened. I did love the feeling of being completely smooth down there, and from then on I shaved regularly.

I'd seen my dad naked a time or two, but never with an erection. I supposed this would be a good place to describe Papa. He is about six feet tall with sandy blonde hair and hazel eyes. He's in great shape for such a geek. He runs a lot and has a home gym he uses almost every day. He has an athletic build, with muscular arms and great six-pack abs. He is also uncircumcised like most Russian men. Sarah always used to tease me about how hot my dad was. I knew he was handsome, but I always got irritated at her, because what girl would ever be attracted to her dad? And then one day it all changed. I was 14 years old at the time. Sarah and I had entered a science fair contest. Well, dad used his considerable talents to help us assemble it and we ended up winning first place! I was so excited that I rushed into the house after school to tell my dad. He wasn't in his office or out back so I went to his room. That's when I heard the shower running. The bathroom door was cracked and I peeked in. I was mesmerized by what I saw. I saw my dad through the glass shower door, facing sideways so he didn't notice me standing there staring at him. And he was stroking his hard 8" cock! Compared to Steve's, it was positively gigantic! Suddenly he tensed up, groaned, and white stuff started spurting onto the shower wall. I shook my self from my reverie and sneaked back out of his room. When I got back to my room, I felt my panties and they were soaked through. I yanked them off, grabbed my brush and plunged it in my little pussy. I imagined my dad's huge cock sliding in and out of me until I started having the best orgasm of life. I was cumming so hard that I didn't hear the knock on the door. Suddenly there was my dad standing in the doorway frozen in shock staring between my legs. He mumbled something about being sorry then took one last look between my legs and backed out the door. That's when I realized what he must have seen when he opened the door. I was laying there with no panties on, legs spread wide in the air, with my hair brush buried in my bald, soaking cunt. I was extremely embarrassed, but at the same time I was really turned on as well. Dad acted as if nothing happened that evening as we snuggled and watched TV. For the next few months nothing seemed out of the ordinary and I was disappointed to realize that he didn't look at me in sexual way. On the other hand, visions of him naked in the shower became the subject of many of my masturbatory fantasies.

Then one weekend, dad rented some movies for us to watch. We made some popcorn, hot cocoa, and got ready for the movie. I was just wearing my pajamas, which consisted of one of dad's shirts that I borrowed and no panties, and he was wearing his boxer shorts. I crawled over to the VCR to put in the tape and start the movie. When I got up and walked back I was amazed to see that dad was trying to hide an erection that was tenting up his boxers. Now I knew that men got erections when they got sexually excited. We snuggled and watched the movie, but I was still trying to figure out what had given him an erection. When I went to the bathroom I turned around and bent over and looked in the full length mirror on the door. The t-shirt rode up and my shaved pussy was clearly visible with the little button poking out of my slit. My God, dad had gotten hard because he was looking at ME! I was so excited and turned on by this new revelation. When I went back I crawled right up into his lap with my legs straddling his. Soon I felt something hard right below the crack of my ass. I stole a few glances and could see the tip of his penis pushing up on his boxers. After the movie I hurried to my room and buried my brush in my bald little cunt and ended up having three orgasms. That night I decided that I wanted him to be the one to take my virginity and I started to put a plan together.

Whenever I changed or showered, I would leave the door open a crack. At night I would wear my shortest "night shirt" and I'd never wear panties. I caught dad looking at me when I got up, and there was usually a lump in his pants. Then I got brave one day and left the door open a crack while I masturbated. I moaned a little bit more than usual, hoping that dad would be watching. When I finished I glanced at the door and I saw a shadow move outside. Dad had seen everything! When I got up, he had gone back to his bedroom. When he came out a few minutes later he looked flushed but happy, and I knew that he had masturbated thinking about me!

I was about to turn 15 and dad had always thrown a big party for me, but this year I told him I just wanted it to be him and me. He asked what I wanted for my birthday and I told him I wanted to shop for clothes and get a glamour makeover at the mall. He bought me a really nice dress which I changed into, and then I had my makeup and hair done. When I looked in the mirror, I barely recognized myself. I'd been transformed from a girl into a beautiful woman. When I came out of the salon, dad was speechless! I even noticed that a lot of other men were checking me out as we walked together. We went to dinner and it felt more like I was on my first date.

When we got home dad asked me what I wanted to do and I told him I was going to take a bath. Then I asked him to wash my back like he used to when I was little. He hesitated and said he didn't know if that was a very good idea. I begged and pleaded and he finally agreed. He started the bath while I went to my room to get out of my new dress. Then, completely nude I walked into the bathroom. Dad turned around and was completely speechless again. I could see him drinking in every inch of my naked skin and I saw a look in his eye I'd never seen before. Of course, with my hair looking so mature I didn't want to wash it, but I asked him to scrub my back. When he was done he started to leave. I asked him why he was leaving if he hadn't washed me all over. He hesitated but slowly walked back to the tub. Then he started scrubbing me, first with a washcloth, but soon with just his big strong hands. Soon his hands had worked up my thighs and he gently brushed my pussy. I let out a moan and spread my legs further. Seeing the invitation he started gently rubbing my clit. I was in heaven and just about to cum, when he suddenly stood up and said in Russian "What the hell am I doing" and he rushed out of the bathroom. I got out and dried off, put the towel around me and followed him to his room. He was sitting on the bed with his head in his hands muttering something to himself in Russian about being a bad father. I walked over to him, put my arms around him, and told him "Papa, I want you to touch me and make me feel good." He said he couldn't do it. That my wanting it didn't make it right and that he was afraid he would go to jail and never see me again. I lifted his face up to look at me and I let my towel drop. I ask him if he thought I was beautiful. He said I was the most beautiful creature he'd ever set eyes on. Then I kissed him right on the lips. Soon he was kissing me back. I'd never kissed anybody in a romantic way before and he immediately got my juices flowing again. Again I begged him to make me feel good. He finally agreed, but told me that it would always have to be our secret. I agreed and he lifted me up and laid me on the bed. He began kissing and fondling me all over. I was in heaven. Then he started working his way down my belly until he was teasing the outer folds of my pussy. It was driving me crazy, so I begged him to please touch me down there. That's when he dipped his tongue into my pussy and then ran it up my slit and circled my clit. It felt like electric shock running through me. He would circle my clit, then gently suck it into his mouth, and then flick his tongue over the top of it. That was all too much and my world was suddenly rocked by an earth-shattering orgasm so huge I thought I was going to pass out. Unlike the other orgasms I'd had, this one didn't stop right away. Wave after wave of pleasure crashed over me as he very lightly continued to flick his skilled tongue across my clit. When he finally stopped I was gasping for breath and couldn't move or talk. He asked if I was alright. When I could finally start to move and think again, I sat up and hugged him and told him it was amazing and I loved him more than ever. Then I told him it was his turn. He slowly pulled off his shorts and out sprung the object of my desire. I touched and gently ran my hand over the tip smearing his pre-cum over his cock. He sighed and moaned as I slowly moved my hand up and down his throbbing, uncut cock. Then I said "Papa, I want to feel it inside me." He sat up and said "No Baby, you're too small and it will hurt you. I don't think you're ready for that yet." Not to be denied, I told

201

him that I'd been using my hairbrush for several years and I really wanted it. He finally said that he would do it, but if it started to hurt he would stop. He laid me back and started caressing me again. I felt him dip one finger in my pussy as a shiver went up my spine. Soon he had two fingers in me and he was slowly fucking my sopping wet pussy with them. When he was satisfied that I was ready he positioned himself over me and very slowly started pushing his cock into me. First the head popped into me. Slowly he fed about an inch into me and then pulled back. Then it was two inches then three. He completely filled me as he slowly pushed into me. I'd never felt so full before, but then it felt really good too. I never did feel the pain so many virgins feel, probably because I'd been using my hairbrush handle for so long. He had been slowly moving in and out of me for several minutes, and then he pulled almost all the way out and asked if I was ready. I nodded and with one quick motion, he plunged all the way into me until his cocked bumped right into my cervix. A shockwave of pleasure reverberated through me even though it felt like he was going to rip me apart from the sheer size of him. On the third thrust, the orgasm started. This one was completely different. It started deep inside me and radiated outward, until my whole body quivered with pleasure. As I started to cum I know my pussy must have clamped down hard on his cock, because he let out a load groan, tensed up, and then I felt his cock getting even bigger inside me. Then I could feel the warmth of his hot juices filling me and spilling down the crack of my ass. As he fell on top of my I wrapped my arms around his neck and said "Oh Papa, I love you so much. Thank you." He kissed me on the cheek and told me in Russian "Happy Birthday, Baby girl". I later found out that he had secretly had a vasectomy before mom had left us, because he was afraid that another child would just be too much for her. With no risk of my getting pregnant we were soon making love often, sometimes several times a day.

Over the next months and years Papa taught me how to pleasure a man and how a truly skillful man can pleasure a woman. Eventually, we tried anal sex, (to this day he's the only one I allow to penetrate me that way) and I even talked Papa into having a threesome with Sarah when we turned 17. We ended up having quite a few of those until we both went off to college. I'll save those stories for another time, but Sarah always told me I was the luckiest girl in the world to have a dad like him.

Now I'm married to a wonderful man, I have a career that I enjoy, and two little children of my own. But, once or twice a month when I see my dad, we make passionate love for hours. Although I adore my husband and he is a good lover, Papa is far and away the best lover I've ever had, and we are extremely close. My husband has no idea about the true nature of our relationship and he thinks it's sweet that we are so close.

My ex from high school

After having moved far away from the city I was from, an ex and I connected again (Facebook of course) and our chatting was friendly but of course flirting had occurred. We had not intended for anything to occur as we each thought the other was happily married. An illness in my family required me to travel back home often and by myself and when I returned my ex (from HS who we will call Christy) and I chatted and sometimes met for lunch/dinner. My story starts about 4 months after we re-connected and is about.... well no need to summarize the next part as I will provide the details.

After arriving back home and spending 4 days and nights in and out of the hospital visiting my sick grandma, I leave the hospital and turn back on my phone. As I walk to my truck as usual the phone goes nuts trying to populate all of my missed calls and texts.

Bzzz - Text and they come in, About 3 from the wife. The usual back and forth inquiries blah blah blah nothing exciting there, one from Christy

"Hey you, know you are probably not eating well or relaxing, come by tonight for BBQ with me and the family NO ARGUING, No is not an option"

I was not sure I was in the mood for any company but hey I have to eat regardless so I sent a simple reply

"see you at 5:00"

Off I went to my brothers showered, shaved, changed and headed to Christy's house. As I knocked on the door I could hear the commotion coming from inside her place, 2 kids already and another on the way in 3 months I surely did not envy her situation as I had no children. However I do like other people's, you can crank them up and leave or give them back for the parents to deal with :) It had been about 3 months since I saw Christy and when she answered the door she looked to be about 9 months preggo and ready to pop any day. I said "Damn are you sure you are only 7 months along?"

She replied "Oh Jay still the charmer, you sure know how to make a girl feel special. And yes I am pretty sure although I am a lot bigger then with the other two.... maybe there is more then one in here" rubbing her belly and winking at me.

Other then her obvious baby bump, Christy carried her self well through her pregnancy, never gained a lot of weight anywhere else. She still looked great. Very pretty face and she did not need make-up, she always had huge tits and they still looked huge but fuller, and proportionate ass to her pre-pregnancy self that did not change as she got knocked up. I always found her attractive and now was no different. Christy always held a special place for me, in our youth we were as much best friends as anything else and we were each others "firsts" for everything.

As I walked through the house following her, as any guy does, I was staring at her ass I was actually getting turned on, I had never thought about sex with any serious thought outside my marriage never mind with a married pregnant woman, but seriously now, My cock was starting to stiffen..... she would see if it kept up. Not long after entering into the living room her other two kids, I am guessing aged 3 and 5 got excited to see me as they had a few months previous, Kids love me and were excited to show me everything they had on the go. This distracted me from having a raging hard on and it subsided, but Christy looked at me and smiled like I haven't seen for years. She did notice..... My mind raced that "She must be checking me out as well"

As the initial excitement from the kids wore off, and we were able to have a drink and chat a little with small talk, the phone rang. She went to answer it, far enough out of range I could not hear but the facial expressions were unmistakable to a fellow married person. She was not impressed at the words coming out of the other end. Upon her return to the table, she sat down and relayed the content of the call.

"So it appears Roger will not be home tonight. He is stuck at the border waiting for paperwork so that he can cross with his shipment."

She was on the verge of tears I could see it and she blurted out immediately after,

"He is cheating on me, I know it. Before I was pregnant he never had "paperwork" issues and hardly ever was late, held up or missed a return home. Now I don't see him for days and he doesn't even touch me or sleep in the same bed"

I grabbed her hand and replied "Maybe he just has a lot on the go, maybe you are over thinking it? I heard woman get extra emotional when they are pregnant, maybe that isn't it at all?"

"maybe" she said " "maybe not, either way we are on our own for dinner, I will go start the BBQ and get these steaks on for us, the kids have been fed and need their baths and they will be to bed early tonight as they have not had a nap today."

Standing up I stated " Point me to the BBQ I will handle dinner, take care of the rug rats and we can eat after they are in bed"

After half hearted protest she caved..... Must have been my seductive eyes and charming wit.... or not. In either event I cooked the steaks like a pro and the rest of the dinner as well if I might say so and after the kids were down we sat for our "grown up" dinner. We had some small talk, Christy kept pumping me full of beers and I was starting to feel slightly buzzed.

"Are you trying to get me drunk to take advantage of me?" I asked jokingly or I thought jokingly.

"Jay I don't think you could handle the sex drive of a pregnant woman. I think I would eat you up and spit you out" She smirked as the words came out.

"That almost sounds like a dare, or a challenge? In either case maybe I would die trying to test that theory"

And there it was again, The familiar tightening of the pants. Where were these thoughts coming from. Sitting across from my sexy high school friend, ex and FWB that I had fucked ragged on so many occasions. She was still sexy as hell if I was single and she were single we would surely hook up again. Now both married her carrying another mans baby my mind kept going back to "how would my cock feel in her hot cunt? How good does her pussy taste still? Can I seduce her to fucking me? Does she want me right now as bad as I want her?"

My thoughts were interrupted by her suddenly as if she could sense my mind trailing off the beaten path to areas of the forbidden forest.

"I have to say something Jay, don't take this the wrong way but, being pregnant comes with certain issues. I need to take care of something and I hope you don't mind?"

Now being that we are pretty open and flirt a fair bit these words should only have generated a witty reply from me. Being the naughty thoughts in my head my reply was short and I can only imagine my face looked stunned.

"uh, ok I am sure I won't"

"Jay.... I really need to get out of these clothes" she winked.

God yes she winked, and paused and then the shit eating grin.

" and into something looser fitting" Still smirking her demeanor changed to casual conversation. "it is brutal wearing tight fitting pants and normal clothing I need to piut on some yoga pants or something so I can relax a bit"

At that point I exhaled, I misinterpreted her meaning (I think) I stammered "Of course do what you have to do"

Rising from the table she said " You almost look like you were expecting something else?" Winking again, Devilish grin she continued "Why don't you make yourself comfortable in the living room, we can chat some more or watch a movie or.... something like that"

"sure" I said "sounds good, I just need to go take care of some of this beer"

As she walked away I knew I could not stand up with the enormous hard on I had without showing it off. As Christy walked away she bent over to pick up kids toys along her route I swear showing off her ass. On the third toy she looked back at me staring at her gorgeous ass she smiled. A smile I haven't seen for years. Once up the stairs I rose and headed to the bathroom. With a huge hard-on there was no way I could piss. Needless to say the bathroom visit took a while longer then I thought and I thought for sure Christy would be back and waiting for me when I finished.... I was wrong.

When I returned from the bathroom to the living room, The lights were dim, the tv was on to a "music" channel and the screensaver images were lighting the room nicely. Not too much but not so you would be tripping over furniture. I sat on the larger of the two couches, "comfy" I thought.

Christy called down "I thought you fell in, I will be down in a sec. I realized my pants had the usual kid contamination and had to change."

"OK" I called back.

This extra time was great, I had talked myself down to attributing my condition and interpretation of the night thus far into my buzzed state, distracted mind and of course being a red blooded man that thinks every woman wants to fuck me. After all a married woman with a nice family, and situation, not to mention with child would not risk it for a random fuck.... no matter how good.

I whispered to myself " Your an idiot" and snickered.

What happened next changed my perspective.

Down the stairs (which are behind me) I heard Christy's foot steps, From my peripheral vision I could start to see her, red something or other and skin, lots of skin. There she was wearing a red teddy, Something that probably fit her loosely pre-pregnancy, now hugging every curve and she had on a small robe that was not even long enough to cover the teddy. All it did was cover her arms slightly. Her tits were pressed into the top so much they were almost spilling from the tops and gorgeous. Her legs still shapely and curved and gorgeous. My mouth must have been open, my tongue probably hanging out one side.

"I hope you don't mind this outfit, most of my other clothes are kid stained and this makes me look presentable. With anyone else I would not wear this but yu and I have history and it seems OK"

My mind racing, I started to clue in quick. This is not innocent, this is pre-meditated. She wouldn't come down here dressed so revealing if she did not want me and KNOW I want her. I told myself " It is time to be your old self, Like you are single and cruising for pussy. Like high school..... That is what she wants SHE WANTS ME like we were in High School"

"Of course" I replied, "I have seen you in the most intimate ways possible and you don't look like you have aged a day since the last time I saw you naked. However you feel comfortable is good for me. If Roger came home he may think something is up and not be as understanding though"

"Don't worry about him coming home tonight, he called while I was upstairs to give me the hotel info where he was staying in case of emergency. Call display doesn't lie and from the area code he is in, he couldn't make it home in less then 6 hours anyways. We have all night to be "comfortable"

With that she leaned back while still standing in front of me, stretching like she was working out a kink. Thrusting her tits way out and when her arms went over her head and her teddy rode up. There it was under her protruding belly, No panties, and lovely pussy. Christy always had a gorgeous pussy, The type I have always compared every pussy to since I had it. Puffy with her lips protruding on either side, when she was turned on her clit would start to protrude and when we were younger, before shaving was the standard she had a thin bush that her juices would always glisten in.

Now I could see she made the effort to shave around her opening, but a top of her cunt where I imagine a landing strip used to be she probably could not reach. She saw me looking, hungrily staring and she held the pose longer because of it.

Not one to miss an opportunity I asked "back sore?"

"not my back, my neck and shoulders"

"Well come here and I will help you out." As I spread my legs and patted the couch between them. "I am a helpful guy like that, never want to see a friend suffer"

She smiled "Ah aren't you sweet?"

she came over as fast as she could turned to me, lifter her teddy just as she was sitting down so it was almost over her ass and nuzzled her ass into me.

"Maybe you should take off this robe so I can do a good job?"

As the words were coming out she was already pulling it off, not that it did much hiding anything. She knew she had me where she wanted, her ass was pressed into my cock, now unable to hide my excitement. I am not a huge guy, 7.5 inches proportionately thick, but the one quality most loved is that I have a curved cock that woman love to ride. As I rubbed Christy's neck and shoulders she would ever so slightly hump back into me. I knew her eyes were closed and she leaned back further like she was melting into me, she started to rub my leg above my knee.

"This is it" I thought "time to go for broke and see what her intentions are"

I leaned to her ear and whispered "you want me to keep going? I know the answer from your body language but I want you to say it. You must know from what you feel in your back I am hot for you?

She turned her head to look me in the eyes "Yes I want you to keep going, I never have stopped wanting you from the second I found you on line. I thought it was just past lustful thoughts but you are the one I compare every sexual encounter too. I want to know if it is just in my head or my reality."

I could see the desperation she had in her face but before i could reply she just kept going, spilling everything in her head to me "I didn't know if you had the same thoughts about me or not, if you were able to forget and move on, I didn't know if you found me attractive especially being pregnant, or if I was hoping against hopes..... Don;t get me wrong although you have a special place in my head and heart I am not looking to fuck up my life and start new with your never ending love. I don't think you and I were ever about that. I just want to be physically with you. I want you to make me feel whole sexually, Take my body and do what you do to me"

With that she kissed me, stuck her tongue in my mouth and instantly i felt 8 years younger. She got up, turned around I could see the wet spot on the leather in from of me, but she straddled my lap, grabbing both sides of my face and pulled me into her mouth again. We made out like two high school lovers, Passionately, like we were just discovering each other for the first time. She was grinding into my rock hard cock through my shorts. I buried my head between her tits and she gasped and I could feel her heart beat in her chest.

"take me upstairs" she whispered "fuck me in my bed so that I can think of you every time I have to endure Roger touching me. or at the very least every time I use my Vibrator on myself since he hardly ever touches me"

"lead the way" I relied.

At that she grabbed my hand and led me up the stairs, throughout the double doors that led to their room and there waiting was a huge king size bed. She pushed me onto it "We need you on a level playing field with me"

She undid my belt and buckle and pulled off my shorts, then came the boxers, then the shirt. Suddenly I was naked sitting on the edge of her bed. As she started to go down on her knees I stopped her.

"All things equal time to lose the teddy"

"No, you don't want to see my belly, I have stretch marks, I am not the woman you knew and I want you to fuck that girl and remember that girl and make me feel like her"

"Nonsense" I said "You are as sexy and gorgeous as I remember, I am not the same guy as back then and neither are you but that is fine. If I am going to fuck you, pregnant, I want to see every gorgeous inch of you."

She smiled, stood up and removed her teddy. Now I have to say. I have not been with a naked pregnant woman before, nor seen one other then magazines. Sure she had stretch marks, what woman can go through 3 pregnancies and not. She was still gorgeous and sexy and other then my wondering how it would feel and how she would respond, I was hot to find out.

Again, she started for my cock. I stopped her ad said "No, you first"

I laid her on the bed with her legs hanging off the end. i spread her legs and got to my knees. As I was about to go to her pussy she said "I thought you didn't like eating pussy?"

"A lot has changed over the years, I have learned to enjoy it and what it does to my partners. Just enjoy it and lets's see where we end up"

For the first time I got a good look at the cunt I haven't seen for almost 10 years. Surprisingly (I don't know why) it was the same as I remembered. Christy had tried to maintain a shaved pussy I learned (not easy being pregnant) and it was appreciated by me. I love shaved pussy. Her lips were perfectly protruding as I remembered and her clit was already very much visible. She had cum everywhere, her lips glistened with her cum, I could visible see it leaking out of her. Not just clear wet lubricant but becoming white cum like I had already fucked it out of her.

After admiring the beauty in front of me, I went for it. Not pussy footing around (no punn intended) I took her entire mound into my mouth.

Moving up to where my tongue could penetrate her and I had her clit in my mouth like it was the nipple of her tit. She moaned and bucked to me. Instantly I felt her gush into my mouth and down my chin. The amount she came I could never hope to consume it all, no man could.

I took her clit, suckling it and flicking my tongue over it. I have a technique where a like to think of my tongue as an artists brush. As every woman is different so is every work of art, Once I find the right strokes, flicks and drawing the right shapes and patterns, the art of eating pussy is revealed. As I would change rythhm, pressures, strokes, Christy's body would move correspondingly to me technique.

"My god Jay........OOHHHHH MY GGOOOOODDDD...... I have never felt anything so god damn amazing....... FFUUUUCKKKKK"

I have never had a woman cum so much regardless of what I did oral, anal, pounding her pussy. Never had I experienced so much. I could even make my wife squirt but that was different type of wet. This was insane. She bucked against my face as her most intense orgasm took her over.

"FUCK don't stop.....wait stop..... no don't stop. FUCK, FUCK FUCK FUCK...... I don't know what to do it's insane... OOHHHHHH MY FUCK......GOD.....Oh My God" What are you doing to me?"

To me to make a woman feel as orgasmic as Christy must be feeling is as much of a turn on as anything. It takes a level of maturity to get to that point in your life I believe. As a teenager I remember being almost selfish and assuming that when I was done my partner was done. Had I made that assumption with Christie I was going to make it up to her all in one night if I could.

"My GOD.....Jay, Fuck don't stop..... I Don't know what is going to happen next but FUCK....... Oh God>... OOHHHHHHH"

Christy was loosing it, I stuck my tongue into her pussy as deep as I could. My chin was soaked, the bed under her soaked, I could feel her cum come in waves out of her. I do not recall her tasting as good as she was now in our youth, maybe I never tapped the well as deep as I had her now. She tasted amazing, Tangy but sweet and so very plentiful I was amazingly aware of my throbbing cock,matching me heartbeat, hoping I would not be a two pump chump when the time came raced through my horny mind when it happened.....

"FUCKING GOD.... OOOHHHHH SHIT"

And an indescribable scream from deep within her soul that could never be transcribed. If her neighbours lived closer they would be over. I do not know how her kids did not wake. She came and cum she did. Her cum just flowed, hot over my tongue, she even started to squirt. Not in quantities I had seen before with my wife but with pressure, and then the milky cum form deep within her pussy. Christy pushed my head back "I can't take it anymore"

Then I got to see her pussy contracting and releasing from all of my efforts.

"My FUCKING GOD ALMIGHTY" she gasped "You have learned a lot since the last time we did this. I have never, never, never ever had an orgasm like that. I know I have been over the top horny when I am pregnant but could never imagine such pleasure being possible. It Is your turn get up here"

I was not about to argue. I laid down on her bed. Christy said "Let me show you the things I have learned over the years. Although even with all my practice on Rogers' 5 inch cock I might not be able to take you all"

With that she sure tried to take it on one gulp. No easing into it for this horny preggo cock fiend, she jammed 5 inches in easily and I felt her throat contract around the head of my cock, she gagged and coughed a little and spit came out all around my shaft. When she came up for air right after she said

"I remember that curved beast now, let me move a bit"

She went from straddling me to facing my throbbing soaked cock sideways. Most woman including my wife do this because of the curvature of my cock. I actually prefer it because it gives me access to play with there tits, and finger their pussies. Christy engulfed my cock again like ti was her let meal. This time she almost got it all, let me tell you sucking cock was always what I loved about her... in the past. She did not disappoint. Drooling all over my cock and playing with my balls, she knew ho to give the best "dirty"porn star blow jobs known to man.

I don't know how long I could last, I could feel my balls tingling my cock was on fire and Christy must have sensed it because she slowed down her efforts to prolong it as best as she could. I knew I had to distract my mind from the impending explosion of Cum from my balls that I am sure she would drown in. I started to reach for her pussy to play with it and she shot up.

"I can't handle you on my clit just yet but how about this" She reached into her nightstand and pulled out a pink dildo about 6" long and continued "Fuck my pussy with this while I suck your cock. I want you to cum in my mouth, we have all night and I know I can get you hard again to fuck me, Let's get the first one off and out of the way"

I didn't need to be asked twice, I knew there would be no need for lubricant as she was dripping. I don't mean dripping like some people describe as a measure of wetness. Her pussy literally had strings of cum dripping from it. She went back to work on my cock, This time fucking it deep into her throat and when that dildo opened her lips and I thrusted it into her she inhaled my cock even more. I knew I wouldn't last long so I matched the thrusting of the fake cock in her to the pounding her mouth was doing on my cock. This was driving her wild and she started to muffle moan into my cock.

"MMUUMMPHH OOHHHH MMYMM MMGOODDD"

With those sounds she started to buck again and I could feel cum running down my hand and wrist. I couldn't take it anymore.

"My god Christy..... OH MY FUCKING GOD .... I am going to cum, Are you ready.... Oh god You Horny preggo slut of mine>...... FUCK"

And with that I blasted stream after stream down her throat. She took the first few shots with out hesitation, the third and following ones must have caught her off guard as she had to pull back, but never taking her mouth off of my cock. When the shooting stopped she took my still hard cock out of her mouth, Opened her mouth and showed me my load on her tongue. She smiled, closed her mouth and smiled.

"My god" she said "you are amazing, I need a drink, for some reason I feel dehydrated."

She skipped off to the bathroom as I watched her sexy ass sway, she looked back at me and spanked her ass and said "I will be right back Stud"

As I lay there I could not help but notice for the first time in as long as I remember. Porbably since High school or maybe college, My cock was still hard, rock hard and pulsating. "Must be a mental memory of the amazing piece of ass I had again fucking me" I thought.

In either event I was not going to waste this chance....

As Christy came back, she too noticed the obvious.

"Is that still ready for action?" She asked

"It would appear so" I shot back

As she laid back down she asked

"How do you want me?"

"I will be honest Christy, I am not sure how to fuck you being pregnant, Can I hurt you? Hurt the baby? Can you do the same types of things?"

She giggled and said " You can not hurt the baby, Your cock may hurt me, but that would be that same regardless. You should also know I had my other two C-section so my pussy will feel the exact same as it did when we were 16. Although I don't know if it matters either way. Riding you may not be as easy but I am just as flexible and able to spread my legs wide and you can fuck me as deep as you want. From behind you wouldn't know I was pregnant so the choice is your sexy."

"Well I want to watch you as I fuck you right now, Lay on your back and let me pound you like you have been missing"

With that she laid down, she propped herself up with some pillows behind her neck and I positioned myself between her legs. My cock did start to deflate a bit but I knew once I was being squeezed by Christy's tight wet pussy I would be my full hardened self. I reached in to kiss her before i was going to fuck her. Our tongues fought in her mouth for dominance and my cock was teasing and rubbing outside of her soaking wet pussy.

She bucked as it hit trying to make me thrust in her. I steadied the head of my throbbing cock against her opening and she moaned

"Please fuck me, I desperately need your cock, It has been so long since any flesh and blood cock has fucked me but I want you. From this day on and forever you can fuck me anytime anywhere. I will make myself available to you and only you."

How could any man argue with that, I pressed into her hot wet cunt. The heat from her was incredible, her wetness would have to be described as legendary. I didn't thrust all of it into her, not wanting any type of pain. I am sure she probably should have handled it, I wanted to feel every inch go in, every fold and muscle inside of her hole as I pushed.

It dawned on me as I was on my first full thrust into her. We had never fucked bareback. The closest I ever came was just wet humping her pussy while she was a virgin. I would rub the entire shaft of my cock while she road me and came on me but never penetration without a condom.

For some reason I wanted her to realize this as well.

"Christy, babe. You feel amazing. I will fuck you anytime and every time I can. Do you realize this is the first time I have been inside of you with out a condom?"

"Oh GOD YES, I know I can't stop cuming on your hard cock, I want to feel you shoot your load into me. Not yet OHH GOD but please..... fuck me... I want to feel you in a week from the soreness of my cunt."

I don't know what it is about a woman talking in such a filthy way, but words can fire me up like no bodies business. I took it almost as a challenge and put her legs over my shoulders. I started jack hammering my cock into her pussy like I was drilling for gold.

"OH OH OOHOHHHHHH FUCK ME JAY. FUCK ME LIKE MY SMALL DICKED SPERM DONOR OF MY CHILDREN NEVER COULD..... FUUUCCCKKK. I wish that small dicked fucker could see what a real man fucks like"

As the words were leaving her mouth so was another wave of cum, if I could describe the sounds of my cock pounding her pussy and the wetness of it all I would win a pulitzer, there may not be words enough to satisfy the description, squishy gushing noises both from the opening of her sopping cunt and my balls slapping against her dripping ass. Mixed with the squirting she was doing I wasn't sure how she would hide the wet mattress from Roger. I really didn't care at that point as these thoughts were merely distracting me from blowing another wad of my baby making juices in Christy.

"OH GOD you fucking stud, You are my sex God Jay. Please let me ride you as best as I can, I remember how much you love to be fucked. If I sit up I can still get good depth with your cock"

With that it was my turn. I laid down and Christy was ready to take her turn. I really am trying to communicate the insanity of it all when I say. As she stood over me, straddling me and readying herself to lower her gorgeous, sopping swollen pussy over my cock. Her cum was dripping, strings of if trailing behind as each drop left her lips and cunt. I am not exaggerating in the slightest as I have never experienced anything like this before or since her. It was such a turn on to know that I made her this way, this crazy, this lustful.

As she was mere inches from me she asked

"Are you ready my fuck god to have my soaking pussy engulf you?"

All I could do was nod and mouth "FUCK ME"

The level of pleasur I was having was legendary. Here I was laying in another man's bed, my wife a thousand miles away, him 500 miles away. His horny pregnant wife my long ago high school fuck buddy, girlfriend now she was my cock slut. Begging me to allow her to be my fuck toy. She was seconds from sticking my throbbing cock inside her pussy and using me to cum again. If there is a heaven it must feel this good. I saw past her belly although sexy and also a whole other level of kinky.

She says "Ready for a surprise?"

Before I could answer She has my cock against her puckered but still soaking asshole and with a plop fucks it all the way in in one stroke.

"OH GOD JAY.... I have never had another cock on my ass.... OOHHHH GOD"

ANd with that another wave and gush came out of her pussy and run down to my stomach.

"Please stud play with my clit, can you reach it I will lean back and fuck you with my ass. PLEASE I WANT TO CUM WITH YOU IN MY ASS"

As far as a pregnant woman goes, she fucked me better with her big belly then I have been fucked on top by anyone. I gladly suffered through to reach her clit, it was protruding far enough I could sneak my hand around the side.

" Oh God OH MY FUCKING GOD>........ OH MY GOD"

This time it was both of us screaming these words. When my cock hungry MILF slut started to go the wetness of it all was insane. She came,,,, and squirted. Had her belly not been there to block the squirting explosion I would have needed a face shield for sure. AND SCREAM

"FUCK FUCK FUFUUUUKKKK"

she fell on me my cock popping out of her ass.

"Fuck Jay, I can't think of anything but your cock. OH GOD I have given everything I have to you, take anything you want. I will suck you, Fuck you with my pussy, my ass my tits, anything anywhere. Promise me you will put your load deep inside of me and I don't care anymore"

"Well Christy, My sex toy, Clean my cock off with your mouth and I will bend you over and pound you deeper then you have ever felt before"

I am not a total pig and would never expect any woman to suck my cock after being in her ass. I can't imagine any woman outside of the controlled environment of porn doing something like that. The reality is I did wiped it off for her. But when I returned from the bathroom Cleaned up but still throbbing hard it resumed.

Without any hesitation that dirty cock fiend gobbled down my cock slurping every but of it, right down to my balls. She faced fucked my cock with out any extra guidance from me.

"Christy, I want you to know you are the best cock sucker and fuck I have ever had"

taking my cock out of her mouth, she looked up at me and said "You too stud, I meant what I said about being your fuck toy anytime. My only regret is you live so far. I hope I motivate you to come home more often then you have in the past"

Quickly shoving my fuck stick back down her throat

"Oh GOD babe bend over for me and get ready for the pounding of your life."

She turned over legs bent and knees on the edge of the bed she shoved her ass and pussy so far back I knew I would be bottoming out on her pelvic bone with my thrusts. I wondered if her baby would truly be out of reach of my cocks wrath of destruction as I attempted to beat Christy's guts out.

I aimed my cock at her cunt and while holding her hips pounded as deep as I could, She took t well Screaming "GOD DAMN" as I pounded off the inside of what must have been her cervix.

"Fuck JAY, Fuck me like there is no tomorrow, CUM SO deep in me I spit your load out. FUCK MY CUNT!!!!"

That was the last straw for me, I couldn't take much more three more thrusts and I grabbed her hips on the final one and pushed till her eyes must be bulging.

"OOOHHHHH OOHHHHHH MY GOD I FELT YOU GROW AN INCH FUCK FUCK FUCK FUCK YOU FUCKING BASTARD OH MY GOD"

and stream after stream of cum shot out of my balls , up my shaft and like a fire hose coated the inside of her burning cunt. That wasn't it though, as I came so did she, I thought she pissed the bed she squirted with such ferocity and the cum leaking around my cock was surely hers since mine could not make it back from so deep inside of her yet.

As Christy collapsed my cock popped out. I had to stand there admiring this sexy woman who I had used and had used me for 2 hours plus. I watched what eventually was my cum ooze out of her and add to the collection of her juices from before.

When the our orgasmic high came down Christy asked "want to shower with me? was my back?"

"Sure, I need one as bad as you"

As we walked to the ensuite she said "I have never came so much, NEVER knew it was possible, It was kind of embarrassing."

I had to laugh "Fuck babe it was the horniest most exciting sex i have ever had do not be embarrassed. What about your bed?"

"Don't worry, If you will help me change the sheets, Roger doesn't sleep in here anyways so we can just flip the mattress and he will never know. My pussy is never used by him anyways, it is yours now"

"sounds good" as we stepped into the shower

After helping Christy clean up the evidence I left for the night. I walked to my brothers leaving my truck as I was probably not in condition to drive. When I went back for it the next day Roger was home. We made small talk he probably though I was a retard for the grin on my face. Why you might ask..... well beside the obvious reason I railed his wife all night and she was going to be my sex slut anytime I was in town as his back was to the house Christy was flossing my her tits and rubbing her cunt in the window behind him..... Thank god for sunglasses and stupid neglectful husbands and wives.

I hope you guys enjoyed the story. It is 100% true, actually it is probably toned down from reality as I am not a professional writer and articulating reality is not as easy as you would think. Words are easy to type but the intention, feelings, and tone of the moment is sometimes hard. I tens to write things as I would say or think and sometimes I am sarcastic or playful and those things do not come through.

I had many encounters with "Christy" over the years. If appreciated I will write more. Although the sex is pretty wild each time, locations and situations change. Not to mention she wasn't pregnant after.

Other then Christy I did eventually get out of my sexless marriage and date. I led another life that has involved a fair bit of swinging, a lot of threesomes with couple friends that I made over the years and also became the lover to a few married older ladies.

A willing housewife

My story starts at the beginning of last summer, when my husband Simon and I moved to a new town in Southern England, along with our two young sons, and into a newly built house on a brand new housing development.

We are both the same age, approaching the end of our twenties, with the big 'THREE-ZERO' looming ever closer. We have been happily married since we were both aged twenty, and our two boys are now aged five and six. We are a couple very much in love with each other, and have a contented life.

On the estate we had moved to, the next phase of houses around ours was still being built and other houses were still being finished. The sparse landscaping around our property left a lot to be desired, and in keeping with the surroundings, our own gardens still looked like a building site.

SUNDAY.

After a month of living in the new house we had finally settled in. Simon had started his new job as an associate at a local solicitors firm, and the boys were enjoying their new junior school. Simon earned enough money from his job, so I didn't have to work while our boys were still young, but as a housewife I looked after the house and boys during the day.

We had finally finished decorating the interior of the house, and it was exactly how we had wanted it to look. The exterior however was not at all as I had imagined. I decided that enough was enough, and that we were finally going to do something about the garden. It was a lovely summer's weekend, and the perfect time to get out and look for something to make the garden look nice. I also wanted a safe place for our boys to be able play. After doing a little bit of online research we drove to the local nursery to get some ideas, and hopefully buy a few trees and plants to get us started.

As we wondered through the seemingly endless rows in the veritable forest of trees and bushes we were approached by a young woman who asked us if she could help us at all. She appeared to be about eighteen or nineteen, very petite and very pretty. She was about 5' 4" tall, with blue-grey eyes, and long light brown hair reaching down to the middle of her back. She wore what appeared to be the standard nursery uniform; dark green polo shirt, with the company logo emblazoned across the chest, along with matching shorts, both looked about two sizes too big for her. She had slender tanned legs, and on her feet she wore an old, scruffy pair of dirty pink and white trainers.

It was a stiflingly hot summer's afternoon; probably in the high eighties, and even with the oversized polo shirt I could tell that she wasn't wearing a bra. I was sure that if I had noticed this fact, then my husband would have as well, so as we followed the girl I led my two boys along, but also kept my eye on Simon, curious to see if I could catch him checking her out.

As we walked around, looking at the various different plants I began to get the feeling that this girl was flirting with Simon. Maybe it was my imagination, but she seemed to be taking every available opportunity to bend over in front of us, seemingly offering him a view down the front of her shirt. On a few occasions, as she squatted down to read the tags on the bottom branch of a particular shrub or bush, she bent in such a way that her thighs opened up, and her shorts gaped open to expose her legs all the way up to where her obvious tan lines started. I was beginning to think that this girl wasn't wearing any panties either!

After a further forty minutes or so we had picked out quite a few different trees and plants; far too much for us to take home by ourselves. The girl led us to the greenhouse office to pay for them, and to arrange for them to be delivered, and also for them to be planted in our garden. Everything was arranged for the following Wednesday. I was amazed they would come over so quickly. The girl completed the necessary paperwork and handed us our copy. Across the bottom she had written, "Thanks! Becky." We said our goodbyes, and she smiled and gave a big goodbye wave to our boys, and we left to return to our car and back home.

Once we were at our car I immediately started to tease Simon about the girl and the way she was dressed, and that she seemed to have been flirting with him. Simon is the shy type, and he immediately blushed, his cheeks turning a bright shade of red. He said that he really hadn't noticed.

"She was just dressed for the weather," he said with a smile. "If you worked there you'd probably dress the same way!"

I continued to tease him.

"But she was very pretty, wasn't she?" I asked.

"Well, I suppose she was cute!" he answered eventually.

"Aha! I knew it!" I shouted.

We had a good laugh, kissed, then headed home.

TUESDAY.

It was around midday, and I was in the house doing some housework as I normally do. Simon was at work and the boys were at school; so I was on my own until at least 3:30pm, when I had to go to pick the boys. I had some music on the stereo as I went about my chores. Suddenly the doorbell rang, startling me. I switched off the stereo, and when I looked out of the window to see who it was, I could see a large white van from the garden centre parked on the driveway.

"They're a day early!" I thought to myself. But then I thought that was okay, and it was better to get the planting over and done with. It would also be a surprise for Simon if he came home to find the planting all done.

As I opened the door I was surprised to see the girl from the garden centre; Becky. She was dressed just as she had been when we saw her on Sunday. It was another very hot day outside. The sun shone brightly in the clear blue sky. She was sipping from an almost empty water bottle. Her face looked hot and sweaty, and I imagined that sitting inside a van on a day like today would not be a very pleasant experience.

"Hi!" she said cheerfully. "Remember me? Becky? I just came by to take a look at where we'll be planting tomorrow. I hope I'm not bothering you."

I said "Hello," and told her that she wasn't bothering me at all, and that I was just doing some laundry, so I could probably do with a break anyway. I invited her inside the house, and as she followed me through to the back door, I told her that my husband was at work and the kids were at school. She nodded and smiled at me, before explaining further that she just needed to check that there would be no problems in our garden before they came to do the work on Wednesday morning. I was a little disappointed that nothing was being done today, but we had arranged for the work to be done on Wednesday, so I couldn't really complain.

Since I had been working inside I was wearing one of my old pairs of denim shorts, and one of Simon's old white work shirts. My feet were bare, and I stopped at the back door to slip on my sandals, before we walked out into the humid heat of the back garden. I pointed out to her where we had put out some wooden stakes in the ground on Sunday evening, to mark the various locations for the new trees and bushes. She looked around the garden, checking the locations, making some alternative suggestions, and making sure that access would be sufficient for their workers. Eventually we wondered back over to the paved patio as we talked about gardening. When I mentioned to her that I had always wanted a vegetable garden, she said that she'd be happy to get me started.

She seemed like a genuinely pleasant girl, and as we chatted some more, I learned that she had been working in the garden centre, which was the family business, in some form or another, since she was twelve years old. She told me that she was about to start her final year at college in the coming September, and that one day she hoped to take over the business from her parents. As we talked she tilted her head back to drain the final mouthful of water from her bottle. As she did this some of the liquid escaped from her lips, trickling down over her chin and onto her neck, running down onto her chest underneath the polo shirt, soaking into the dark material. She giggled with embarrassment, and lifted her hand to rub the water into the sweaty skin on her neck and chest.

"God! It has been so hot these past few days, hasn't it?" she moaned.

237

She noticed that I was now staring at her as her fingers continued to slowly rub and stroke the smooth, tanned skin on her neck. I froze for a second, shocked that I had been caught looking at her like that.

"Well," I stammered, pointing at the empty bottle in her hand, "why don't you let me refill that for you?"

She smiled and nodded, and we walked back into the house and headed for the kitchen.

Moving from the intense heat of the midday sun into the air-conditioned coolness inside of the house gave me a shiver, and made my nipples instantly harden. As I had thought I would be at home on my own for most of the day I hadn't put on a bra, and my erect nipples pressed against the material of my shirt, making me feel a little excited. As we reached the fridge I turned to take Becky's water bottle, and I couldn't help glancing down, noticing that she was in exactly the same condition as I was, with her little buds poking out against her damp T-shirt. I also noticed that she was looking at straight at my nipples.

I was beginning to feel a little strange. I had never been with another woman before, and had never even fantasised about it. I suppose that like most women, I'd wondered what it might be like, but had never thought about trying anything. Now, here I was, getting turned on by this young girl. Or maybe it was just the heat outside that had made me feel a little light-headed.

I stood for a few seconds, watching her as she watched me, before finally reaching out my hand and taking her water bottle. I filled it to the brim, and also filled a glass of water for myself, and we both took a long cold drink. There was an odd kind of tension in the air, and I needed to say something to try to break it.

I smiled and joked, "You know, my husband thinks you were flirting with him yesterday!"

Okay, so I stretched the truth a little bit.

We both giggled nervously.

She looked at me right in the eye.

"I wouldn't do that," she said. "I don't flirt with men!"

It took me a minute to realise the meaning behind what she had said, but before I could respond she swiftly stepped forward, raised herself up on her tiptoes, and kissed me quickly on the lips, before stepping back away from me again. I was stunned and scared half to death, but at the same time I felt shivers of excitement coursing up my spine, and shock waves ran through my whole body down to my toes. My nipples tingled, becoming even harder. I don't remember deciding to do what I did next, but I somehow moved to her and bent my head down and returned the kiss. It was the softest, sweetest, most tender kiss I had ever experienced. At first it was just our lips gently touching, but Becky slowly opened her mouth, and I felt the tip of her tongue gently trying to make its way into my mouth. It was like no other kiss I had ever had. My whole body trembled, and I wanted to kiss her so very much.

I surrendered and opened my mouth for her, and soon our tongues were twisting and dancing together, and I lifted my hands to cradle her head gently. She reached up and cupped one of my breasts in her hand, whilst letting her other stray to the back of my neck. Her hands dropped abruptly, grabbing at my waist, pulling us closer together. Our bodies touched, our curves moulding together. We held each other, kissing passionately, for several moments, before she let go, breaking the kiss. She backed away a few steps and hoisted herself up onto the kitchen worktop. She sat there facing me, a wide smile on her face as she stared into my eyes.

I swiftly stepped forward towards her, making up the ground between us, and as she parted her knees wide allowing me to stand between her thighs, we kissed again. She lifted her legs, wrapping them around me, trapping me, digging her heels into my backside. I felt her fingers on me, skilfully and methodically unbuttoning my shirt at my chest. I made no attempt to stop her, and she eventually reached the last button; unclasping it, pushing the material to the sides and off my shoulders, exposing my upper body and naked chest. As my shirt slid down my arms, dropping to the floor, she broke our kiss and, without pausing for a second, trailed her tongue down across my neck, before lowering her lips to my breasts. She slowly and delicately licked and sucked on each of my hard nipples, finally settling on my left, which she gently tongued and nibbled between her teeth, while her small hands worked on both breasts. I quivered at each light touch she made, a warm glow starting to build deep inside my body. I could not remember ever being as excited as I was at that moment. Looking down, it just turned me on even more that it was another woman doing this to me, and not my husband. My breathing was now reduced to long, deep, shuddering pants. I arched my back and moaned, and she enjoyed this.

I had to quickly grab hold of the wall cabinet to keep my balance, as my legs were beginning to feel a little weak. Her hands slowly skimmed down my sides, delicately sliding over my skin, and across my hips to the front of my shorts. I knew where she was heading, and I didn't want her to stop. Her fingers fumbled a little with the top button, but soon it popped open, and I felt the zipper sliding down and then her warm fingers slithering past the waistband of my panties. Electricity bolted though my body to my pussy and clitoris, and I moaned out softly. I clumsily pushed my shorts down my legs for her with my own hands, and kicked them off my feet to my side, leaving me clad now in only my powder-blue coloured panties. She immediately slid her hand further down under the delicate lacy material toward my centre, and I felt her fingers brush through my short pubic hair, and to the top cleft of my pussy. She moved lower, her fingers sinking into my slit. The sheer amount of wetness she found there must have been incredible. I was turned on in a way I had never ever experienced before. I felt a shiver going up and down my spine as my most private feminine place was being explored and caressed by this girl.

Becky began to move her fingers up and down my through the folds of my pussy and over my clitoris, before eventually pushing two fingers inside me, making me groan out loud. She moved her fingers in and out, making a wet, squishy sound in my wetness. I pushed my hips against her hand. She pushed the full length of her fingers into me, and sucked a little harder on my nipple. The combination of stimulations; her mouth on my breast, her fingers buried deep in me, her heels pulling against my bottom; was overwhelming. I was whimpering at this point, and it only took three or four more strokes of her fingers in my pussy, before I began moaning and clinging onto her for dear life. I came so hard and so suddenly that I nearly dragged us both crashing to the kitchen floor. It was the hottest, strongest, most amazing climax I had ever had.

She held on to me as I tried to catch my breath and regain my composure. I leaned against her and the kitchen worktop on which she was still sitting, and we looked deeply into each other's eyes. We kissed gently and laughed. I could hardly believe what had just happened to me. I felt drained, but at the same time filled with an intense feeling of excitement and desire. I knew I had to make this girl feel just as wonderful as she had just made me feel.

We continued to kiss, and my excitement kept growing and growing. Each kiss became deeper and more sensual, and my hands began to roam around her young body; over her back, trailing my fingers down her spine to squeeze and caress her bottom. I moved up to her front, finding her small round breasts and gently squeezed and fondled them through her polo shirt. I lowered my hands, grabbing at the hem of her shirt, and she threw her arms above her head, like a child would when someone is pulling off their T-shirt. I quickly tugged it over her belly, past her bare chest, and up over her head, before tossing it over my shoulder and onto the floor behind me. There she sat before me. She was absolutely gorgeous; her breasts weren't big, but instead were perfectly sized for her age and slender frame, with reddish-brown areola and nipples like pencil erasers. Her flat stomach raised and lowered with excitement. Her skin was tanned, and glistened with a fine covering of sweat.

With trembling fingers I reached out and touched the flesh of another woman's breasts for the first time in my life. They were soft and warm. Her skin was so velvety. I pinched and pulled and twisted at her nipples gently, and she let out a little moan. I hoped that she was enjoying this

242

as much as I was. We kissed again, long and deep, while I continued to knead her breasts. Slowly I traced my tongue down over her neck to her chest and into the valley between her breasts. I gently rubbed my face between those breasts, feeling her sweat cover my cheeks, before I slowly kissed my way to her right nipple. At first I only flicked across the tip with my tongue, but was soon overcome by the urge to suck it into my mouth. I loved the feel and texture of the tiny goose bumps and wrinkles. I sucked and nibbled like I was a child, and her nipple was my favourite kind of sweet.

Becky was breathing hard and her body was squirming around. I looked down and realised that she was trying to shimmy herself out of her shorts as she sat on the counter.

"You're going to have to help me with these," she giggled. "I think I'm stuck!"

I hesitated for a moment. I wasn't sure that I was ready for this, but the look on her face propelled me to take what was clearly the next step. I quickly hooked my fingers in the waistband of her shorts and, while she lifted herself up of the worktop, I began to peel her shorts down her thighs. I could have easily passed out as her wet pussy appeared, pointing straight at me, seeming to thrust up in my direction. I stared straight at it, as I finished pulling her shorts down her legs, past her knees, then down to her ankles, and finally off over her trainers. I was right about the other day. She wore no panties.

Dropping her shorts to the floor, I stood and again stared at her small, delectable body, now completely naked. Her legs were smooth and perfectly shaped. Her thighs looked soft and inviting. What struck me as most captivating however, was seeing that her pubic area was completely clean-shaven. While I usually trim my pubic hair, hers was completely bald. It was stunning. I couldn't take my eyes off her.

Her whole body was so beautiful, and I wanted to run my hands all over it. I slowly slid my fingers across her belly until I reached her pussy. It was hot and slick with her juice. I moved my finger back and forward over its plump lips. I slowly got down on my knees to get a better look at her, and she spread her legs for me and shuffled forward so her bottom rested near the edge of the worktop. My face got closer, and I could see every wonderful detail of her. The skin around the puffy lips was slightly darker than the rest. Her labia where swollen and full, and they seemed to almost pout out at me, soaked with the dew of lubrication. She was very wet indeed.

If I had any doubts about myself and my ability to do what came next, they were quickly erased as I inhaled her scent. I had never smelled another woman's pussy before, and it was an intoxicating mixture of perspiration and musk. There was nothing artificial. No perfume, no cologne or powder; just the raw, natural, sweet aroma of this girl's lust. I leaned in closer and inhaled deeply. The odour filled my head and made me dizzy with desire. I had to have her. The urge to lean over and taste this girl was overpowering.

I bent forward, touching her pussy with my mouth, and slid my tongue between its dewy folds. I was tentative at first, but the slippery, salty taste made me press on. I stretched out my tongue as far as it would go and licked her glistening slit from the bottom to the very top, not neglecting to tickle her little clit. Becky giggled and moaned and squirmed as I got my first taste of another woman. She was sweet and tangy, not unlike my own juices, which I have tasted a few times. But there were subtle differences that I couldn't quite put a finger on. But this wasn't a wine tasting, and I didn't waste any more time trying to compare flavours.

I slid my tongue back inside her, wriggling it around while my teeth lightly nibbled at her wet pussy lips and clit. She started to make little animal sounds. It made me feel incredibly sexy to think that I was getting this girl so excited. Her sounds urged me on and made me feel more aggressive. I started sucking on her clit while driving my tongue deep into her.

I could feel her shifting her body around, and I looked up to see what she was doing. One by one, she had lifted both feet up, placing them flat on the worktop next to her, opening herself up to me further. She reached down under her bent legs and gently spread her lips apart with her fingers, holding her pussy wide open for me, exposing her inner depths. At that moment it occurred to me what a sight we would have made if Simon had walked in on us right now. Here was this gorgeous girl sitting on my kitchen worktop, naked apart from those grubby little trainers. And here I was; an ordinary housewife, on my knees in front of her, naked except for my now soaking panties, with my face buried in her wet pussy. Of course at that point I doubt I would have even noticed if anyone had walked in. I doubt I would have stopped even if the house was on fire.

I returned my full attention to Becky's pussy, slurping and licking at it for all I was worth. All my inhibitions were being forced out of me and I displayed all of my passions. I slid my tongue over her fingers, and she began moving them, rubbing herself. I licked away at her fingers and pussy as we both slid up and down her open slit. Dropping lower I tongued her hole again. In and out I went, wiggling my tongue as I lapped at the insides. I was at the heart of her femininity and she had nothing left to hide. She began oscillating and grinding her hips against my face, in rhythm with my tongue, her breath raging and uncontrolled. She watched as I sucked all of her young juices, and God did I love them! I was out of control, and began drooling saliva out of the sides of my mouth, as my tongue stimulated her young sensitive pussy.

I was really worked up myself by now, and I slowly slid my hand down across my belly to my soaked panties, grabbing at the waistband, pulling them so that the material rode up into the folds of my pussy. I slipped my hand down the front of my panties, my fingers finding my own slit throbbing and soaking wet. I plunged two fingers inside myself and started to hump against my hand as I intensified the pleasure my mouth was giving her.

I had just about fingered myself to a second intense orgasm when she started to squeal and thrash about. She was getting red faced, and her eyes seemed glazed.

"My God," I thought. "I'm making her cum!"

That just about did it for me, and I came all over my hand, rocking and squeezing on my clit. Seconds later, her sweet juices splashed all over my lips as she orgasmed. Shuddering, she moaned loudly, closing her thighs, squeezing them onto my cheeks. She bucked her hips, pushing forward against my face, her whole body shaking. I glanced up at her, seeing her face puckered in the pleasures of satisfaction.

As her soft moans died down and her hips finally stopped bouncing up and down, I looked up at her again, this time letting my gaze travel across her entire body. Her pussy glistened and her tummy quivered and heaved as she panted. Her mouth was slightly open and beads of sweat had formed on her upper lip. She looked down at me and smiled contently.

I helped her hop down from the worktop and she collapsed to the floor beside me. We were both wasted, and we sat, wrapped in each others arms, gently stroking each others skin.

After a few minutes the spell was broken by the abrupt sound of a mobile phone ringing. Becky jumped as though she had been stung by a bee, and scrambled to get at the phone in the pocket of her shorts. She answered it, listening to whoever it was that had phoned her, before she eventually stammered something into it in reply, saying that she had just stopped off to look at another job, and that she was on her way back. She hung up the call.

"I'm so late!" she said, as she clumsily threw on her clothes.

On very shaky legs I walked her to the front door, paying no attention whatsoever to the fact that I was nearly naked. She kissed me quickly on the lips, smiled, and said that she really had to hurry.

"But," she said, grinning, "I know where you live!"

With that she ran out and quickly got into the van, started the noisy engine and reversed off the driveway.

As I watched her drive off I wondered if what had just happened was real, or if it might have been some very sexy dream. My head was spinning, and all I could do straight afterwards was take a long, steaming hot shower, and try to clear my mind. I still felt incredibly sexy; so sexy that I could barely keep my fingers out of my pussy as the hot water cascaded over me, pounding against my skin. I had to masturbate several times just to relax myself, the entire time recalling in my mind what had happened. I was tense for the remainder of the afternoon, as I pottered around the house, waiting until it was time to collect the kids.

Later that afternoon Simon arrived home from work, and it was as if we were back to normal. I remained a little uptight for the rest of the evening, but Simon didn't seem to notice anything untoward.

Early on Wednesday morning, the garden centre crew arrived as arranged, and expertly planted all of our trees and shrubs. Becky wasn't with them.

I have been fantasising about Becky ever since and cannot get her, or what we did on that amazing day out of my mind. On several occasions, whilst alone at home, I have dialled the number of the garden centre, only to run out of courage and hang up before anyone answered. One afternoon I even drove over to the nursery, but left without ever getting out of my car. Maybe one day I will have the courage to see her again.

A new haircut

It was a Wednesday morning and I was laying in bed, my wife Jane had taken the kids to school and was then going for some 'Retail Therapy' with two of her friends. The house was quiet, as it would be for another four or five hours. I had waked up with a massive erection and with the house being so quiet I thought I'd treat myself to a nice slow wank.

I reached into my wife's bedside drawer and pulled out the tube of lube I bought about 2 years earlier. Our sex life had never been the most dynamic and after 10 years and 2 children, it was almost nonexistent. Hand relief and a good fantasy was the best I could hope for most of the time.

This time my fantasy focused around one of our friends 'Jo'. She was a really attractive, petite brunette who had just turned 40. You wouldn't know it to look at her, she was slim, had great skin and one of the best arses you could ever wish to see. She had cut my wife's hair a few times and we knew her well. I've always got on great with her and we always had a great laugh at any parties we both attended. I always cum really hard when I fantasies about her... little did I know that fantasy would soon become reality.

I had applied the lube to my cock and was slowly rubbing it, enjoying every stroke and savoring every second of my fantasy. It was one of those messy wanks that you occasionally get to indulge in, one where

You can cum as loud as you want to.

All of a sudden there was a knock at the door... "Shit", I hurried to my feet. Had the missus come back for something? I quickly wiped my hand on a towel Id found on the floor and threw my robe on. I was still pretty hard as I made my way down the stairs towards the front door, I snagged my robe on the hand rail and heard a muffled 'Rip' sound, I looked down but couldn't see any hole or tear so I moved towards the door and opened it.

I opened the door to find Jo stood there in her Hairdressers garb "Hi hun". If only I could've saw myself, I was still hot from my moment upstairs and it must've showed. "Are you alright?, you look kind of flustered" she said "I'm fine hun, I was just asleep and I had to rush around trying to find my robe. Anyway, whats up hun?"

She had come to drop off some hair treatment stuff for my wife "Is she home hun?" she asked "No love, shes gone to do some shopping with her mates, your'e more than welcome to come in for a brew though", she accepted and moved through the door into the kitchen.

She sat down at the kitchen table while I put the kettle on to make us both coffee. We indulged in general chit-chat for a few minutes until I sat down, placing the cups on the table. We chatted for a few minutes but all the while I couldn't help noticing her eyes kept darting downwards. I looked down to see a rip in my robe "Oh shit, Im sorry hun. I ripped it rushing down the stairs".... "Its alright, I was just catching a cheeky glimpse of your cock" she said.

My cock was still a bit swollen from before and as I hadn't wiped the lube from it, it was glistening with pre-cum at the end. "You weren't asleep at all were you" she started laughing "You were having a wank you dirty bastard". What could I say? I could've brushed it off but instead I just smiled and said "Well you've caught me out, I was having a really nice wank until you knocked at the door". She was still looking at my cock, she seemed to now have a lustful look in her eye like she wanted to just kneel down and suck on it. "Well it would be a shame if you didn't finish yourself off hun" she said with a slightly seductive tone. I could've cum there and then, the very woman I had just been fantasising about was now basically telling me to wank myself right in front of her. I hesitated for a moment trying to decide if she was being serious or not, then before I knew what I was doing, I reached inside my robe and pulled out my semi-hard cock.

I gave it a few strokes and due to the situation I found myself in, it was fully hard again within a matter of seconds. She watched intently "You have a really nice cock" she leaned forward to take a closer look "This is making me so wet, Ive always wanted to see your cock". I stared straight into her eyes as I stroked my length. "So jo, are you just gonna sit there and watch me wank or are you gonna give me something to wank over" she smiled and sat back "I suppose I could help you get there quicker".

She stood up and started to unbutton her blouse revealing her pale skin and a black bra. It was one of those bras that pushes the tits together and hers looked amazing. They weren't huge, but they were perfectly formed and the sight of them made me even hornier. She then undid her trousers and slowly lowered them to the ground. "Oh my god" I said, It was like that scene from Austin Powers where his 'Inner monologue' just comes out. She looked at me and smiled "Does this help at all?", she turned around and revealed the arse that I'd wanted to grab hold of for years. She had a black thong on so it revealed her entire arse..... oh my god what an arse. It wasn't too big or small, it was round and pert, one of those arses that you just look at and think "God I could play with that all night".

She walked towards me and turned around, pushing her arse towards my face. She pulled her cheeks apart revealing a tiny bit of her labias and arsehole. I leaned forward and pushed my face into it "Easy tiger" she said. She then slowly peeled her thong off revealing her pussy, just as I was about to start working it with my tongue she moved away and sat back down. She spread her legs and started rubbing her clit, I could see how wet she was and due to the sight of it I could feel myself coming close to cumming. We both sat there for the next few minutes, watching each other until it became too much for me, streams of hot cum spurted from the end of my cock in all directions. Most of it landing back down onto my stomach, hand and cock, the sight of it obviously turned her on as her body started spasming as she started to climax. "Oh god" she whimpered as she came hard on her fingers, all the while looking straight into my eyes.

We both sat there for a few minutes with satisfied smiles on our faces. Just as I was about to get up to clean myself off she said "Don't go anywhere, I'm not finished with you yet" and with that she moved onto the floor and crawled over to me. She opened her mouth, slipped her tongue out and started licking the warm cum from my cock and fingers. It didn't take her long to lap up my come and she was soon sucking on my dick like a woman possessed, determined to get me hard again. It worked, I was hard again within a minute or so as she continued to slurp away at my ready-again cock. My god she was good at sucking dick, she was one of those women who you could tell really enjoyed it. After 10 minutes the sucking stopped and she stood up, she moved forward pushing her tits in my face. She slid down my body, the cum on my stomach sliding in between our bodies. She gently lowered herself onto my hard shaft, the tip teasing against her labia. She slid down onto the head of my cock then moved off again, she repeated it again, this time taking more of my length inside her. I resisted the temptation to pull her down onto me and let her control the speed.

After a few minutes of teasing me like this she slid up off my cock then slammed hard down onto it, god it felt amazing, her pussy was nice and tight and I knew I was going to cum deep inside it. She started riding me slowly but would quicken the pace every now and then. This was heaven, the woman who id been wanking over an hour earlier was sat on my cock with her pert tits in my face. After 5 minutes her body spasmed again as she came hard, her pussy muscles clamping down on me. I gave her a minute to catch her breath then pulled her off and stood up, I wanted to fuck her from behind "Bend me over and fuck me" she growled. I obliged, as I pushed her over the table I looked down to see her arse "Fuck it" I thought "I wanna taste that before I'm finished". So I bent down and started lapping away at her pussy and arse, she tasted so good. "I said fuck me" she growled again, being the gentleman I am, I had to oblige her. I stood up again and pressed the head of my cock against her now soaking pussy, it offered no resistance as the walls of her wet hole welcomed my cock.

I was in control now, I was going to fuck her like a ragdoll.

I started off slowly, grinding my hips against her whilst I rubbed her clit. She moaned as I pulled out my length slowly then powered back inside, her body jerking as I did. I did this another four or five times before I took things up a notch. I started fucking her hard and fast and she loved it. "Oh god yeah fuck me" she screamed as I fucked her like a man possessed. We were both sweating heavily which seemed to make the whole thing feel more sordid and dirty. I was now banging her so hard that the table was rocking back and forth, the motion of it helping us find rhythm. "Oh god yes" she screamed as her pussy clamped hard down on my cock as she came for the third time, this time it was too much for me and with a heavy grunt my cock started twitching as I emptied my hot load deep inside her. Cumming at the same time is one of my favourite things and this was evident by the amount of cum I unloaded into her. We both stood there totally fucked, cum dripping from her pussy, I reached down to rub her clit but she cringed "I'm sore now haha, you fucked me so hard my lips are stinging".

We went and sat down on the sofa for a while, gently playing with each other as we chatted.

Ive seen her since at various parties and dinners and we always just smile at each other, Were each others 'Booty Call' now though and I hope were gonna see each other again soon.

I needed to be dominated!

"Do you love me?" I asked Jeff.

My name is Jennifer. Jeffrey, Jeff for short, and I are best friends. We lived close to each other since birth, attended the same schools, and hung out together. Jeff shared everything with me and talked about anything that came to mind, including his past loves. I was the one to patch him up after each one when he came to me with his broken heart.

Jeff had several girlfriends and had gone all the way with some of them. We would talk about his experiences. He would ask me about what turns girls on and I would reply what I thought other girls would enjoy. I even gave tips on how he could improve himself. Through it all, I never shared my deepest desires or how hot it got me.

Jeff was athletic, strong, and a natural leader both on and off the football field in high school and college. Watching him take charge made me weak at the knees. It also made me wet!

I had a crush on him since the fifth grade. I had needs and didn't know how to share that information with him. I had a few dates, but earned a reputation as an "Ice Princess". The reputation was well deserved. While many of my other classmates lost their virginity, I didn't let the boys get to second base with me. I just couldn't trust myself. I knew once that I got started I would surrender completely to my needs and the will of my Master.

I needed to be dominated!

It was the beginning of summer and Jeff and I just graduated from college. We went to the same college, I majored in bioengineering and Jeff went into finance. We both had job offers with local companies so we were staying close to home. I was working for a startup company using nano-technology for medical applications. The company could not pay well and instead gave me stock options.

Jeff worked with a local investment firm and his decision-making skills proved to be valuable to his clients and his firm. He was quickly a rising star with his company and was well liked and respected by everyone. It also helped that he kept himself trim and looked hot in his outfits.

We were hanging out in my bedroom listening to music and talking. My mother never remarried after Dad died. She was out for the weekend on a business trip. She trusted me to be home alone and trusted Jeff. I think she secretly wanted us to be together and would be happy for us to be a couple.

There was a lull in our conversation when I asked Jeff that question. "Do you love me?"

"Huh?" he exclaimed in surprise.

"A simple question," I explained. "Do you love me? We've been friends forever."

He thought about it for a moment and then said, "Of course! I'd do anything for you!"

I pounced on this, "Really? You would do anything for me?"

"You know I would," he replied quickly with a smile on his face.

I paused for a long moment and then said, "Ok, I have a favor to ask."

"Sure, what do you want?" he quickly responded.

"It is a very, very big favor," I said with a warning tone in my voice.

"Ohhhhkaaay," he said cautiously.

I took that as an ok to go on. "First, I want to explain something to you that I haven't talked to anyone else. You know I don't fool around on my dates. It makes it hard for me to get dates, but that is my rule. And you always wondered why, right? Well, I'll tell you why.

A lot of my friends think it is because I don't trust the boys, but that is not the completely true. It isn't the boys; it is myself I don't trust. The reason that I don't let the boys touch me is because I get excited by certain things that would make other people disgusted. And I know that if I let myself go even a little bit, there would be no turning back."

"You are confusing me, Jenn," Jeff said. "What are things that get you off and why would there be no turning back."

I sighed as was quiet for awhile. Finally, I reached over to my bedside table, pulled some items out of the drawer and silently placed them in his hands. He examined them carefully. They looked like alligator clips, the type used in our physics lab with our wiring experiments.

"What are these?" he asked.

"Those are clips," I said quietly. "I use them on my nipples and sometimes my clit when I masturbate in bed. Do you know those dreams people have, where they are in class and they realize to their horror and embarrassment that they are naked? For me those are wet dreams." I went on, "most girls think of a movie star or a rock star when they masturbate. I think of Harrison Ford in Raiders of the Lost Ark, except he is using the bullwhip on me while I have an orgasm!"

I was crying now, sobbing uncontrollably. Jeff, gather me in his strong-arms. His musk overpowered my senses and I could feel myself getting weak. I felt compelled to surrender myself completely to him and while enjoying his power over me.

"Jenn, it's ok. Everyone has fantasies," he said. "If I told you half of my fantasies you would think I was a degenerate. These fantasies don't make you a bad person. I still love you and I don't think badly of you."

I could feel my heart beating wildly in me. I was hoping he would be the One. Drying my tears I said, "I knew you would feel that way."

"Then why were you so worried about telling me?" he asked. "Why were you crying?"

"Because I've never told anyone this," I said. "And besides, I'm not done."

"What else do you want to tell me?" he asked in an understanding voice. Hearing these words I felt comforted but also compelled to continue.

"Jeff, it's not just that I have these fantasies," I said. "Remember the psychology class we took? Remember we laughed about domination and submission? I am a submissive and need to be dominated. I am reluctant to take the initiative, which is probably the reason why I am paid at the lower end of my company. I need someone to take charge and make decisions for me. The thought of a strong master using me as his sex toy makes me wet and I can almost come thinking about it.

Nothing is too extreme. He can fuck me in the mouth, pussy and ass in the same session and I would enjoy it. Nothing is too perverted. If he wanted me to clean him after sex or even after he pees I would willingly suck his cock clean.

While in school, I could keep the boys away. But the feelings are getting stronger. Without the school environment, someone will figure me out and in all likelihood take advantage of me and may seriously hurt me. If I don't do something before then, I won't care. Being dominated and forced to serve will fill my thoughts and needs to such a point I won't care about my well being, just my needs and the enjoyment of my master. Even now, just thinking about it is getting me hot and wet while giving me a happy, giddy feeling."

After a long pause, Jeff finally asked, "So what can I do for you?"

"Jeff, I need to know what it's like to be with someone that loves me, that cares for me, and will do what I need, but still think about me. Jeff, between now until next year, I want you to own me."

"Own you?" he asked, shocked.

"I promise you that if you do for me, I will never say no to anything you ask of me. I will be your slut, your fucktoy, your plaything," I said with a deliberate voice.

"And why do you want me to do this?" he replied with an incredible look on his face.

"I want you to fulfill my fantasies; it is all that I think about now. If I don't do something affirmatively to make this happen, I will fall for the first guy that treats me strongly and dominates me. If he hurts me, beats me, and permanently scars me, I will like it and beg him for more," I replied with a slight pleading in my voice.

Jeff was quiet for awhile and I thought I lost by best friend. "Please Jeff, do you hate me?"

He smiled at me and looked straight into my eyes. He could see directly into me, like I was naked in front of him. "No, Jenn, I don't hate you. This is a lot to ask of me. On the other hand, this is every man's fantasy. I'll admit it turns me on, but if you want me to do this you are going to tell me exactly what you are looking for."

My heart raced, I started my rehearsed speech, "One, I don't to be permanently damaged. I am on the Pill, so pregnancy is not an issue, but I don't want to be disfigured in any non-reversible way.

Two, don't do anything would make you lose respect for me. If you want a slave for your personal enjoyment, to serve your every pleasure, that is fine with me. It would also turn me on a lot and I would enjoy it. But if you ever ask me to do something that causes you to lose respect for me, I'd rather have my fantasy left unfulfilled that have you lose respect for me."

Jeff though for a minute, then said, "I am new to this and you must be patient with me. I could live with those conditions and I'll add one more. Your fantasy begins when you say, 'My fantasy begins now!' and ends when you say, 'My fantasy is over'. Whether you say it after ten minutes or after a year. That way you will have ultimate safe word and have confidence that you would never get in over your head."

I couldn't believe he was willing. He even understood me so well and though of my well being. Jeff's third condition proved the psychology class was correct. The power of the relationship belongs to the submissive and this was a real-world example. Here he is thinking of my benefit, even beyond what I proposed. He was so caring and so totally understanding of my need that I blurted out, "Does this mean you will do it."

"Not just yet," he said with a wry smile. "Jennifer, do you have something to say to me?"

I looked at him confused, then it dawned on me, my hear soared and I shouted, "Jeff, my fantasy begins now!"

I shivered and my pussy released a surge of fluids. I may have even had a mini-orgasm, all from four little words – my fantasy begins now. For months I had been contemplating this, and now I was committed. Could I go through with this? Could Jeff? I loved Jeff like a brother or a platonic friend and trusted him completely, but we would start a new relationship. I just signed my body over to him. I gave him carte blanche. I know he is my best friend, that he loves me. However, I just handed him the keys to my body.

The more I thought about it, the hotter I got. I realized that Jeff owned by body and in all likelihood he would be fucking me in moments and take my virginity. Just thinking about it was getting my pussy slick with my juices.

"Stand-up," Jeff said, snapping me out of my reverie.

I stood up in front of him.

"Take off your clothes," he said in a no nonsense tone. I started to awkwardly, but in my best demure fashion, follow his orders and strip off my clothes.

"No, no, no!" he exclaimed. "If I want a sexy striptease, I'll take you to a strip club and have the professionals teach you on the stage. Now just take clothes off."

I quickly complied and removed all of my clothes like I was preparing to take a shower at the gym. Jeff signaled with his hand for me to turn around. I turned in front of him, as he appeared to evaluate my body. I kept myself in shape and was proud of my body. My B-cup breasts were symmetrical and could fill certain C-cup style bras. My breasts were firm and the nipples sensitive to my ministrations. Sometimes I could just come by playing and pulling my nipples.

"Go stand in the corner with your nose touching the corner of the room," Jeff ordered me.

My mouth dropped open. He was sending me to the corner like I was a naughty girl. I went to the corner, naked. I should have felt embarrassed, but I felt my pussy getting slick with fresh juices. I was getting excited! I heard him leave the room and then come back. Then I heard him rummaging through my drawers.

"What are you doing?" I asked.

"Did you tell me you would do everything I asked of you?" Jeff said in a harsh voice.

"Yes," I responded in a soft voice.

"Then shut up and keep your body pressed against the wall," Jeff replied in a no nonsense tone.

I pressed against the wall, tears dripping from my eyes. It had already started. He lost respect for me. Then I realized I was dripping from my pussy.

"Ho, ho!" he exclaimed, "What have we here?"

I heard a familiar buzzing sound. He found my vibrator! The few minutes I heard other drawers open and a variety of activities as he continued his search as he continued his search through my most intimate possessions. Through it all, I could begin to catch a scent of my pheromone as this complete invasion and surrender had an effect on my body. My nipples were becoming erect and more sensitive. My clit felt engorged and I desperately wanted to touch myself.

"I have few questions to ask you," Jeff said. "First, tell me what you've done in your life, sexually

"You know what I've done," I replied, still facing the wall. "Not much at all. I haven't let a boy fondle my tits. I've kissed a couple of times but that is it. I plat with myself, but just on the outside. My hymen is still intact. I've played with my ass a little but I've never put anything in. I've never seen a real life grown-up's cock."

He seemed to consider that for a little bit, then he ordered, "Turn around."

I turned and saw what he had been doing. There was a box on my bed and some clothes were in it while others were scattered around it.

"I put all of your clothes that I did not like in this box," he told me. "You will put it away and not open it until this fantasy is finished. I think you will find most of your underwear gone. You can look at what remains to see what is acceptable." I saw that what remained were thongs and g-strings.

He handed my vibrator to me saying, "You may use this but only when I am around. You may cum as often as you wish I want you to enjoy your fantasy. I'll also buy you additional toys that I'll enjoy using on you." I shuddered at that last statement and could feel a tingle originating from my clit, spreading through my body.

"Drop your hand," he said. He was clearly evaluating my body. He briefly touched my pubic hair and said, "This will have to go." Then he spun me around towards the bathroom and announced, "Time for a shower and your first lesson."

The warm pulsing water always relaxed me, especially now that Jeff was in the shower with me. I giggled when I saw the water streaming off of his penis. It looked like he was peeing in the shower, even though I knew it was just water.

The giggle wasn't lost on Jeff who said, "The first lesson is you will learn to love all fluids from me." That was an odd statement, but before I could think about it, Jeff wrapped his arms around me and he hungrily, passionately kissed me. Relaxing, I opened my mouth and accepted his tongue. His wet tongue explored, tickled and stimulated me. The moist saliva lubricated him and I knew I could learn to love it. In return for receiving I also shared this dance within my mouth. My tongue touched and explored him, feeling his warmth and passion flow from him.

With the symphony of attack on my senses, the warm pulsing spray, Jeff's passionate kisses, I could feel my body begin to respond. My nipples and clit became more sensitive and erect, wanting more. I became light-headed and felt like I was floating in the sea of stimulation.

Jeff broke through the reverie and said, "Your second lesson is you will learn how to keep me clean without your hands." Again that sounded odd when Jeff pointed to his chest with the water droplets on his skin. Adjusting the showerhead so the water hit the wall besides us, it created a sauna effect. "This will be easier in the beginning and I will be patient. You may start by licking the water off of my chest."

I was glad for the order and started to lick the water droplets off of his chest with relish. Licking the water felt almost as if I was tasting him. Emboldened I worked my way lower until I came up close to his cock. The cock had texture along from the skin and veins. The underside had a central tube that was sensitive to the flick my tongue. The shaft felt huge in my hands and I wondered if it would fit in me. Working my way to the tip I noticed the spongy feel and then flicked my tongue around his piss-slit.

"I will take your three cherries," Jeff said out loud, "the first of which, will be your mouth. You will learn to suck my cock. You must trust me and give into me. Do not panic, I will be firm and gentle with you. If you trust me and give your body complete to me, you will enjoy the experience."

I felt his hand touching my head, guiding me. I opened my mouth and took it in. It was soft at first and I flicked my tongue along his sensitive underside. I could feel the cock harden! It was wonderful and turned me on so much I knew I was dripping and wet from my own fluids. Bobbing my head up and down the shaft I could feel all of the ridges and textures. I could tell Jeff was getting excited and I delighted knowing he was using me.

"Precum will come out of me first," Jeff warned me. Remember my rule.

Precum leaked into my mouth, the fluid was salty and warm. It almost pulsed in as I felt his cock beginning to strain and harden as a steel rod. Now he was beginning to drive into me, using my mouth as his instrument.

Giving in completely, I relaxed my throat. On one of his thrusts I felt his cock reach down into my throat. I was deep throating him! Surrendering completely I took my hands and wrapped them around his ass, giving him complete access to my mouth. Now he took his hands, grabbed my head, and started to fuck my mouth. I knew he was closing to coming.

The more he pumped into me the hotter I became. I didn't think I could come this way but Jeff's passion inflamed me. More and more he pumped his cock into me and more and more I oozed more of my own fluids. Then in a final burst he pushed deep in, spasming and shooting is sweet cum directly into my throat. He withdrew slightly so the head was in my mouth. I could taste his sweet fluid as he continued to pump his semen into me. Feeling his pulsing cock in my mouth triggered a mini-orgasm within me.

I felt a little dizzy and the warm pulsing water felt good. I closed my eyes to enjoy the spray and tasting his sweet cum. Jeff held me for a moment and then slipped out of the shower. "After you finish drying, come to bed," he told me as he was leaving the bathroom.

I quickly finished the shower, then dried myself including my hair, preparing myself for him. After leaving the bathroom, I obeyed Jeff's instruction and lay down on the bed. Jeff came over and with my sash tied it firmly covering my eyes. With my eyes blindfolded, I found it heightened the rest of my senses. I became more aware of my body, my breathing, the sounds, the scents, even the feel of the bed and room became more intense.

"I wonder what Jeff is doing?" I wondered silently to myself. "Will he take my virginity now?" I could feel my nipples becoming more erect in anticipation; my pussy felt slick with new juices even though I just finished showering. My pussy released more pheromones and the room became thick with my scent.

"You will learn you are mine," Jeff's voice instructed me. "Your mouth, breasts, pussy and ass are mine for my enjoyment. Through me, as you learn to trust and give yourself to me, you will find the enjoyment, ecstasy, and peace you are seeking."

Suddenly I felt Jeff roughly grasp my left nipple and felt the familiar alligator teeth clamp onto my areola. In my heightened state the clamp felt firmer, stronger that I remembered. Although the clamp bit into my breast my mind did not register it as pain. It fed my desire more. Then he roughly attached the second clamp the nerves were sending constant signals to my brain. I wanted more!

"Spread your legs," Jeff ordered me. I quickly complied, exposing my sex to him. "Will he take me now? Will he just thrust himself and take me?" I wondered. Suddenly I felt his hot breath on my pussy. "OMG, he is going to eat me!"

"Ahhhhh," a slight moan escaped my lips. I can't believe the feelings and sensations of Jeff's lips and tongue on me. Even his hot breath was stimulating my nerve endings causing more juices to flow. Each lick along my pussy sent small jolts of electricity throughout my body. Like an orchestra conductor, Jeff was coaxing my body to respond to him in ways I never though possible. He was such an expert I knew I would follow and obey him, just like my body was following, responding, and obeying him.

I felt his arms reach under and around my legs lifting me up. He continued to eat me then went higher to my clit. Then his hand reached over and grabbed my nipples. CONTACT! "OHMYGOD, OHMYGOD, I AM COMING SO HARD!" I yelled. My tits and clit became connected through Jeff's hands and mouth. The simultaneous stimulations took me over the edge with one of the biggest orgasms I ever had.

Jeff continued to hold me firmly in his hands and mouth while I spasmed around him. He then slowly licked lower to my ass and started to lick my sensitive anus. In my heightened state, his licking on my erogenous zone took me over again. "I Am Coming Again!" I knew my ass was opening and closing around his tongue as it spasmed through the orgasm. The wonderful sensation of his soft tongue was unbelievable as I felt it penetrate me and caress my sensitive opening.

He then released me and I felt him spreading my legs as he came up higher. His cock was stroking along my pussy, coating my slick juices along it. It felt enormous and didn't even penetrate me yet. Gently and firmly he held me in his arms. "When you are ready," he whispered to me. "Yes", my mind screamed out, "Yes", my body yearned for him. My pussy was oozing rivulets of cum; heat emanated from my body. I wrapped my legs around his waist, "I am ready", I replied back.

Jeff then firmly and steadily pushed his cock passed by labia. After going part way in, stopping before my hymen, he pulled back. He advanced again, this time I locked my legs around him and pulled him into me. "Yaaah!" I exclaimed, the brief moment in pain escaped my lips. "You are mine," he told me. Yes, I am his, he took me and I willingly gave myself to him. In all manner of mind and body I am his.

He then firmly and deliberately started to fuck me. It was a wondrous feeling, his cock skin sliding along my walls. I could feel his cockhead reaching deeper and deeper with every stroke. His cock touched my cervix at the apex of his stroke. His penis stimulated all parts of my womanhood. My clit was tugged as he stroked back and forth, the G-spot felt the pressure of his cock, my vagina, though firmly gripped his cock, gave way with each incoming stroke. More and more the symphony started to build, more and more my body reacted to his direction. Yes, yes, I could feel my orgasm building. "Don't stop, that's it, yes, yes, I AM COMING!" and again my body reached an apex of ecstasy. By surrendering to Jeff I could achieve so much more.

Jeff didn't come yet, instead he lifted my legs higher and aimed his cock towards my ass. "I am ready," I said to Jeff. His cock and my ass were coated with my slick juices and I felt his pressure against my anus. I relaxed my opening and he firmly pushed in. His cock pushed past my external sphincter then he waited, letting me adjust to him. Then he pushed further past my internal sphincter and I felt him completely in me. I felt so full. His cock was so huge.

Slowly and firmly he worked his cock in and out of my ass. My tight orifice gripped him firmly but the slick fluid lubricated him so he could easily slide in and out. They say there is an A spot in the ass, similar to the G spot in the vagina. He reached it and I could feel another orgasm building within me. Faster and faster he pounded into me, slapping my ass with his thighs. More and more I felt the heat building in me until I cried out, "I AM COMING AGAIN!"

The anal orgasm took me higher than I thought possible. Convulsions wracked through my body and time stood still. Jeff brought my body to new heights and pleasure I ever thought possible. My ass milked his cock until I heard him exclaim, "I A COMING," and immediately I felt his hot fluid coat the inside of my walls. That triggered another mini-orgasm within me as I continued to contract around him. Our muscle spasms were in synch and we mutually bathed in the afterglow of our ecstasy.

My pussy continued to ooze fluids, something I never was able to do when I masturbated. A sheen of sweat coated both of our bodies as we breathed deeply to recover from our intense effort. Jeff gently removed the clips from my tits, allowing blood to flow back into them. He then lay beside me breathing deeply and cuddling with me. The tingle of pain blood returning to my tits was dulled by my body's endorphins, which still circulated and gave me a feeling of floating softly and gently above our scene.

I remembered my earlier lessons and Jeff's prophetic words from the earlier shower. I immediately knew my duty. He was right, it was a lot easier in the shower but now I turned around and faced his cock. After lovingly kissing the tip of his cock, I made an "O" of my mouth took his entire shaft down to my throat. Bathing his cock with my tongue I cleaned it without my hands and at the same time drinking in all of his fluids.

I felt Jeff gently stroke the back of my head and he said, "I am proud of you, you have learned your lessons well." Hearing Jeff's praise my pussy leaked a few drops of fluid and I had a warm feeling deep within my core. "I am so happy and glad that Jeff was willing to be my master," I thought quietly to myself.

After completing my task I curled up and spooned against him. He spoke quietly and lovingly to me, "I have now taken all three of your cherries. All three of your holes will be accessible to me whenever and wherever I want. You must keep your body prepared at all time for me."

"Yes," I replied and silently fell asleep within his arms. "I will do everything he asks and willingly give myself to him whenever he desires me," I thought to myself, hypnotically implanting these commands deep within my subconscious as I drifted into sleep.

Shortly after Jeff agreed to help me live my fantasy, I told mom that Jeff and I started a new relationship. Mom muttered something like, "about time", kissed me and said she trusted both Jeff and myself.

Almost as quickly as I started living my fantasy, I almost ruined it. The following week, Jeff surprised me and came over. Since mom was busy working I did what I could to maintain the house. I was in the midst of dusting the furniture when he came in.

"Hi Jenn, you look good, you would look sexier naked," he said cheerfully with a wink.

Unfortunately dusting was not one of my favorite duties and I replied curtly, "Hi yourself, what you do you want."

His tone changed immediately and became stern, firmer, more in command, "I came to you and you will be sexy doing that naked. Strip now," he said in a no-nonsense tone.

I was still naïve in our new relationship and hesitated to comply with his command. I didn't understand why he wanted me to do this. Instead of trusting him completely and doing what he asked, I hesitated.

Jeff didn't hesitate. In a fluid motion he came to me, sat in a chair, and pulled me over his lap. He was going to spank me!

"Jeff, I am sorry!" I begged.

"You will learn to trust me completely. There will be times when I want your opinion and insight. In those times you may speak up. When I have made a decision you will honor it immediately, passionately follow me. Your failure to obey me in this simple task, to strip in the comfort and security of your own home in front of a man you wanted to own you. It is my failure to teach you properly. I will correct that now. I am spanking you to make you better in this relationship. You will receive ten spanks, count them out loud as you receive them."

He then stripped off my pants and underwear and struck me hard on my ass. "One....I-am-so-sorry-I-won't-do-it-again," I cried out.

"Did I tell you to apologize? I gave you a simple task to count as I spanked you and in this you failed. I'll add another ten for this, Now Count!" Jeff spoke.

"Pack, pack, pack" came the strokes and promptly I called out the numbers. Around ten I realized that he was not hitting me out of anger but out of love. Love for me, love for our relationship, love to make me a better submissive. At that point I started to give in and accept the punishment. My pussy started to ache. Each stroke was now like a jolt of electricity, sparking and turning on my body. After the tenth one I blurted out, "Ten, Green light!" Jeff paused for a moment and then continued on. By eighteen I was dripping and almost had an orgasm on his lap.

After the twentieth stroke, I almost regretted it was over. He then pulled me off his knee soaked with my pussy juices and said, "You have a job to do." I quickly got off his lap, stripped off the rest of my clothes, and licked my pussy juices off of his lap. I wanted to go higher and looked up at him expectantly. He shook his head and said, "You haven't earned it today, continue with your chores." With that he left the house.

Jeff called me the next week. "Jenn, we are going for a drive and enjoy the day. Wear your blue mini skirt, a tube top and no underwear," he told me. "I'll be over in 10 minutes."

"Ten minutes," I said to myself. "At least the choice of clothes made changing easy." Just thinking of no underwear made my pussy slick with anticipation.

Right on time, Jeff came over. I was dressed in the clothes he specified and he took me to his car. He lined my seat with a towel, I though that was odd at that time but learned to accept whatever he did. We started down the interstate at a leisurely pace when we slowly caught up to a large 18-wheeler came along our right side.

"Pull down your top and let him see your gorgeous titties," Jeff ordered me. I immediately complied and flashed both my tits and a bright smile to driver. He must have appreciated it because we heard a loud blast of his horn and he gave us a thumbs-up. As we past the truck Jeff told me to put my top back up as we continued down the freeway.

A few more miles down the road we came across another truck. As we pulled along side Jeff ordered, "Pull your skirt up and start playing with your pussy, show him how wet you are." Eagerly, I pulled my skirt up and stuck my fingers into my vagina coating them with my juices. Then I brought my fingers up to my mouth to suck and clean them while using my other hand to furiously rub my clit. The driver must have also enjoyed that show and blasted his horn, too.

By this time I was so close to cumming I didn't realize we passed that truck. We continued to drive on passing driver after driver and they could all see me rubbing myself. The drivers all honked their horn and smiled appreciatively at us.

When I was about to come, I begged, "Jeff, Jeff, please...."

Jeff generously responded, "You may cum."

"THAAAANKYOUIAMCUMMING!" I yelled and enjoyed one of my largest orgasms. I must have squirted because the front of the towel was moist with my juices.

"Thank you, Jeff," I said, "That was one of the most wildest experiences I ever had." I appreciated him looking out for me. We were safe in his car, yet I could be as wild as I wanted and act out one my fantasies. The rest of the ride I fell asleep exhausted, clinging to his arm with a smile on my face.

The next few weeks were an adventure in discovery. I kept myself ready for him, my ass was always clean and lube and I was ready for him to fuck me in any hole. Under Jeff's careful and protective orders I learned more about myself. I didn't have any limits or Jeff was able to anticipate them for me. He was firm and patient with me. With each new discovery I learned more about my needs, how I benefited from the relationship, the wondrous joy and ecstasy I could feel, and how I could grow and expand my horizons. I learned under Jeff's careful tutelage and I knew this relationship was becoming more than an experiment and a temporary release for me.

Later in July, mom had to take another extended business trip. Jeff came over to keep me company and help with various home repair and maintenance projects. It was late in the afternoon, Jeff came in from mowing our lawn. He was hot and sweaty and the smell of his musk acted like a pheromone to me and I could feel my pussy leaking juices in response. I knew he would enjoy a refreshing shower so I dutifully grabbed a set of towels for him. He had already started his shower when I came in. I wordlessly stripped and joined him. I still giggled when I saw the water stream off of his cock like he was pissing. I remembered his commands to me and my mind was swirling with thoughts of engulfing his cock, while pretending it was really piss!

I kept my hands and mouth busy and soaped and scrubbed most of his body. After rinsing him off, droplets of water still clung to his body like sweat. Hungrily, I started to lick them off his chest, alternating between light flicks and broad sucking with my tongue and mouth. I worked my way lower and knew I was having my desired effect on him.

I looked up at Jeff and asked wordlessly if I could suck and service his cock. With a nod he gave his permission to me. Jeff's cock was growing longer and harder. It was so beautiful as it grew to its full length. With my careful ministrations, I soaped and cleaned his cock, delicately pulling back the foreskin then rinsing the soap away. At full strength, his cock was like an antenna to me, sending me signals directly to my brain and body, compelling me to serve him.

In obeyance, I was on my knees and lightly kissed the tip of the cock head. Then I started to work down the side, lightly kissing every inch. When I reached his scrotum, I delicately took it into my mouth and bathed it in my warm saliva. Lovingly, I used my tongue to clean and touch all parts of his nut sack.

I continued my cleaning by lightly flicking my tongue along the underside of his cock. His urethra tube, which functioned like a canon to shoot his semen deep within me, was sensitive to light flicks of my tongue. Up and down the tube I fluttered my tongue, acting like a living vibrator for him.

"You have learned well," Jeff said has he gently stroked my head.

"You are a good Dominant, I am happy you have accepted me, " I replied.

I was rewarded for my ministrations with the first of many drops of his precum. Curling my tongue into a tube, I accepted his gift and let it slip along my taste buds so I could savor the full flavor of it. The first drop cleansed the inside of his cock and always had a complex flavor.

With the tip of my tongue I teased his piss slit and was rewarded with more precum. This time I opened my mouth to engulf his cock, letting the slippery fluid mix with my saliva in my mouth. I then used it to coat his cock, making it slippery for next phase.

"Jenn, I am going to fuck your mouth," Jeff warned me.

He firmly grabbed my head with his two hands and started to stroke his cock with my mouth. Surrendering myself completely to him, I relaxed my jaw and throat. With complete submission my throat opened up and with the slick precum fluid mixture, his cock easily slipped down into my throat. Back and forth I felt the full length of his cock along my tongue. In and out I felt the cock slip past my mouth into my throat.

Jeff considerately adjusted the spray to hit the side of the walls, creating a sauna effect. I could look up into his eyes while he fucked me. My arms reached around to grab his ass cheeks, giving him complete, unhindered access to me. I was rewarded with my subservience with stronger, more urgent stroking of his cock. My mouth was his sex toy and he was using it for his pleasure. More and more, firmer and firmer, he grasped my head and banged my lips and tongue against his body.

With each stroke, stretching my throat, my nervous system reacted with signals of its own. It sent tiny shocks to my tits and clit. Each stroke was another shock and as he was going faster and faster, the shocks also increased in speed hurling me towards my own orgasm.

I could feel his balls tightening, signaling his oncoming orgasm, and I knew I would be rewarded for my service. Firmer and deeper I felt his cock pound me when at the apex of his deepest stroke, he firmly ground my lips to his pelvis and he came in my throat, shooting his first shot of wad directly into my stomach. Retracting slightly he continued to shoot his cum into my mouth allowing me to savor his sweet semen. Feeling is cock pumping in my mouth was enough to push me over the edge with a small orgasm as my pussy contracted rhythmically in time with his pulses.

I remembered my duty and continued to suck gently from his deflating cock, taking in the final drop that were still in the tube. Jeff then adjusted the shower spray, which broke both of us out of our post orgasmic bliss as we both finished our shower.

After drying I turned to Jeff and asked, "You have worked hard on the yard, please allow me to massage you."

He assented and led me to my bed. He lay face down and waited for me. I grabbed by body lotion and spoke softly to him, "My dear Jeff, you have given me so much and taught me so much. I know I should wait for your instruction but I want to give and share some of the pleasures you have given me. Please allow me to service you and your body."

"Jenn, thank you for asking, you may use your imagination and your heart to guide you, I will trust you in this," Jeff responded.

My heart soared and I then warmed the body lotion and started to massage it into his muscles. I started at the neck and shoulders working and massage all of his muscles. My hands and fingers worked and kneaded the muscle fibers, searching and relaxing every knot. Along the back I continued down and I noticed Jeff was becoming visibly relaxed. Emboldened, I continued and worked the outside of the thighs, calves and feet, making sure his body every inch was serviced. I then worked my way up the inside of his thighs and came back up to his ass.

I massaged his ass cheeks and in doing so his rosette center was open to me. I remembered how he kissed and made me feel. I drew myself closer and could feel his heat. Extending my tongue I used the tip to gently tease along his opening. I was rewarded with a slight groan from Jeff. Taking this as permission, I parted his cheeks and pushed my face flush to his tush. Using the tip of my tongue I fluttered it up and down his crack.

282

Since we just took a shower it smelled clean but even if we didn't I would have enjoyed his earthy smell. I dove further into my work and started to use my tongue in earnest. Although I didn't have a cock I could use my tongue to piece his opening. With persistence and determination I pushed and thrust my tongue as deep as I could. Using my spit as a lubricant I continued to push, lick, and flutter around his rosette opening.

I thought I knew Jeff well. He recently came from the blowjob in the shower and men normally take about an hour in their refractory period to recover. Jeff was a superman. I felt a drop of precum developing on the tip of his cock. Then I heard a small grunt, I realized it was becoming uncomfortable for Jeff with his stiffening cock. He signaled that he was turning over and allowed me to move out of the way.

As Jeff turned over, he looked me straight into my eyes and nodded and smiled. He understood me so well! This was my gift to him, a gift given out of love as much as my desire and need to serve him. He knew he could have me and willingly I would do his bidding. By nodding and giving me permission, he showed he understood and appreciated my gift to him. We were both in synch.

"Thank you, Jeff," I said, and quietly mounted him cowgirl style. My pussy was slick with my juices and his cock slid easily, naturally inside. I prided myself by keeping in shape and routinely did my exercises, including Kegels. Using my pussy muscles alone, I was able to milk his precum into my hot box.

"Please use me to give you pleasure," I begged Jeff.

"Jenn, thank you, I will honor your gift. Today we will make love together," Jeff replied lovingly.

I was naively confused by Jeff's response but trusted him completely. Jeff had taken all of my cherries; we had sex numerous times. All I knew was I would follow him anywhere and do anything he asked. I wanted to show and demonstrate that to him the depths of my feelings for him.

Together we kissed passionately, then I started to ride him in earnest. Jeff's cock rubbed my G spot perfectly and his girth pulled by clitoral hood back and forth over by clit. He used his hands to rub by body, massage and pull my nipples, and pull me down to him. We spoke, we moved, we were in synch. My pussy juices were flowing and I felt many mini-orgasms rip through me. Suddenly Jeff grabbed my hips with both hands and pumped by body up and down his cock. I could feel the tightening in his body, his oncoming orgasm sent an energy bolt through me causing me to squeeze and grasp him firmer. Following his lead, my body bounced up and down until at the crescendo of his stroke, he thrusts his cock to the entrance of my cervix. Deep within me, within my core, I felt his pulsing cock shooting his hot sperm deep within me. It caused my body to convulse in time with him and I also convulsed rhythmically with him. Now I understood his statement.

I collapsed on his strong chest and both of us breathed deeply recovering from our exertions. His entire body started to relax and his cock slid out of me. I knew my job and dutifully cleaned him then curled up beside me to bask in our afterglow. We spooned and his cock was tucked snugly between my asscheeks.

A few hours into our nap I felt his cock grow and push firmly against my ass. I recall looking it up one day, it is called nocturnal erectile tumescence, and is used as a test if a man has ED. In a man's semi-conscious state their cock will spontaneously become erect. Jeff certainly didn't have ED and his cock was growing larger and more insistent against me. I was glad I kept by ass lubed, ready for him whenever he wanted. I relaxed my opening and gave myself to him.

I felt his cock glide into me. My heart started pumping firmer and faster when I realized in his semi-conscious state, he desired me. I pushed back against him helping drive his cock deeper into me. Then I felt his arm come around me, helping to push my ass back and forth on his cock. This was raw emotion and desire on this part. He wanted my body, he wanted me! After a few more pumps I felt him begin to stiffen and I felt his hot come bathe my interior. His heat permeated by body and a warm glow that started from within me spread throughout my body. He then relaxed and I felt his cock slide out. I remembered my duty and cleaned him then continued to cuddle beside him.

The next weekend Jeff came over and helped with some repairs around the house. That day was especially hot so I prepared ice tea for us and made sure we were well hydrated. After he completed the repairs that he affectionately dubbed, "Honey Do List", he went to take a shower. I felt daring and wanted to do something special for him and followed him to the bathroom. He was about to take a pee when I asked, "Can I help you with this?" I then held his cock gently in my hand and pointed it down to direct the flow into the bowl.

I know I surprised him with my action. He looked at me and smiled. The he gently caressed my head, relaxed and let his stream go. Holding his cock like that was so wild for me; I also started to get wet. I was careful to make sure to direct the stream into the bowl so it wouldn't make a mess. Doing so forced me to look closely at his cock and feel the piss shoot out of his cock. It was so wild! When his flow slowed, I knew he usually gently shook his cock. Instead I remembered my duty and used my mouth to take in the final drops. His fluid was salty yet sweet, probably from the ice tea.

After that we took a shower together. When I saw the water stream off his cock again in the shower I went down and engulfed it, reliving our wild episode earlier.

The rest of the summer was hot in the temperature, in our passion for each other, and in our business. My body was always ready for him and he safely guided me to new sensations and experiences. I wanted to show him my gratitude and would surprise him when I took the initiative and wild sex adventure for the two of us. Under his love, guidance, and protection, I grew stronger and had more confidence in myself.

My new found confidence also helped me at work. I was willing to speak out and suggested solutions when our team hit a roadblock. My approaches were not tainted by previous discoveries by other scientists and my ideas helped our company find a new way to treat many medical conditions without surgery. Because of our finances, I received stock options instead of a cash bonus for my contributions. Our company was in the midst of a groundbreaking nano tech project and it was capturing the attention of larger medical equipment companies. Our approach was so novel that no one had any projects remotely like ours. We held all of the intellectual property rights without challenge and any company that wanted to use our technology or ideas had to work with us. One large company in particular decided that the easier way was to buy us out and own all our patents. They hired Jeff's firm to negotiate the sales. If the transaction was successful Jeff stood to make a hefty bonus from the transaction fee and I would become an instant millionaire because of my stock options.

Nature provided the backdrop and like the change in season our relationship also started to change. It was October and we were in the middle of fall. Jeff noticed the change in me first. After a torrid session initiated by me, Jeff said, "Jenn, I love you deeply and dearly. You have gained a lot of confidence in yourself. We started this relationship because you wanted to safely explore your fantasies and be dominated. I have fulfilled my part by helping you to explore this side of yourself safely. I also enjoyed guiding you, but you have grown so much in these past few months. Do you still have the need to be dominated?"

"Jeff, I have grown so much because of you," I said quietly. "If I have strength, it is because you were there to provide it for me. I realize that this started when I said 'let my fantasy begin' but I do not want this to end. I am afraid that if I say the words, 'my fantasy is over', you will leave me. I love you so much I would do anything to be beside you. I offered to let you own me and I mean it. If want me to call you Master, I will please let me be part of your life." I was sobbing and tears were streaming down my cheek.

"Jenn, as a true submissive you must trust me completely," Jeff said while caressing my cheek and drying off my tears. "Trust me now."

I looked at him with my eyes shining and moist. He was right, I needed to completely let go and trust him completely. "Jeff, my fantasy is over." I looked up at him as tears welled up in my eyes.

Jeff reached over and grabbed a small case on the nightstand. He gave it to me. Inside was a gold choker necklace, almost like a dainty collar. Jeff said, "Jenn, I love you. Let this necklace be a symbol of my love to you. We started this relationship with your desire to be submissive to me, let this necklace remind you of that. Later, we will go shopping for a more traditional ring and I'll ask you to be my wife." With that he took the necklace out and clasped it around my neck.

I cried as we hugged and kissed. I heard him whisper, "We started this to meet your needs and fulfill your fantasy, we will now begin a new journey with our lives and live this fantasy together."

The sweet smell of Stephanie

I met Stephanie at a club a couple years ago. We were both drooling over the same hot guy we knew we didn't really have a chance at. After Mr. Hot Guy left we started talking, gossiping really, about the girl he left with. She got pretty drunk. I don't know why, but for some reason I would have felt terrible if I'd just left her at the club, she might have driven herself home- last thing I wanted was to read about a drunk driver hitting a tree and killing herself in the morning edition of the newspaper.

Instead I got her to come to my house. She trusted me, not that I wasn't one to be trusted, and I let her stay on my couch over night to sleep it off. When I asked her about getting her car she said she had walked to the club with some friends (they'd left without her I assume) so cars weren't an issue.

In the morning, when she woke up, I had breakfast sitting on the table. She thanked me, especially for the coffee. We ended up talking for a long time. My niece was to be over for a haircut not long after Steph and I ate; I told her she was more than welcome to stay as long as she didn't mind watching me cut my niece's hair. She said it was no big deal; she thanked me again for letting her stay at my place for so long. I had no problem with it, she was really nice and we'd hit it off immediately.

Allie, my niece, knocked on my door about twenty minutes later. She gave me a hug and a kiss and greeted "Ms. Stephanie" politely. I asked her how short she was cutting her hair and she told me that she wanted it cut to her ears. I was a bit shocked, her hair had never had a major cut, a trim here and there, but nothing quite as much as this. After all, Allie's hair was grown down her back until it nearly touched the small of her back.

I agreed and sat her down in the living room. Steph came out and watched. It took about forty-five minutes; I kept making sure that she really wanted to take off so much, she kept saying that's what she wanted to do.

After I finished she thanked me and gushed about how amazing it looked- and, honestly, it did look really good. She said goodbye to me and Steph before leaving.

After I left Steph asked if I was interested in working at a little beauty shop.

"You're being serious?" I was in disbelief.

"Yeah, right now I'm the owner and the only employee. Not only do I get lonely between appointments, but business is declining because I get booked on the same day a walk-in 'desperately' needs a cut o whatever."

I hugged Steph, my friend of less than twenty-four hours who was already my lifesaver-as I was possibly hers.

My arms were around her neck. Hers were on the small of my back. I leaned my head back so I could see her face but didn't pull away. The space between us was full of electricity.

I hesitated for only brief moment, then, without really thinking, I stuttered out "I- I think I want to kiss you."

Her hands fell down to my ass, she gave it a squeeze. A lusty look filled her eyes. "I dare you," she whispered.

Of course, being that my ass is very sensitive, I moaned because her touch was so unexpected. I leaned in, our foreheads touched. I could feel her warm breath on my lips. Then her nose skimmed mine.

There was no hesitation. We didn't start off slow. Oh no, this went from zero to maximum in a split second. Our lips didn't lock until our tongues twirled.

Things moved even faster, time seemed to sped up. My hands were under her shirt, undoing the front clasp on her bra. I loved the feeling of her hard nipples on my palms. I kneaded her breasts while we kissed. I think her legs were going to give out from the tension between them- I know that's how I felt, so I figured it must have been the same for her- so we moved to my couch. Somehow, my shorts and panties had come off. Her shorts were off too.

She was under me. Our bodies pressed together, my pussy juice was leaking onto her panties.

"Let me taste you," she whispered. One of her hands slipped around my waist, in a slow, VERY teasing way, and pressed lightly on my slit. When my pussy lips parted I moaned, if her hand had to breath it probably would have drowned in my wet snatch. She pushed her middle and index fingers into my tunnel. Her thumb found me clit. My hips jerked and she gave me a naughty smile.

I had been kissing her neck, but now I was mostly sucking on it between moans. It was amazing. I'd never really realized how amazing it would be to be with another woman- imagine, somebody who knows how your body works because theirs is the same! It was intense.

She slowly began to pull her fingers out, I squirmed. "No, please," I begged. "Steph, I need you, don't stop!"

She gave me a wicked grin, pulling her fingers all the way out and bringing her hand to her lips. She licked her fingers slowly, it was a very sexy image. I was turned on beyond belief.

She made her way from underneath me. Not accidentally, my legs were hanging over the couch. She hiked them both over her shoulders and kissed my thighs. I was squirming like crazy, so tempted to just grab her head by her hair and forcefully pull it up to my pussy. At the same time, I was enjoying the feel of her lips, her tongue, on my legs to make her stop. Her hands reached up and went underneath my shirt, trying to find my bra. I quickly pulled them both off, hands shaking form the pleasure.

She pulled and pinched my nipples. She was kissing the lips of my pussy, not pushing her tongue farther. I tried to move meg legs in a way that would make her slid her tongue into me. But she would have none of that. Steph liked being in control. She looked up at me, devilish grin on her face, naughty look in her eye.

"Tell me what you want," she instructed, pinching my nipples.

I moaned. "Please, Stephanie, I can't take this!" my pussy was so tense I thought I might explode. "I need you to relieve me, please eat me!"

"Talk dirty to me babe." Her body moved so gracefully as it slid up mine at our lips locked again. Her hand found my love tunnel again, she pushed just one finger inside me. I was going crazy, I'd become so tight that just that one finger felt like three. My pussy was so tense, it was amazing. She knew all the right places to touch me, I was in heaven. I reached down. I was so dazed with lust I couldn't remember if she'd taken off her clothes. But when I'd finally gotten my head enough to realize I should give her some attention too we were both completely nude. It was crazy, and I was going crazy.

I trailed my hand down her body, I think her eyes rolled back in her head a little. I parted her lips with my first and third fingers, finding her nub with my middle. She cried out and I pulled back her hood with my thumb and pressed her finger to it. I was worried I'd somehow hurt her.

I started to pull away. "Are you alright?"

She grabbed my wrist. "Please," she nearly begged, and I could see the lust in her eyes. "Do that again."

We were both sitting on the couch. Her chest, I estimated a C cup, was pressed to mine. Our lips were locked. She scooted her ass forward on the couch, I knew she was setting up for a scissor. I moved my legs so it would work. Our pussies rubbed together, her warm juices on my tunnel, on my clit, felt so good. We pressed together.

We must have scissor for at least a half hour- minimum. I couldn't get enough of her warmth. It was amazing. That's when she stopped. I thought I was going to go crazy, I'd climaxed at least once while we were scissoring, but I'm kind of multi orgasmic so I couldn't be sure.

That's when she put her hands on both sides of my face and told me it was time for me to clean her up like a good girl. I was about to slid off the couch and put my head inbetween her legs when she shook her head. She just pushed away from me so she could stretch her legs out in front of me. She propped herself up on her elbows and shook her head again. I had wished she'd've been more straight forward, I was dying to climax again.

"Come sit on my face." She laid back again. I was confused, I thought she'd wanted me to clean her up. I didn't object though. I put my pussy over her face. She started to eat me, I shuddered with lust. She stopped, I felt like the world was going to end.

"Please, don't stop," I moaned. "I'm begging."

"Then get down there and copy me like a good girl."

I smiled, my first 69. I leaned forward, laying on her stomach. I parted her lips with my fingers and started lapping at her sweet pussy.

She started again on mine, and I couldn't help but moan.

We didn't stop until her both noticed how hungry we were, which wasn't for a very long time. I climaxed on her face after she started sucking my clit, getting a similar response from her when I did the same- but to make it more interesting I fingered her too.

295

My best trip

After a long day's drive Paul and his mother-in-law, Sharon, find themselves enjoying one another in a quite unexpected manner.

It was hot, and we were barreling down the Interstate in the biggest U-Haul truck I was able to get. My mother-in-law was riding with me, my wife and two sisters-in-law were driving in a car as we drove from Chicago to San Antonio.

It wasn't our intention to keep the two vehicles in close proximity during each day's drive. Instead, we had agreed upon the end-of-day stop where we'd all have dinner and spend the night.

The passenger distribution was determined by the fact that I like to travel early--on the road each day by 5:30. My mother-in-law, Sharon, is the only other "morning person" in the group. So we left early, expecting to get to the stopover location about three o'clock ... we'd probably be about three hours ahead of the car.

Riding with Sharon was OK with me. I like her better than any of the others, including my shrew of a wife.

Yes, shrew! I thought I had found a great potential mate when we were dating, but soon after we married she turned into the most demanding, most selfish person I know. I hated staying with her, but--frankly--didn't want to begin my financial life anew ... she'd find a way to "get it all" if we divorced.

Sharon and I stopped for lunch about 11. She phoned her youngest daughter, Marcy, and found that they had just gotten in the road--they were over five hours behind us. I heard Sharon say, "Well, we'll see you at the motel this evening, but you're getting in late enough that Paul and I aren't going to wait to have dinner. It's hot, we'll need showers when we arrive and we'll be hungry long before you get there."

When she got off the phone I said to her, "Boy, I'd never get away with saying that to Nancy." Sharon responded, "Nancy's my daughter, Paul, and I love her. But she's not a very nice person. You're a great guy. Look at you driving this truck so we can move Marcy from college to her first real job; a half-continent away." She paused and then continued, "Yes, you're a great guy and--frankly--you deserve better." I was amazed that Sharon would say that ... Not amazed she might think it, but truly amazed she'd actually say it to me.

That began a conversation that continued over the next three hours or so. I shared my frustrations about Nancy, Sharon shared her frustrations about my father-in-law, Alex. The words just kept tumbling out and pretty soon we each mentioned our sexual frustrations. "Love making is never as good when you don't respect your partner, is it Paul?"

And I'm thinking, "Too bad I didn't marry the mother!"

We got to the motel and each headed to our respective room for a shower and change of clothes. We agreed to meet in the bar in an hour.

In the shower, I kept thinking of Sharon's comments about sex. She's right, far better when you respect your partner. Then I began thinking about Sharon in another way. I thought about her great body.

Sharon is only 11 years older than me. She works out every day and has maintained her figure. And, she has the prettiest blue eyes I've ever seen.

I thought about what it would be like to cup one of her breasts in my hand. How it would be to grab her ass and pull her to me as we kissed. Wow! What thoughts were these? Did I really just stroke-off to the thought of my mother-in-law? Yup, and I enjoyed it.

When I walked into the bar it was such a nice surprise. There sat Sharon in a yellow sun dress. She was beautiful.

"I brought this along to have something to wear out for dinner after we got settled in San Antonio. I love the Riverwalk there. But after today's conversation I thought I'd dress in something a bit more special than jeans and a T."

Although I'm still not sure why I did it, I leaned in and kissed her-- tenderly on the lips, with my own lips parted just slightly--then said, "You are gorgeous; and I'm lucky to be with you."

We each had a drink. Sharon ordered a white wine. I ordered a Scotch, neat; with a club soda on the side. As soon as I ordered Sharon decided to switch her order to the same as mine. The first drink, was followed by another, then one more. There wasn't a lot of talk. We just sat next to one another and enjoyed the closeness.

As we neared the end of the third drink I put my arm around Sharon's shoulder and said, "Thanks for this, I'm enjoying it."

Sharon looked at me and then leaned for another kiss. This time her tongue flicked against my lips.

She whispered, "Paul, let's go to my room and make love."

I couldn't believe my ears, then I decided I'd heard correctly. I asked for the check and paid for the drinks as quickly as possible.

On the way up to the room, we kissed in the elevator. No longer sweet, gentle kisses. Needy, passionate, body-grinding kisses where we became almost ferocious in our desire for one another.

Damn these electronic door locks. Half the time it takes me several swipes of the key to open the door ... yes, it happened now. Sharon had gotten her key out and I took it to open the door. It didn't open; it didn't open, again; or again. Sharon grabbed the key and tried and it worked. She looked st me with a smile and said, "I must want it more than you."

We tumbled into the room. Kissing, caressing, and mutual exploration led to shedding of clothes. Almost immediately we were naked and in the bed. Then time seemed to stand still.

All movement stopped. We kissed as though we'd never kissed before. A long, luxurious kiss; I caressed her face, ran my hands through her hair, and gently explored her neck. She moaned and then softly said, "Oh my God, Paul, I've wanted this for so long. So very long."

My hands were now on her body. Yes, cupping those breasts I'd fantasied about only an hour earlier. My hands, everywhere. Followed by my lips, leaving a thousand brief kisses.

I pulled the small of her back to bring her closer to me, and she arched to get even closer, as though we were trying to become one.

My hands then trailed down her legs to her feet and then back up her inner leg. As my hands--and lips--continued their journey up, Sharon spread her legs, opening that treasured spot. Oh, that wonderful slightly perfumed smell; so very enticing!

I was as excited as I'd ever been as I rubbed the outside of those beautiful pussy lips. Sharon squirmed then opened her legs fully and thrust her pussy toward me. When my tongue hit her clit, she bucked like nothing I'd ever experienced. She continued to thrust; seven, eight, nine, ten times. She grabbed my head and pulled my face into her heat, alternatively groaning, moaning, screaming, crying. With a final huge thrust she began to squirt and I let her drench my face.

It took Sharon a few minutes to come down from that incredible climax. I held her as she wept. I dried her tears as she sobbed that she'd never before felt so good.

Then, she disentangled from my embrace, smiled and said, "It was too good ... we can't just quit now," and she grabbed ahold of my stiff cock.

"Oh, yes," she said, "this is exactly what a woman wants ... it's a perfect size. It will fill me, but I can still get it in my mouth."

With that Sharon took my cock in her mouth. Slowly at first. So slowly that I thought she might not take much; that I'd be disappointed. Not so. Slowly, Sharon took every bit of me. Her faced pressed into my pubic hair as she relaxed her throat to engulf me. I could feel her throat muscles working, fighting to allow my presence. She looked me in the eyes and began to move up and down. In and out. Shallow one moment; incredibly deep the next. Always looking into my eyes.

Just when I thought this couldn't get better, she added her hand, stroking me as her mouth moved up and down. Then, she began to hum. I was so close.

As Sharon sensed I was close to cumming she sped up, adding more suction. I was in heaven. A beautiful woman sucking my dick, deep-throating me.

I was at the very edge. Then, I felt something else. Her finger at my asshole. Circling, then pressing slightly. I moaned to show my pleasure and she drove that finger home. That did it. I shot four huge ropes of cum down her throat.

After Sharon came up for air we continued our kissing and caressing. I can't imagine how but I remained hard.

I heard her whisper in my ear, "I can't imagine anything in the world that would feel as good as having you inside me. Please fuck me." I didn't need to be invited twice.

I rolled over onto her and mounted. Her cunt was incredibly warm and velvety soft, like nothing I've ever felt before. She lay there, legs spread wide with feet in the air while I thrust, and she responded to each and everyone of my moves. Then, I withdrew and rolled her over, entering her doggy-style. I cupped those beautiful tits, slapped one gently and then gave her ass a good smack. One good smack fallowed by another, followed by another. With each she grunted in slight pain. I was pretty sure she liked it, and became certain when I heard her say, "do it again," and "again." She did like it!

I pulled her to the side of the bed and had her put her feet on the floor. Then standing behind her I began to pound her ... hard. After a few minutes, I stood her up pulled her to me and began to fuck her standing up. We made our way to the wall for a bit of support and I pounded her as hard as I've ever down anyone ever.

We came at exactly the same time. Sharon screamed, I just grabbed and pulled her close? Holding her until we each recovered from our climax.

Then we kissed, gently and sweetly like the first time.

We'd been in the room for an hour. It smelled like sex and each of us feared that one of Sharon's roomies for the night would be suspicious. So we decided to get another room for Sharon and the two daughters with whom she was sharing. We then each went to our rooms and reshowered, then met for dinner.

Sharon and I held hands going into the restaurant. We ordered. I offered a "toast to our new relationship." And my phone rang. It was Nancy, my shrew of a wife. She told me that they were about two hours out and asked if the hotel was OK. Talk about a damper.

After I got off the phone, Sharon again took my hand and thanked me for the afternoon. "I never in my life felt this good."

"You don't need to thank me," I said." "I loved it, and I love you." Sharon responded with, "uh, now what are we going to do?"

"Well, I said, we've got about two hours ..."

An unforgettable mother-in-law

this is a true story about the affair I had with my ex fiances mom.

let me start with some back story. Ashley and I had been dating for about a year and a half when she was diagnosed with a kidney disease. long story short, she was on multiple prescriptions that totally depleted her libido which before this was pretty high because she was only 20 at the time. myself, i was 21. Ashley and her mom, Lindsey, had a great relationship. Lindsey was 17 when she had Ashley so the age gap wasn't too drastic. they talked about everything from fashion to sex. in fact Lindsey once told me "don't buy the cow without first drinking the milk." I took this as permission to fuck her daughter and that i did!

Ashley was about 5'10", probably around 150lbs with big c's and a decent butt. her body was tone and tight. she was a FREAK! she was down for anything; facials, ass to mouth, 69, you name it she'd try it. Lindsey was about 5'8" around 155 or 160 if i had to guess. she was a little bigger than her daughter. her tits were definitely bigger!

my attraction to Lindsey was very early on and i was open about it. in fact, i used to joke with her all the time. even her husband, James, would laugh at me blatantly hitting on her. any whom I was so attracted to her that I often would do anything I could to get my nose in the crotch of her dirty panties. id sneak into her room, id rummage through the hamper, find the dirtiest, wettest pair, and smell them as I rubbed my cock. often times id explode my cum all over them. I absolutely loved the way that pussy smelled. I would do this every chance I got!

one day, I went over to Lindseys house to use the printer. Ashley was at school and James was at work.

the house was unlocked because she was expecting me. I walked into the house and heard the shower running. I knew right away that Lindsey was showering therefore there'd be fresh panties for me to smell. I went into her bedroom and found a pile of dirty clothes laying on the floor making a trail to the bathroom. it took everything i had not to try and sneak a look at her naked body in the shower. instead I pulled my pants down and began to rub my cock while inhaling the sweet smell of her pussy.

after i finished, i went to use the printer as i had planned. a few minutes later, Lindsey came into the room in nothing but a towel. apparently she caught me looking her up and down because she called me out for it. i tried to play it off but she knew as well as I did that I wanted to see what that towel was hiding from me...

a few days past and nothing was mentioned about that day. i was at work when I got a text from Lindsey. it said "I noticed my panties were moved the other day. hope you enjoyed them. ;-)" me, being the uber flirtatious type replied "absolutely I did." Lindsey replied "I know any kind of sex with Ashley has been lacking lately but I appreciate you being so understanding. my panties are yours anytime you want if it helps you relieve some sexual frustration." I was pretty blown away when I got that but decided to see how far i could take it. i said "Id love to get my nose in a pair that are super wet..." to my surprise, Lindsey replied "anything you want, come by the house tomorrow morning around 9 and ill leave you a pair thatll make you cum instantly."

the next morning i did exactly as i was instructed. on her bed I found a hot pink thong and a vibrator. I immediately went to town on the thong after figuring out Lindsey had worn the panties while masturbating. after I finished, I text Lindsey a simple "thank you."

that entire day, all I could think about was Lindsey and how bad I wanted her. I decided to be bold and tell her. at that point I figured it was worth a shot. "I can't get you or those panties out of my head." what shocked me the most was her reply. "come over tonight while Ashley is at work."

when I walked in her house that night I found Lindsey in a tank top and some incredibly short shorts. I looked her up and down and swallowed hard before mustering up a "hello." Lindsey welcomed me on and offered me a glass of wine which i could tell she had already been enjoying. I took the glass from her soft and warm hands as she looked me in the eye and said "you've got two hours before James gets home. you can look, but don't touch. Don't touch me, you can touch yourself all you want."

At that moment Lindsey pulled the tank top off revealing her big tits and dark brown nipples. she groped herself as I stood there trying to process what was happening. next, she slipped her shorts off to reveal her hairless cunt and round ass. as I reached out to feel her skin, I was quickly reminded of the rules. I could not help myself. I spent what felt like an eternity examining every inch if her body. naturally, my cock started to swell and Lindsey was starting to notice. "pull it out" she said. I freed my cock from my shorts and held it in my hand as she sized it up. she seemed impressed. I had to release a load. I asked her to sit on the couch and sprwad her legs so I could see her pussy as I rubbed myself. within minutes i had cum all over the floor and couch. Lindsey seemed to enjoy her show and i enjoyed every second too.

I began to pull up my boxers and pants as Lindsey began to get dressed. I hated watching her cover up her body but she insisted that there'd definitely be more for me later.

A few days later I began getting anxious for more. I didn't just want to jack off to her naked body, I wanted to feel her body with my hands and my tongue. I wanted to feel her and taste her but most of all I wanted to fuck her and pump her pussy full of my cum. I couldn't help myself any longer so I shot a text to Lindsey telling her how bad I wanted to be inside of her.

the very next day i went over to her house to see just how much I could get away with. being that I'm not an idiot, I know women like being dominated so I decided this would be my approach this time with Lindsey. I walked into the house and pushed her up against a wall and began kissing her. she made no attempt to stop me so it was game on.

As I was kissing her I let my hands explore her body. I pulled her hair and felt her tits. after a brief minute, I had to get her clothes off. I pulled my head away and pulled off her shirt and bra. as soon as I saw her nipples began to suck on them. she started moaning so I knew I was doing something right. I undid her pants and let her pants and panties fall to the floor.

that's when I started to really get brave. As li was still sucking on her tits, I slipped a finger inside of her and started to feel around. By now she was shaking and I thought she was going to collapse so I grabbed her by the hand and took her to the room. I laid her on her bed, with her legs still on the floor, and began eating her pussy. Never in my life have a tasted anything as good as that pussy. I licked it until she was begging me to stop. Even with her asking for me to stop, I kept going because I loved the feeling of her thighs squeezing my head every time she came.

Finally after enough begging me to stop and fuck her, I took full advantage of her wishes. I stood at the end of the bed and pulled her to me. Her legs were now on my shoulders as I slid my rock hard cock deep inside of her dripping wet pussy. It was a moment that I'll never forget. It was hands down the best pussy I've ever been inside. It was tighter than I'd imagined and it just swallowed me up. I began to slide in and out of her and listen to the moans she was making to know I was doing it right.

After a minute or two, I flipped her on her knees so I could stare at her ass as I fucked her. Her ass was simply amazing. Round and soft and her asshole looked just as good as id imagined. As bad as I wanted to slide my cock deep inside of her ass, I decided that was best left for another time.

After a few more hard pumps, I couldn't hold back and blew my load deep inside her cunt. My legs went numb and I collapsed on the bed and pulled her onto me.

We both laid there for what felt like an eternity and caught our breath and bring ourselves back to reality. After it sank in what I'd just done I couldn't help but smile ear to ear. I gave her a kiss and proceeded to put my clothes on and get out of the house before we managed to get ourselves caught.

We had many more sexcapades after that one. That was two years ago. About a year and half ago Ashley and I broke up but Lindsey and I kept enjoying each other's talents for months to come.

It's been almost six months since the last time I filled lindys pussy with my cum, but I still think about it every day. Every now and then we will send some sexts back and forth and remember the fun.

I   miss   that   pussy...

One night at the dancing club

I met Debbie, when she was eighteen, in a small mountain town in Colorado. Long blondish hair, almost to her waist. Hazel bedroom eyes. Gorgeous face, with sexy lips and a mouth that looked like it was begging for a hard cock to suck. Big, ski jump, 36C tits. Her aureoles are about two inches in diameter. Her nipples about 3/8" in diameter and 1/2" long when aroused. Her waist is 26 inches and her hips 37 inches. Lying on her back, naked, you can see her abs and rib cage. Her pubic mound is extremely prominent, so much so that her clit is accessible without her spreading her legs! She can be fucked without spreading her legs! Her pubic hair is sparse. Her legs are shapely and her ass firm and round, just a tad large proportional to the rest of her body, with the exception of her tits. She has sexy size 6 feet.

Upon asking around town about her I found out that she was a virgin and that a lot of guys have tried to fuck her, without any luck. A few had felt her tits and ass. (After we were married she admitted to putting a shy family friend's [Mike Mosburn] hands on her tits and letting him feel

310

her tits for about a half hour while she made out with him. She had on a thin stretch knit bra she'd worn for the occasion and let him get his hands under her blouse. She said she like being felt up and usually wore a padded bra and that Mike was the only guy she trusted to play with her nearly naked tits and not rape her or tell everyone in town what she'd let him do, and how much she'd enjoyed it. She had on thin white cotton shorts and a thong and he played with her ass.)

I asked a chick I was fucking (Cheryl Hawkims) about Debbie. She didn't like her, said she was a cock tease and too good to fuck around. She said there was a rumor that Jack Timer (Debbie's senior year boyfriend) had gotten Debbie's cherry but that she denied it. Cheryl loved to fuck. I was one of a few guys that would eat her cunt. Maybe because she fucked so many cocks. I love eating pussy! Cheryl could deep throat me. She had ski jump tits, bigger than Debbie's. But they hung a little. Debbie's didn't. They were perfect. Cheryl liked it up her ass. I'd never gotten into anal. A couple years later I wished I had! Cheryl had long, sexy legs, tall at 5' 10", but a flat ass. She was pretty.

I took Debbie out twice before I kissed her. The third time we parked and made out. I got to feel her tits. The fourth time I got her blouse open and bra undone and felt her naked tits. She said no one had ever done that before and it felt good. I told her she had the most magnificent tits I'd ever felt. Two dates later we were on my bed making out. She let me dry hump her and strip her from the waist up and see her with the lights on. She told me to look at her. I told her how exquisite she was and she loved it. I kissed her and felt her tits and sucked them. My hand found its way between her legs. She was HOT and her pussy was gushing! I slipped my fingers up the leg of her shorts and caressed her pussy, lovingly, through her soaked panties. I put her hand on my hard cock and she stroked it through my pants while I stroked her pussy.

The next date we wound up on my bed and I stripped her to her panties. She stripped me to my underwear and we felt each other all over our bodies. With the lights on. She laid there on her back with her legs spread and let me look at her while I felt her tits and cunt. She sat up and stroked my hard cock through my underwear. She slid her hand inside my underwear and stoked my cock, grinning at me. She said, "Like that?" I groaned in appreciation. She said she had no idea guys dicks got so big and hard. I was pretty drunk and out of my mind horny. I started taking my underwear off and Debbie helped me get naked. She told me my dick was beautiful and that she wanted me to look at her pussy. I stripped her panties off and she spread her legs, laying there totally naked for me. She felt her tits and rubbed her pussy, saying it really turned her on for me to look at her naked. Her cunt lips were splayed completely open. Pussy juice oozed from her hot wet fucking cunt and ran down onto her virgin ass hole. We lay next to each other and explored, Debbie stroking me and me feeling her tits and cunt. My finger found her opening and slid carefully in. I'd never been with a virgin before and didn't want to take her cherry with my finger. I got my finger almost all the way in when Debbie gasped, pressing her cunt into my hand for a few seconds and said to stop. I backed out and masturbated her. She came within a minute. And again. She came four times and begged me to stop, saying she was so sensitive she couldn't stand it anymore. She asked me how her pussy looked after being finger fucked and masturbated. I told her she had the tightest, sexiest pussy I'd ever seen or felt. She spread herself wide open and held her cunt lips open. She said she loved being looked at naked. She looked at my precum oozing cock. Debbie said she wanted me to take her. I asked if she was a virgin and she said yes. Chivalrous drunk me said we should wait until tomorrow when we weren't so drunk. We felt each other all over for a while and I took her home.

The next night we kissed for a few minutes, stripping each other. I ate her cunt. She watched me eat her cunt and came, telling me to eat her. She came hard, grabbing my head and fucked her cunt into my mouth. We fucked our brains out. For hours. Fuck, Debbie was the tightest fuck ever, and I told her so. We showered and she sucked my cock. She watched herself in my dresser mirror while she sucked my cock. She was a natural. She ate every drop of my come. She said it was bitterer than she expected from talking to her girlfriends, but liked it. We both got off on watching her suck cock. We watched ourselves fuck in the mirror. After I came Debbie turned her spread open cunt toward the mirror and we looked at her cream pie. Fuck! Talk about nasty! She said, "Look at what you did to me!" Debbie had a sluttish grin on her face. She was the wildest fuck I'd ever had. She told me to finger her cum filled pussy and masturbate her. We watched my cum be forced out her cunt by my finger and spread all over her cunt and clit. It ran down onto her virgin ass hole. She came repeatedly. I held her swollen red cunt open and we could see her clit. Her lips were plastered wide open. Her clit was stuck to her right cunt lip. It was half an inch long and an eighth of an inch thick. Debbie masturbated herself for me for the first time. She said she'd been masturbating since she was twelve, but had never seen her clit before or cum that hard before. She bucked her hips into the air when she came.

We looked at her in the mirror. Her crotch was drenched in cunt juice and cum. Debbie pulled my head into her cunt and I ate her while she watched. I could taste my cum mixed with her cunt juice and liked it. It

313

tasted like fucking!!! Debbie exploded. She grasped my head and fucked her cunt with my mouth, grinding it into my face. My tongue was in her cunt. I stuck it as far into her as I could. She exploded again and screamed with orgasmic pleasure. Her crotch was sliding up and down and around on my mouth. I licked and sucked all of her cunt juice. Her virgin ass hole pressed into my mouth and tongue in her gyrations. I could tell from her gasps that it really set her off. Finally she planted her ass hole onto my tongue. She fucked her ass hole directly onto it. It was covered in cum and cunt juice and slid in easily. She pulled my head into her ass like she wanted my whole head up her ass. She screamed for me to eat her ass. She held me there and I worked my tongue in and out. No woman I'd been with had ever cum so hard as Debbie did then.

We fucked. And fucked. For two more hours. Debbie screamed every time I came in her. She wanted cum in her cunt. I shot off in her until I was depleted. We rested and savored our sex. Debbie sucked my cumcoated prick. And watched herself in the mirror. She said she couldn't believe I'd cum for her so many times.

It was 2:25AM when we dragged ourselves into Brown's cafe for much needed nourishment. Mike and Marsha (Mots) Milles were there after being in the White Horse dancing. We sat with them and Marsha could tell, immediately, that Debbie'd gotten her brains fucked out. Marsha had "B" cup bullet shaped tits, with huge puffies. I'd had a hard-on for them from the first time I saw her. Mike loved showing her off and let everyone know he kept her tiny little cunt shaved. He liked fucking her "little girl" pussy. Debbie saw me staring at Marsha's tits. Marsha had on a stretch knit top that molded to her tits, perfectly, showing their exact size and shape, including her puffies. When we got home she commented on Mike liking to show her off and said I could look all I wanted if it made me horny and I fucked the shit out of her after looking at Marsha's tits. Which I did. Debbie said she'd been looking at guys' crotches since she was twelve and it turned her on to see big bulges. The next day half the town knew she was finally putting out. And loving it. Debbie didn't seem to mind. Half the guys in town were asking her out. She turned them all down. We fucked constantly. I bought her sexier, more revealing clothes than she was used to. She'd always liked guys checking her out and teasing then. It still took her quite a while to become comfortable wearing them. She'd started getting tits when she was ten. She was a large "A" cup at twelve. Boys and men were looking down her blouse at her bra, but she'd never had sexy, revealing bras before. She'd worn short skirts, but with panty hose. I bought her thigh high, stay up by themselves stockings. I hated panty hose. I bought her seamed butt panties and her skirts draped seductively into her ass crack while she danced.

The more Debbie fucked and sucked my cock, the more she liked it. She became insatiable. We fucked when we woke up, her sucking my cock to wake me up. She got off on putting my soft cock in her mouth and feeling it grow hard. We fucked on my lunch hour and when I got home from work. And after dinner. And when we went to bed. Beta Max and VHS had just come out and we rented porns. We both really got off on women sucking huge cocks, stretching their mouths to the limit and getting fucked in the mouth while the guy held their heads and rammed into their mouths. She loved cum shots all over their faces. I'll never forget the first anal sex video we watched. Debbie said that was the nastiest, sexiest thing she'd ever seen. The woman's ass hole gaped open and cum gushed out. She'd been taken anally and his cum ran down into her spread open cunt. I liked watching it, but wasn't into it, as I said before. We watched a gang bang video, five men and one woman, and I told Debbie that as horny as she was she'd probably love being gang fucked and that it would probably take ten guys lining up on her for about four hours to satisfy her. That was the first time I saw Debbie blush. Then she turned crimson! The woman in the video did double and triple penetrations. The woman took at least twelve loads of cum. Debbie was incredibly turned on and fucked my brains out. All five of them had fucked the woman one after the other. She said she couldn't even imagine being fucked that hard and fast and deep by five huge porno cocks up her pussy and getting those heavy loads of cum shot into her. At the end of the video they all jacked off onto the woman's face, tits, belly and held open cunt. Debbie masturbated while she watched this scene.

We got married in June.

We went to Denver for a weekend, arriving about 7:00PM Thursday evening. I'd researched some motels and found one with mirrors in the rooms that catered to horny couples. It had a good, slightly expensive restaurant, and private, members only, dance club down the street that was a pretty much no holds barred swingers club. I wanted to watch people fuck. And I got off on showing Debbie off. Debbie loved the room.

We fucked at the motel for an hour. There were mirrors everywhere and we watched ourselves fucking, Debbie commenting on how much she liked watching herself fuck and suck. Like the women in the pornos. Debbie wore an incredibly low cut bra and blouse and a mini-skirt when we went out. Her turquoise tulip bra was underwired and had push up, push in pads that started at the middle of the bottom of her tits and wrapped half way up the outsides of them. The pads were covered in satin. The rest of her bra was sheer with small lace rosette appliqué. It exposed her tits right to the edge of her aureoles at the top and the insides of her tits. The pads arced up and were only two inches wide at the widest part, exposing most of her tits through the sheer bra. It was the most cleavage she'd ever exposed and it turned us both on. Looking down her blouse, from just the right angle, I could see inside her bra. Half her naked aureoles were exposed to the edge of her nipples. She'd never let anyone but me see her naked aureole and nipples and said she'd have to be careful. Her panties were matching turquoise sheer lace in the front with the rosettes and totally sheer in the back. String bikini, tiny in the front, showing some cunt hair, and only covering half her hot fucking ass. Her blouse was burgundy, sleeveless and only went down to just above her belly button. It was a wrap blouse and gaped open when she was twirled when she danced. Her wide set tulip bra straps showed out the shoulders of her blouse and her bra showed out the sleeves of the arms holes of her blouse when she raised her arms while she danced. Her blouse was scoop necked, exposing her chest to a quarter of an inch of her bra top when standing upright. Bent over, everyone could see down her blouse to her sheer bra, aureole and nipples. Debbie's skirt was mini, dark grey, thin satin, see through with the light behind her, mid-thigh, draping into her ass crack. Sitting down, it raised up to just below her pussy. Dancing, with her arms up around my neck, it raised up to the bottom of her ass cheeks. She wore sheer dark grey thigh-high stocking and platform heels that aligned my cock with her cunt while we danced.

We'd had almost two bottles of wine while we fucked. We were pretty fucked up when we went to the motel restaurant. We drank more wine at dinner. The waiter (another Steve) devoured Debbie with his eyes while he served us. He recommended a dance club (the swingers' club) and said to show the doorman our receipt and we'd get a free membership which usually cost $50 per couple. It was 10:15PM when we got there. We were seated clear in the back at a two person table on a side wall. A guy was seated directly across from Debbie at another two person table, giving him a direct shot up her skirt. Another guy was at a table to the side of our table, giving him a shot up her skirt every time she got up to dance. At 11:15PM the waiter and a friend of his showed up and sat with the two guys at the tables across from us. Our waiter and his buddy had a clear shot up Debbie's skirt while she was sitting and the other two had a clear shot up her skirt when she got up to dance. We were both drunk and horny by that time. They switched tables for different views of her panties. They took turns dancing with Debbie, looking down her blouse when they came to ask her to dance. They looked up her skirt from about five feet away when she got up.

All the women had on sexy revealing outfits. Some of the women were being felt up. The men weren't bothering to hide their hard-ons. They were grinding their crotches together. Women were getting their asses humped when they entered and exited the dance floor.

At the midnight break we went to our car and smoked a joint. Debbie was horny and sucked my cock. I fingered her to three orgasms. Her cunt lips were spread wide open, ready to fuck. She smelled of wanton sex. We commented on how much they could see of her. She said there was no way for her to keep them from seeing up her skirt. I told her they'd already seen her panties and she might as well not worry about it. Debbie said she'd shit if anyone she knew ever saw her like this, or if she ever ran into these guys again. She'd dirty danced and slow danced with them while I danced with various women. She said they all had hard-ons and pressed their cocks into her crotch. She said our waiter had a huge curved cock and it lined up perfectly with her cunt with her platform heels. She said he must not have underwear on because it went between her legs and she could feel it on the entire length on her pussy and clit. And that it was all she could to keep from humping into it.

At the 1:00AM break we smoked another joint. She asked if I'd noticed they were taking her hand in their hands holding it next to her right tit when they slow danced. She said they were pressing the backs of their fingers into the side of her bra and moving it around, trying to feel her tit. She said she let them do it because they could only feel her bra pad, mostly. They occasionally ran their fingers across the whole outside of her tit. And they pushed into the side of her tit a lot. She said one of them was always dancing right next to her, on her left, looking at her chest when they did it. Debbie said they were running their hands across the top of her panties, which was at the top of her ass cheek, right at the top of her ass crack, and feeling to the sides of her panties. She thought they were trying to figure out what kind of panties she had on. Then she said they'd all danced with her right in front of their tables and had slid their hands down her ass half way and she'd pulled their hands up. They'd moved their hands around the top of her ass. She thought they wanted to show each other how much of her tits and ass they could feel. She wanted me to watch them try to feel her up. To watch her tease the fuck out of them.

I disappeared into the crowded dance floor and watched them dance when we went back in. Sure enough, our waiter was pressing his fingers into the side of her tit while one of them, dancing a foot away from her, looked down her blouse. He slid his fingers almost to her nipple and back to the side. Fuck! He'd pulled her blouse open and pushed her tit out of her bra, exposing her entire aureole, nipple and all, to his buddy. His hand went over half way down her ass, right in front of the other two guys watching at the tables. She pulled his hand up while he ground into her cunt. As she pulled his hand up he slid her skirt up, eventually exposing almost her entire ass through her sheer panties, five feet away from the guys at the tables. They took turns on her, dancing and grinding into her cunt and exposing her tits and sheer panties to each other while I watched, hidden in the crowd.

We were both totally fucked up and turned on. Our eyes met. Debbie arched her back and pressed her cunt into Steve's hard curved cock. I could just imagine how his cock felt on her horny spread open, just finger fucked cunt. Debbie's entire cunt with a hard thick curved prick pressing into it, moving to the music and rubbing into her clit, sticking out of her up turned, prominent pubic mound. Debbie watched me watch her be molested. They all felt her tits and ass, exposing her nipples and ass. They dirty danced and humped their hard cocks into her cunt and her ass crack. She shoved and ground her cunt and ass into their hard cocks while I watched. Everyone watched. Debbie watched other couples grind their crotches together while Steve ground his hard curved prick into her cunt.

We got back to our room and attacked each other. I told her how sexy she looked and how proud I was to be with the sexiest women in the club. Debbie said the guys had felt her tits and ass. And seen her panties up her skirt. She asked if that turned me on as much as it did her. I told her I almost came in my pants. She said every guy she danced with had a hard-on. I said I couldn't blame them, that I had one all night. We fucked! She said she knew some of the guys were talking to each other about her after she danced with them. And, that it was a good thing none of them knew us. She said she'd love to have heard what they were saying about her. I had her put her bra and blouse on and showed her how they were showing her naked nipple to each other and told her she needn't worry about other men seeing her nipples any more. She just about shit and wanted to know why I didn't tell her. I told her I couldn't get to her and they'd obviously been looking at her naked aureole and nipple for over an hour already. She couldn't believe they'd done that to her without her knowing. Her nipples were hard as rocks. She devoured my cock while I savaged her tits. I told her what an incredible cock sucker she was and how she had the most perfect tits in the world and how I couldn't blame them for showing her tits to each other and feeling them. She asked if I was mad about them seeing her nipple. I said "No, of course not!" I told her about them sliding her skirt up her ass and showing each other her practically naked ass. She put her skirt and panties on and I slid her skirt up while we watched in the mirror. We slow danced and she ground into my cock, asking if I'd be pissed if Steve wouldn't let her back away from his cock and made her cum. I told her it wouldn't be her fault and I could just imagine the guys watching her have a monumental orgasm right in front of them. We both laughed.

The next morning we fucked and planned our Friday evening escapade. We went shopping and bought Debbie a thin, semi-sheer white spaghetti strap top and mini-skirt outfit. Her blouse exposed the top of her big, wide set, outward pointing tits to the top of her aureoles and about an inch of the insides of them clear to the bottom of her tits. The color of her aureole and nipples was obvious. It draped seductively between her tits and around the outsides, displaying the full height and width of her tits. Her period was starting Monday and her aureole had swollen, puffing her aureole to twice their normal size (and sensitivity). It went down to two inches above her belly button. The slightly sheer mini-skirt barely went to mid-thigh. With light behind her you could see the silhouette of her legs through it. It draped into her ass crack. We'd found a pussy pink stretch knit, sheer g-string that molded to her pussy. Debbie modeled it in front of the mirror in our room. Half her cunt hair was exposed. Debbie danced in front of the mirror. Her tits jiggled seductively. Her skirt rose up to her g-string, exposing her thighs to the point where they curved inward toward her pussy, making a fucking gap with her thigh-high stockings squeezing the tops of her thighs. We watched in the mirror while we slow danced, me holding her hand in mine, pressing my fingers into the side of her braless tit. She asked how her tit felt. I said, "Naked." I easily worked her blouse to the outside of her naked nipple. She said it was going to be an extreme turn-on, knowing that they were feeling her braless tits and seeing her naked nipple this time. We fucked. We went shopping again and bought her pair of really tall, black, spike heels and "tall" shear black, stay up by themselves, thigh-high stockings. They went clear up to her crotch and the bottom of her ass cheeks, squeezing her thighs, creating an even larger gap between the top of her thighs and her cunt. Debbie commented that Steve's big curved porno cock was really going to be able to stroke her pussy the way her stockings squeezed her thighs open. She modeled the outfit and I bent her over the end of the bed, pulled her skirt up, g-string aside, and fucked the shit out of her.

We went to dinner and our waiter, Steve, from the night before, got an eye full of tit. We had a couple glasses of wine and Debbie was loose. As was I. It was 9:00PM. Steve gave us our receipt and said he'd see us there. He saw Debbie's sheer pink pantied pussy when she got up to leave.

At the club we went to the booth at the back of the dance floor with the same two men at the tables across from it. Two more guys, that our two friends obviously knew, sat at another table close by a while later. They ordered us a round of drinks. I told the waitress, "Scotch on the rocks." There weren't many people there yet and we had the whole and back third of the dance floor to ourselves. Debbie danced with the two guys from the evening before. Her braless tits bounced and swayed and jiggled. Her skirt twisted with her hips, rising to the bottom of her crotch, showing the tops of her thigh high stockings. She sat back down with me and asked how she looked. I said, "Fuckable!" We slow danced, our crotches glued together. The guys kept drinks cumming to our table. We were both pretty drunk. She danced a few more fast songs with them and a slow song came on before she got back to the table. I was dancing and watched her partner steer her to the back corner of the dance floor. Two of the guys, dancing, blocked my view of her, except for part of her head. Occasionally I could see her smiling face. Once I saw her upper torso from the side and it looked like the guy she was dancing with's hand was at her tit level, a slutty grin on her face. The guys blocking my view, whose faces I could see, were grinning. Then I saw them looking down at her ass level, grinning lewdly. I immediately wondered if she was getting her tits and ass felt. I knew Debbie was pretty drunk and how much she liked being felt up. I also knew how well her tits and ass felt. I was struck with jealousy. I also felt an INCREDIBLE ache in my hard fucking cock! Fuck. Was Debbie being felt up? Where did he have his hands? My cock involuntarily ground into the crotch of the girl I was dancing with. She pressed back into me. Debbie went back to our table and bent over, reaching for her drink at the back of the table. We could see the bottoms of her tits and ass.

Steve got there at 10:45 and the show was on! It was crowded and he danced Debbie in front of his buddies with a lot of other dancers blocking my view. Debbie tried to make eye contact with me, but it was impossible. They took turns dancing with her. Occasionally I got a view of her fast dancing, her skirt swirling up above her cunt and ass, g-string exposed. Them pulling her braless right tit into their left hands when she twirled back to them. I could see their fingers open and knew they were getting a handful of her tit every time. They always slow danced with her by their tables. I saw their hand on the outside of her braless tit. Fuck, were they running their fingers over her braless nipples??!! It looked like they were sliding her skirt up her ass, exposing it for each other. The woman I was dancing with was braless and pressed her tits into me. I imagined Debbie doing the same. She ground into my hard prick.

Debbie was sweating when she got back to the table. She said she needed a break to cool off. It was the 11:00PM break and we went out to the car. I told her I was getting drunk. She said she was well on her way, feeling no pain. She said she'd seen me humping the last chic I'd danced with. I told her it was because I'd just seen her with a lewd, sexy grin on her face. She laughed and said Steve had pressed his hard-on into her crotch and told her he wanted to fuck her. She said it was a real turn on getting to tease them, knowing they'd never see her again. I asked if they'd all told her that. She said he was the only one bold enough. I told her, from the look on her face, it must have turned her on. She said that his hard dick felt really good pressing into her pussy and that Marsha had explained that the greatest compliment a man could give a woman was to get a hard-on and tell her he wanted to fuck her. I told her she had three hours to get complimented all she wanted and to tease all she wanted and then we were going to the room and I would demonstrate her greatest compliment! She asked me if I meant it. I told her I wanted her horny out of her mind when we fucked. She asked if I didn't mind them wanting to fuck her. I told her I wanted to fuck her the first time I saw her and I expected that any normal guy would want to fuck her, especially in her sexy, revealing outfit. I asked her if they'd all seen her panties getting out of the booth. She said she she'd made sure they had. I asked her if she knew when she bent over, leaning over the table, that her tits and ass were exposed. She said that was the general idea! I told her it was our next to the last night here. She kissed me, deeply.

The woman I'd danced with before found me again. She talked dirty to me and said her husband was watching us. And that he wanted to watch me feel her up while we all watched my wife tease. He was next to us and watching us and Debbie. Debbie was at the back of the floor, dirty dancing. My partner and Debbie were shaking their tits and asses. Her husband was watching his and my wife. A slow song came on. Her cunt pressed into my cock. I could tell by the look on Debbie's face that Steve's cock had found Debbie's cunt and ground into it. His hands went half way down her ass and she left them there, all five of them watching. Shirley's husband, Bob, maneuvered his partner where he had a better view of Debbie.

After the song was over we sat at their table and Bob said Steve had her skirt clear up to the top of her ass for half the song. I told Bob and Shirley the guys didn't know we knew what they were doing to Debbie. And how they'd looked at her nipples the night before.

The four of us went to our car and smoked a couple of joints at the 1:00AM break. Debbie was fucked up and wanted to know what they said about her. And if they'd seen her ass hole! Shirley said she would to dance with them and ask them about her. Shirley and Bob said they came here all the time and really got off on Shirley exposing herself and being molested. Bob said that on Saturday nights she went totally commando and exposed her tits, pussy and ass to everyone there. She got finger fucked and stroked cocks while a lot of people watched.

Fresh drinks were at our table. Debbie drank half her drink before she was asked to dance again. She was three sheets to the wind and I pretended to be. She danced really sexy in our corner. Tits bouncing and swirling. A few of the guys got girls and danced with them by their table, blocking my view half the time. They took turns with Debbie and I danced with a few girls besides Shirley. I watched and when two of the men got up from their table I disappeared into the men's room. I hid in the last stall and heard the two of them saying how good her hot ass felt and that she had no idea they were lifting her skirt clear to the top of her ass, by their table, for them to look at. They said her ass hole looked inviting and wondered if she took it up her ass. And that she was drunk enough that she'd let them all run their fingers over her tits and expose her nipple. Steve was going to try to feel her tit and butt hole and pussy. He was going to try to make her cum. Shirley reported that the guys had all felt Debbie's tits and humped their pricks against her cunt and ass hole and they and wanted to fuck her. And that Debbie liked being felt up and humped by their hard pricks. They all said she humped her cunt into their pricks.

My mind whirled. I could see them feeling her scrumptious tits and her enjoying it. I could see her exposed ass hole and crotch in her sheer pink g-string, cunt hair sticking out, and them devouring her visually. Wanting to fuck her. I couldn't blame them. Fuck, I was setting her up to get totally molested and loving it. How far would Debbie let them go? Thank God we'd never see any of them again and no one we knew would ever find out what she did here. Shirley and I danced while we watched Debbie.

Debbie was sitting at the edge of the table, legs spread preparatory to getting up to dance. Steve was blocking her exit, talking to her. Two couples were between us and Debbie and no one noticed us watching. I knew everyone at the tables across from ours had a clear shot of her sheer, soaked, g-string and spread open cunt. Debbie was looking up at him. Then she looked over at the guys at the tables and grinned knowingly at them. He stepped back to let her up and I could see the size of his cock. It stood out in the pleat of his pants. It had to be nine inches. Thick. Curved. She stared at it before she got up to dance with him. She smiled up at him and looked back down at his prick. Debbie studied it. She spread her legs invitingly, giving him, and them, a clear shot of her cunt in her skimpy g-string, half her cunt hair exposed. Debbie got up and Steve was behind her immediately. His hard cock was pressed into her ass crack as they moved to the dance floor. Debbie moved slowly, letting him hump her ass, pressing back into his hard curved cock while they worked their way to the dance floor. And the other guys watched. Debbie's arms were around his neck and in her five inch heels her cunt aligned perfectly with his hard prick. It sank between her thighs. It was a fairly fast slow song and their bodies moved to the music. He stroked her cunt to the music with his hard fucking prick and she stroked his cock with her sopping wet cunt to the music while the guys at the tables watched. Their hips rotated in a fucking motion. They talked. I could read their lips when they said the word "fuck". I could read Debbie's lips saying, "Fuck me". It looked like she said," suck your cock". And, "fuck my ass". Debbie was oblivious to everyone on the dance floor. Their crotches ground together. His hand went up to her blouse and her eyes closed and her head tilted back in pleasure. His other hand went down the back of her skirt. The guys at the table were enraptured by the show. I could see his hand slide across Debbie's ass and find her butt hole. Her entire body jerked. She said, "Fuck yes". She grinned at him. She looked around and found me. She mouthed, "Oh, shit!" He pulled her into his huge curved prick grinding hard into the entire length of her gaping cunt lips and swollen clit while his left hand obviously was molesting her entire tit. Debbie gasped and groaned as Steve's huge cock stroked her cunt to the music. She ground into his prick and then back into his finger on her butt hole. I was mesmerized, as were the guys at the tables. It was only a minute into the song. Debbie came, hard! Her face contorted into an expression of sheer orgasmic pleasure. She'd been cumming for about five seconds when his hand slid down her ass between her drenched thighs, to her gushing cunt. She rammed her cunt back and forth into his huge cock, masturbating her cunt from the front, and into his fingers ravishing her sopping cunt from the back. His hand slid between her cunt and her ass hole. She convulsed orgasmically, totally immersed in her desire to saturate herself in the exquisite simultaneous pleasure of his prick thrusting against her cunt and his fingers masturbating her cunt and virgin ass hole. He let go of her tit and pulled Debbie's hand down to his hard prick. She automatically wrapped her hand around it, savoring the length and girth of it. She stroked it. Shit, Shirley had her hand wrapped around my cock, stroking me hard. Thirty seconds later the song ended and we went to Shirley's table. Debbie'd cum so hard she'd almost collapsed. She shook her head, trying to get her senses back. She staggered back to our table, still shaking with her intense orgasm.

Debbie said she was ready to fuck. She wanted her brains fucked out. All the guys were looking at her. Fuck, she was horny and drunk. We watched Steve let the guy he was sitting with smell his fingers. Steve looked at us and licked his fingers. Debbie was embarrassed. Shirley laughed and said they looked like they'd both thoroughly enjoyed themselves as much as we'd enjoyed watching them. She wanted to know if Steve had gotten his fingers up her cunt or ass hole. Debbie said, "No, thank, God." Shirley wanted to know if she always came that hard and long, saying she was envious.

We fucked immediately at the room. We both exploded almost immediately. She devoured my cock, cleaning it and crammed my face into her cunt and ass hole. I eagerly sucked up my cum from her cunt. Her ass tasted incredible mixed with her cunt juices and my cum. Like fucking! Debbie exploded on my tongue in her ass hole. She said it really turned her on to let them see her in her g-sting. And see her tits jiggle and bounce around. She said Steve masturbating her cunt with his prick and hand at the same time, and feeling her asshole and braless tits and her jacking his huge cock while we all watched was the sexiest horniest thing imaginable. She slid her fingers up her cunt and put them in my mouth. It had really turned me on watching Debbie. And, she hadn't actually fucked another guy. I could live with her being felt and fingered. Especially by men we didn't know and wouldn't see again. Probably. Until tomorrow night!!!

The next day Debbie said she couldn't wait to go dancing that night. I told her she should leave them something to remember her by. She looked puzzled. I said, "Your final tease of the weekend." Her panties!! Saturday night was commando night and everyone was supposed to go

329

commando at midnight. And, if anyone was caught with bra or panties or underwear on, their partner had to take them off on the dance floor. Debbie said it would be a real turn on to let me watch Steve reach up under her skirt and take her g-string off in front of everyone. We went to Frederick's and bought her a totally sheer pale pink stretch nylon g-string that only covered her cunt, barely. All of her cunt hair was exposed. The top came to a point and spread out over her cunt, molding to every wrinkle and her lips, sinking into her cunt. It ended in a point right at the bottom of her fuck hole. Her clit was swollen and obvious. The strings were barely a sixteenth of an inch thick. It came with a matching halter bra. It exposed an inch of tit on the bottom, two inches of the outsides and three inches insides and the top of her tits to the top of her aureoles. We found a sheer white halter top. It covered all of her tits and molded to her swollen puffy nipples. It didn't distort her tits and allowed them to jiggle and swing as if they were naked. A hot pink, semi-sheer mini wraps skirt. Short, short. No hose and her super high heels. Friday night all the women were really showing off and Saturday night was supposed to be really wilder. When she was sitting the right side of her skirt lay down between her thighs, exposing her entire naked outer thigh and hip. You could hardly see the string of her panties.

We had dinner and got our receipt to get in free, went back to the room and Debbie changed into her new outfit. Fucked up, we got to the club at 10:00PM. Four hours to play!!! Swingers!!!!!

There was no mention of Debbie's cunt and ass being felt the night before. But plenty of anticipation of what tonight would bring. Bob and Shirley were there. Shirley's top was totally see-through. Short skirt that barely covered her cunt. It put Debbie at ease with her revealing outfit.

We took our seats in the back. Steve was there waiting when we arrived. He joined us and bought a round of drinks. He told Debbie how sexy she looked. They danced, humping slowly to the music. They fast danced, Steve swirling her around, showing her g-string. They took turns with her, all catching her tit when she swirled back to them and feeling her ass and humping into her butt.

The midnight break came. Bob and Shirley went out to our car and smoked with us. Debbie told them she was leaving her bra and g-string on so Steve could take them off while we watched. She asked how women took men's underwear off without getting them naked. Shirley said they just undid they guys belt and unzipped their pants and pulled their underwear down below their balls. Shirley said they'd heard there was something special tonight that they'd done a few times before. And that all the locals had talked the owner into doing it tonight. And that Steve was in on it and Debbie was going to love Steve's underwear. We went in, anticipating when Steve would take Debbie's g-string and bra off.

Everyone danced, dirty. We watched. Shirley fuck danced with one of the guys at the table across from us. The girls got into a competition on who danced the sexiest. It didn't take long before they were practically fucking on the dance floor. They got their cunts and asses dry humped. About six couples were watching and cheering them on. Eight horny women were fuck dancing. Husbands danced with other wives. Shirley's big tits were felt. All the women got felt up, Debbie included. Her eyes closed and her head tilted back. Steve's cock was sticking out, pleated pants. He humped her cunt and she humped him back. Her short skirt rose above her cunt. Steve was humping Debbie through nothing but her sheer g-string, which we could all see. Debbie came hard. She sat with me, panting. We watched Shirley get felt up and fingered. A lot of the women got fingered and stroked their partners' cocks. Debbie and I watched the debauchery. Shirley grabbed me and we danced. Nasty. She stroked my cock. Steve led Debbie to the dance floor. He humped her ass. He slid his hands up her skirt, exposing her naked ass.

The commando police showed up. Debbie still had her bra and g-string on. We smiled at each other. Steve was going to get to take her bra and g-string off of her. While we all watched. Oh, shit. They were led to the middle of the dance floor. An emcee announced that they'd caught commando violators. Their punishment was that they had to strip each other to their underwear and dance in the cage for half an hour. Shirley laughed as we made our way to the cage, telling me that this was the "something special" and to wait until I saw what Steve was wearing.

I could tell Debbie was surprised and a little embarrassed. But also incredibly turned on. Steve and Debbie entered the cage and it was lifted to where their crotches were just below eyeball high to everyone on the dance floor. Steve eased Debbie's halter top up over her big fucking tits, his hands lingering on her tits and squeezing them. She closed her eyes and arched her back, offering them to him completely while we all watched. He knelt and unbuttoned her skirt and slowly slid it down, caressing her ass. His finger teased her virgin ass hole, naked except for the thin string. She pressed back into it. He stood and turned Debbie around, slowly, twice, exhibiting her for everyone.

Debbie took Steve's shirt off and licked his nipples. She knelt in front of him. Our eyes met. Filled with lust. She undid his belt and pants and eased his zipper down, slowly. She worked his pants down his ass. His nine inch cock popped out, hitting Debbie in the face. It was huge, thick and curved. Everyone cheered. Shirley laughed and stroked my hard, pulsating cock. Steve had on a white, totally sheer, stretch knit ball and cock sock. His cock oozed precum. Debbie stroked Steve's huge curved cock and ran her finger across his prick head smearing his precum around his cock head. Everyone was yelling for her to suck his cock. Steve's cock was poised directly in front of Debbie's mouth. He pressed the head against Debbie's lips. They parted and we could see her tongue lick Steve's prick head.

Shirley said Steve was a regular there and had danced in his ball and cock sock many times with many unsuspecting wives. And, that it had been arranged that he would dance with Debbie in the cage on Thursday night. She also said that all the regulars wanted to see Debbie naked. They all wanted to see her tits and pussy. Debbie had been set up.

Debbie got up and they danced, dirty. Steve's cock ground into Debbie's practically naked cunt. He placed his cock head directly against her fuck hole. He felt her tits and ass. Steve turned Debbie around and humped her ass. He got his cock head right on her butt hole. He got half of his head into her butt hole. All that stopped him was her tiny string. They danced wildly for half an hour. Men reached into the cage and felt Debbie's ass. The cage was lowered so that her tits could be felt, also.

Steve stuck his cock between Debbie's legs from behind. His big curved cock stuck out in front of her cunt about 4 inches. It curve to up and stroked her entire cunt and clit. Debbie rapped her hand around it and stroked it, pressing it into her cunt and clit. Steve stroked Debbie's cunt and she stroked his cock with her cunt and hand. Debbie came all over Steve's cock, really hard.

They dressed and Steve took Debbie's bra off, caressing her naked tits, his hands inside her halter top. The cage was raised to just above eye level. He knelt and put his hands under Debbie's skirt. He lifted her skirt, tucking it into her waist band. Everyone could see her pussy and ass. Steve worked Debbie's g-string down to her butt hole. And, then the front of her g-string. His right hand was between her thighs, his middle finger stroking her sopping wet naked pussy. He moved his drenched finger to her virgin butt hole. He slid his entire finger up her ass. Steve pulled Debbie's cunt into his mouth and ate her to a monumental orgasm. Everyone cheered them on. Steve was ramming his finger in and out of Debbie's ass hole. Debbie came and almost collapsed onto Steve.

It was Debbie's turn to take Steve's underwear off. The cage was lowered to just below eye level. Debbie opened Steve's pants and his big cock and balls sprang out. The elastic of his ball and cock sock was really tight and Debbie was having trouble getting it off of him. She knelt in front of him and put both hands on the back of his balls. His huge curved cock was right in front of her face. It was then that I noticed Steve was uncircumcised. Debbie's hands were all over Steve's balls as she worked the ball sock off. She unrolled the cock sock off just like a rubber, her hands on his naked cock. Her thumb pressed into the bottom of his prick, milking his precum out the tip of his cock.

Shirley had her hands down my pants and Bob's, stroking our naked cocks. Steve pulled Debbie's head into his prick. Debbie licked the precum from Steve's naked prick head. He forced his hard fucking cock into her mouth. Debbie instinctively sucked Steve's dick. He came in less than a minute. Everyone cheered. Debbie was embarrassed, but turned on.

Back at our table Shirley told Debbie how sexy she's looked being felt up and finger fucked in the ass, and especially sucking Steve's cock. We all went to our car and smoked. Shirley sucked Bob's cock. And, when she came up she put her lips to Debbie's lips and forced Bob's cum into Debbie's mouth. She told Debbie that now Debbie had eaten two men's cum in 15 minutes. And we still had an hour to go.

We went back in and Debbie danced with Bob in the cage, letting everyone see her naked cunt. Bob humped Debbie's cunt and ass. He felt her tits. A lot of women had their naked tits out, being felt up. Debbie limited her dancing to the six guys by our table. They felt her naked tits and pussy and asshole. They all put her hand down their pants, and she stroked their pricks. A woman with D cup tits danced topless in her g-string in the cage. She was felt up and finger fucked. Everyone wanted to watch Debbie and Steve dance again. Debbie finally relented. Debbie was really fucked up. She let Steve fuck his cock against her naked cunt and ass hole. Debbie masturbated with Steve's prick pressing against her cunt. Steve pulled her halter top up over her tits. She stroked his big curved prick through his pants with her cunt and came. Steve took his naked prick out and Debbie stroked it. He tried to fuck her, lodging his cock head into her fuck hole. She told him "No". Steve kept pounding into her and got half his cock into her fuck hole. She said, "Fuck yes, fuck me Steve" and wrapped her legs around him and pulled him into her. At least seven inches of Steve's prick was buried up Debbie's cunt. Everyone was yelling for Steve to fuck Debbie. Steve pounded Debbie's cunt, gradually impaling her with his entire nine inches. Debbie frantically fucked her cunt into Steve's thrusting prick. She finally got her wits about her and twisted away from Steve's prick. Debbie knelt and sucked his cock for the second time, thinking that was better than him fucking her. Everyone cheered her on. She gave Steve her sluttiest blow job ever. When Steve was ready to cum he held her head and fucked her mouth. His cum gushed out of her mouth. She couldn't swallow it all. And it ran down onto her big tits.

Debbie came back to our table and Shirley sucked Steve's cum from Debbie's blouse. Debbie was embarrassed. Bob and Shirley told Debbie how sexy she looked fucking and sucking Steve's big cock. Debbie looked at me and I told her that Steve had raped her mouth. Everyone was really drunk and horny and it wasn't her fault. We danced and everyone looked at her big almost naked tits. All six of the guys danced with her and uninhibitedly felt her tits, ass and pussy. Steve danced with Debbie again. He put her hand down his pants. She stroked his hard thick curved uncut prick. While we watched, knowing he'd cum in Debbie's mouth twice while everyone watched. Steve felt Debbie's naked tits and her naked ass and cunt. A crowd had slowly gathered around Debbie and Steve. Steve had her halter top up over her tits. Debbie was dancing and letting everyone look at her naked tits, bouncing and jiggling. Steve lifted her skirt up and tucked it into the waistband of her skirt. Debbie's tits, ass and cunt were exposed. Shirley was egging Debbie on. Steve felt both of Debbie's tits. Then he felt her ass. Debbie took Steve's prick out and stroked it, again. Six couples and five single guys were watching. Steve tried to fuck her again. Debbie knelt and sucked his cock again.

Four guys lifted her up and dumped her on an empty table, on her back, her legs spread, and ass hole and cunt invitingly exposed. Steve's cock slid easily up her willing horny fucking cunt. My wife was being fucked in front of me and a bunch of total strangers. Steve's nine inch cock was slamming in and out of my wife's cunt, stretching her out like never before. Steve jack hammered her cunt. Debbie was telling Steve to fuck her. Steve fucked my wife's cunt while we all watched. Steve shot his load up Debbie's cunt and pulled out of her. One of his buddies mounted her and fucked her. He came in her cunt in two minutes and another guy fucked her. This went on until all five of them had fucked her and cum in her cunt, each only taking two or three minutes to cum up her cunt. By this time, at least ten couples were watching the action.

Steve dipped his finger up Debbie's cunt. He lubricated her ass hole with her cunt juices and their cum. He finger fucked her ass hole. Debbie squirmed, working her ass back in to Steve's finger. The lights came on announcing that the club was closing in ten minutes. Debbie was bent over the table with her skirt up over her ass and Steve finger fucking the shit out of her ass hole with two fingers.

We fucked our brains out at the motel. Debbie said she couldn't believe that she had sucked Steve's huge cock. She asked how she looked with his big prick her mouth. I told her she looked very sexy sucking his cock. She asked me about how she looked when Steve had his cock up her cunt. I told her she looked really stretched out. Like the women fucking huge porno cocks. I asked her how it felt. Debbie said her cunt felt really filled. It totally stretched her opening and almost made her cum while he worked his cock into her pussy. She said it stretched her cunt like never before.

Debbie said it was an incredible turn-on letting me and everyone watch her and see her naked tits, ass and pussy. She said she understood why women liked being gang fucked! And dancing naked at strip   clubs.

THE END...OR NOT?

Made in the USA
Las Vegas, NV
10 September 2022

55056221R00204